Seeing the World In 20/20

A SouthWest Writers Anthology of Award Winning Stories

SouthWest Writers
Carlisle Executive Offices
3200 Carlisle Blvd N.E.
Albuquerque, New Mexico 87110
www.southwestwriters.com

Seeing the World in 20/20
Brenda Cole, Contest Chairwoman
RMK Publications, Editing & Formatting
ISBN: 9798668022847

SouthWest Writers

The 2020 Writing Contest

The motto of SouthWest Writers is "Writers Helping Writers." We do this through classes, conferences, workshops and a membership of more than 370 people—many of whom are published, well-known authors. Twice monthly meetings offer insights and opportunities for networking.

The Annual Writing Contest offers an important step in an author's development. It focuses on short pieces of poetry, non-fiction essays and genre-driven short prose. The contest allows both budding authors and seasoned writers to sharpen their skills. Seventeen categories were offered, and awards were given for First, Second and Third place in each.

Many new authors need a challenge in a supportive environment where they can feel comfortable discussing their work. A true success story begins with being courageous enough to put your skills in front of others. Our words are our children, so we need to understand that constructive criticism does not condemn, it helps us mold and grow out talents.

Seasoned published writers can fall into a rut. Contests such as this one channel their minds and talents in different directions, freshening their skills and pushing their boundaries.

Here you will enjoy winning entries in each category. All entries were previously unpublished, however authors had the right to pull their work from this anthology if they chose to retain first publishing rights for use elsewhere, and some chose not to add their biographical information.

These stories are fun, or sad, or factual, or surprising, many of them are all these things. The genres are randomly mixed through the book. Pay attention to the names of the authors-you will probably see them again!

ACKNOWLEDGEMENTS

SouthWest Writers is fortunate to have members who are not only published authors but also editors, photographers, proofreaders and formatters. The following members contributed these skills to the production of the 2019 SWW *Winners Anthology.*

Writing contest organizing committee:
Brenda Cole, Chairwoman
Dan Wetmore
Rose Marie Kern

SWW Manuscript Copy Editors
Kathy Schuit, Kathy Wagoner, Patricia Walkow, Jacqueline Loring
Brenda Cole, Dan Wetmore

Office Support: ReVaH Loring
Cover, Interior Design and Layout by RMK Publications

To learn more about what SouthWest Writers has to offer go to:

www.southwestwriters.com

WRITING CONTEST TEAM

You can tell a lot about a writing contest by the quality of its judges. SouthWest Writers is honored to have a team of award winning published authors and professional editors that cross all genres. We want to thank them for the hours they spent judging the entries and leaving constructive criticism for all participants.

Parris Afton Bonds
Brenda Cole
David Corwell
Larry Greenly
Melody Groves
Loretta Hall
Joyce Hertzoff
Rose Marie Kern
Robert Kidera
Kathy Kitts
Dino De Leyba
Jacqueline Murray Loring
Ralph McCormick
Sam Moorman
Evelyn Neil
Paula Paul
Sarah Rowe
Jeanne Shannon
Happy Kay Saw
Kathy Schuit
Rob Spiegel
Patricia Walkow
Dan Wetmore

Table of Contents

SECTION ONE

BIOGRAPHY/MEMOIR

Our most popular category with 61 entries. Sit back and wander through exotic locales and travel down old pathways.

BIOGRAPHY/MEMOIR   GOLD MEDAL
JOE BROWN

HEY COACH

I have fond memories of coaching youth in football and baseball, but one young man and our shared times are a little more special than most. We met when he was playing on a team in the Antelope Valley Youth Football League. That league was for youngsters before they were old enough to be on a high school team. His name was David Flaugher. He was the same age and a teammate of my older son. I saw potential in him, but he lacked discipline, and that meant he could not be depended on to execute his part of the play. I couldn't always attend the practices because I was coaching at the high school, but on one of the days I was at their practice, I took David aside.

"I'm Coach Jackson, and I enjoyed watching you today. You're David, right?"

"Yeah, who are you?"

"As I said, I'm Coach Jackson, and I coach football at Desert High. I watched you today during your practice."

"So, why should I care?"

"Maybe you shouldn't. But I wanted to know if you planned to play for the high school next year?"

"Yeah, probably. If we are still here. I gotta go." He turned and walked away.

That was my first experience with the young man. His attitude told me volumes, but it also created questions. I hoped to see him next year.

* * *

"Well, David, welcome to your first practice on the Desert High School Junior Varsity team."

"You're that guy I saw at a practice last year. Aren't ya?"

"That'll be me. Aren't you, Coach Jackson? Or aren't you, sir?

13

"You can pick, either one works."

That was the start of our time together, covering the next four years of our lives. David became an excellent high school football player. He was big, so he became an offensive lineman. But where he grew the most was in his self-control. His respect for himself, his teammates, and the adults in his life became his trademark. I was his coach for those years, and the team was successful in winning enough games to make the state playoffs every year. But David's senior year was special and what made it special started in a football game in Bishop, California.

There are four quarters in a football game. You play two and then break for halftime. It was getting close to halftime, and neither team had scored. After we had kicked to Bishop's team, David came running off the field, red-faced with his fists clenched...

"Coach...Coach..." He had a crazed look in his eyes.

"What Flaugher, what's wrong?"

"He's calling me girly, and princess and some names I won't tell ya."

"Who is?"

"Their middle linebacker, number fifty-five."

"That bothers you, David?"

"Yes sir, he's making fun of my hair."

David had beautiful long red hair that flowed out under his helmet.

"What are you goin' to do about it?"

"What do ya mean, Coach?"

"I would never tell any player to break the rules, but why don't you KICK HIS BUTT."

"What? How?"

"When we get the football. On the first play, you fire out and knock fifty-five to the ground. I mean to knock fifty-five into next week. Do you understand.?"

"I think so, Coach. What if the play called has me doing something else?"

"David, for this one play, you go get that guy. Got it?"

"With a big grin on his face, he said, "Got it, Coach."

I went directly to our head coach, who called offensive plays, and said, "Leroy, call your first play with Mayfield running off right guard."

Leroy looked puzzled and asked, "Why, Coach?"

I grinned and said, "Flaugher is going to settle a score with the middle linebacker."

"Sure, we can do that."

Mayfield, our running back, was fast and talented.

We got the ball back about forty yards from Bishop's goal line.

Leroy called the play, and David exploded toward number fifty-five. You heard the sound of the impact of David's block throughout the stadium. The Bishop High coaches had to help fifty-five off the field. Mayfield ran those forty yards for a touchdown. That play gave the team a spark, and we won the game. The best part was when David came off the field after that play. He was beaming.

"Coach, did ya see it? Did ya? Boy o' boy, did ya?"

"I sure did buddy, and I doubt you'll hear another word out of him tonight."

He didn't. Fifty-five didn't make a good play for his team for the rest of the game. Mayfield had one of his best games running behind David.

The best night of that season for David and me was still to come.

* * *

It was a cool and beautiful Friday night in late November 1989. I had been coaching football at Desert High School for a decade by that time. Something wonderful and unexpected was about to happen.

The team was dressing in the locker room for the final home game of the season. There was electricity in the air mixing with sweat, liniment, and excitement. The team had already qualified for the post-season playoffs, and now we wanted to end the regular season on a positive note.

It was Senior Night with its ceremony at halftime. Each Senior on the team remained on the field. Their parents come out of the stands. The players give a rose to a parent during the ceremony. That always is touching and adds a great memory to any season. This Senior Class of players had been one of the most successful in decades. Everyone expected a packed stadium.

I was the varsity offensive line coach going over my lineup and plans sitting in a corner of the locker room when I heard a familiar voice say, "Hey Coach, can we talk?"

"Sure, David, what's on your mind?"

"You know tonight's Senior Night, right?"

"Yes, and I look forward to meeting your folks."

David was one of my best linemen standing well over six feet and weighing 240 pounds. Towering over me, he looked almost embarrassed as he stared down at his feet, saying, "Come on, Coach, how long have you known me?"

"Since you were in junior high."

"That's right, and have you ever seen either my mom or dad?"

15

"Well, no, I haven't. That's why I said what I did."

"Coach, they're not going to be here, that's why I wanted to talk to you."

"OK."

"Coach, would you be my dad tonight during the ceremony?

I practically melted. I knew we had become close over the years, but David asking me that far exceeded anything I could have imagined.

I said, "David, it would be my honor, are you sure?"

With tears beginning to show, "Yes, Coach and thanks."

At halftime, I counted the people forming the two lines of parents and players so I would arrive with David. I had not had any chance to let the announcer know what David and I planned, but there was no need. Roger Bean, the announcer, knew David and me very well and had figured it out because when we got to the head of the line, you heard across the stadium. "Next, number 78, David Flaugher, starting right guard and his friend, Coach Jim Jackson."

The stadium erupted in applause, and I experienced a moment I will never forget as this big bear of a guy hugged me and whispered, "Thanks, Coach, this means a lot to me. "

*   *   *

Joe Brown enjoys writing memoirs and historical fiction. He retired from his military and civil service careers in 2010 as a Senior Analyst advising the Commander, Air Force Flight Test Center. He advised on strategic issues collaborating with senior national leaders across the DoD Test and Evaluation Enterprise.

Biography/Memoir Poetry   Gold Medal
John Cornish

RENTAL

Workweek done, I return home, find the old
farmhouse a bee grave, exterminators
packing nets and sprayers' needle nozzles:
"Stay away!," they roar, then floor their Bug.
The landlord is an ugly man. These bees
never bothered from the front porch pillar,
so what reason has he fabricated
to rend them, they surely better tenants
than any of us transient sophomore
degree seekers who leave doors unlocked,
don't smarten the premises, and lounge
leafless on the front porch roof while claiming
nine-tenths of the law: The bees never stung.
The hive had housed itself here long before
we came, maybe since the days when city
smudged horizon in a farmer's field
of vision. Now I witness witless death.
The bees' crooning quest to make honey
had defied apocalyptic stillness.
Yes, <u>evil</u> landlord! Three small swarms cling
to porch screens and flex like lungs, single bees
arc above the shattered dead and swarming,
their moan flat. When I step on bees they snap.

* * *

John Cornish

Retired college administrator and English instructor, I am looking for critique partners to exchange draft novels or several shorter works. These days I write urban fantasy, but appreciate all prose genres, including non-fiction. Poetry is welcome too! jcornish643@gmail.com. Go Dems!

Biography/Memoir   Silver Medal
Melinda Smith

THE GIRL IN
PATAN DURBAR SQUARE

I felt a light hand on my forearm. I turned and saw a slim girl of about twelve, with dark silky hair, dressed in jeans and a red tunic. She flashed a handful of cheap necklaces at me and started following me. "Ma'am, do you want to buy these beautiful necklaces? I can give you a good price."

I didn't want to engage with her, but her persistence interested me. I asked her name.

"I'm Riya Timilsina."

Riya was one of a swarm of children peddling their goods to the few tourists who found their way to Durbar Square, the heart of the ancient city-state kingdom of Patan. Tourism had faltered in Nepal due to the uncertainties of life during political instability and armed conflict.

It was 2005 on a hot Sunday morning in August. I had arrived in Kathmandu a few weeks earlier to take a job with a UN agency. The Maoist insurgency was in its ninth year. Though the fighting was confined to rural areas, life in Kathmandu was disrupted by weekly protests, strikes, and curfews. The city was swelling with migrants—families and young men on their own, displaced by the war and looking for work.

I had just reached Patan Durbar Square. Walking along a narrow market street cluttered with clothing shops, I choked on the brown exhaust fumes from motor bikes and my head buzzed from honking horns. Men's heads bobbed up and down as they walked in their *topis,* envelope-shaped hats woven in geometric patterns of red and orange.

When the street finally opened onto Durbar Square, I was astonished to see a vision of living antiquity. The square was filled with stone and brick architecture from many centuries and styles—white granite temples adorned with statues of Hindu and Buddhist gods, multi-story red-brick pagodas with carved wooden columns and undulating erotic figures, and stupas guarded by open-mouthed lions. Women glided past in their traditional *shalwar kameez*, trousers, tunics and long scarves of vivid contrasting colors and patterns. Sidewalk merchants sat crossed-legged on the paved red bricks, hoping to sell a few pieces of clothing piled in front of them.

Riya had interrupted my first moments in the square, as I drank in the panorama of another era. I relented and gave her my attention. "How often do you sell jewelry in the square?"

"Every day. I've been doing it for four years to help my mother. I know how to sell necklaces in six languages."

"What languages?"

She proceeded to run through her sales pitch in English, French, German, Spanish, Japanese, and even Chinese.

Charmed by her linguistic prowess, I let her shadow me past two lions standing guard in front of a large pagoda. Normally I escaped street sellers or gave them a little money without buying anything. But she was so young and determined, and I was thinking about my daughter. I always sent her jewelry from the countries I worked in. She was in college several continents away, and she didn't have to sell anything to help support me. Perhaps I could reward Riya with a sale and send some baubles to my daughter and her roommates.

I asked Riya to show me the necklaces. She led me to a stone bench and laid out the necklaces: one with a metal mandala, another with imitation turquoise and coral stones, and a third with yin and yang inlay.

Riya's asking price was 300 rupees, about three US dollars. She hadn't made a sale in two days. She admitted that the jewelry was made in nearby workshops, not in Tibet as she usually claimed. Her candor made me smile. I asked about her family.

"My father drank too much and died four years ago. My mother doesn't have very much money. I come here after school and some mornings with my sisters." She said business was much worse since the Maoist insurgency had intensified.

I asked Riya about school. Her face lit up. She was second in her class. With this information, I decided to buy five necklaces—my daughter could share them with her friends. I picked out a silver filigree perfume bottle, a mandala, a pendant with yin and yang inlay, and two necklaces with turquoise stones. We easily agreed on 250 rupees each. I wanted her to make a handsome profit. Riya glowed with her success.

After our transaction, Riya led me to the other end of the square to meet her mother, who was sitting on the sidewalk with a pile of clothing in front of her. Ambika was a handsome woman with a full face, aquiline nose, and dark, straight hair drawn back and fastened at the neck. Her tired, rounded body, wrapped in a rumpled sari, gave her the look of a grandmother, though I guessed she was much younger than me. She made a living selling underwear and socks, but with so many other women doing the same, it was a wonder she made anything at all. Riya said something to her in Nepali, no doubt recounting the morning's windfall sale.

Another girl joined us, and Riya introduced her older sister Anju. Prettier than Riya, Anju had fine features and dark eyes rimmed in black eyeliner. The girls began to tell me about the tourists they had met in their four years of selling on the square. For my amusement, they performed the multilingual sales pitches Riya had recited earlier. They said sometimes tourists were rude to them. Anju added, making a face, that occasionally they were propositioned. They assured me that they rejected all such offers. Riya said that they didn't like selling on the square, but they had no choice.

Ambika whispered something to Riya in Nepali, and the girls told me their mother wanted me to visit their home. I promised to return as soon as I could. Riya wrote down my email address. I didn't expect her to have access to a computer, let alone an email address. But about a week later, I received a brief email from her, probably sent from an internet café.

Hi mam
How r u?
How is ur days going on?
Where r u?
When r u coming to see us?

I replied immediately, promising to visit as soon as I could. However, my job demanded most of my time, so it was many weeks before I could return.

I was thrust into work I had never done—assisting countries in South Asia prepare plans for the continuity of education during armed conflict or natural disasters. This seemed an impossible task, even if I had been trained in humanitarian work. I was what was known in the UN as a "generalist," a person with a long résumé of program management who could pick up expertise along the way.

The countries in South Asia I was responsible for assisting were beset by instability or outright war. Many were recovering from the devastation of the

Indian Ocean tsunami. Afghanistan was exhausted by the US war against the Taliban and Al Qaeda. Sri Lanka was mired in the bloody Sinhalese-Tamil conflict. Pakistan was embroiled in its own war against the Taliban, and recent earthquakes and floods destroyed what armed conflict didn't. India was in the midst of its own Maoist insurgency. Bangladesh was beset by an intractable conflict between its major parties as floods and cyclones created millions of refugees. The Maldives was literally sinking under the weight of climate change and political instability.

Restarting education seemed a formidable undertaking during these catastrophic events. Education had not been a priority in emergencies compared with urgent needs of food, shelter, water, sanitation, and security. Yet when refugees were asked what they needed, families said they wanted schooling. It provided a glint of hope for the future to people facing the hardship of disaster and displacement.

My job in Nepal was temporary, but it had given me a place to land. I wasn't looking for a career in international aid. It was a means of leaving the US during the Iraq War. I couldn't bear to be an American any more while my country waged an immoral and unprovoked war that brought suffering and destabilization to millions of people. I wanted out.

In Nepal I became a spectator in a different kind of war. I had a front-row seat to a revolution. After decades of conflicts of class, caste, ethnicity, political power, and economic inequality, Nepal's lurch to democratic governance was incomplete. People demanded change. The Maoist movement took up arms, seeking to win the hearts and minds of the Nepali people with a promise to create a republic and end the monarchy. Riya's family and the country's poor were supposed to be the beneficiaries of this revolution. But the immediate impacts were food and petrol shortages, unemployment and insecurity.

Two months passed before I returned to Durbar Square. I had emailed Riya in advance and we arranged to meet where her mother sold clothes. Ambika lit up when she saw me. A few minutes later, Riya and Anju appeared, smiling at me. They spoke a few words to their mother, and Riya took my hand.

"My mother wants you to come to our house." With Riya steering me, we walked behind her mother and sister down one of the narrow streets where tourists never went. She guided me down a passage into a small courtyard paved with worn red bricks.

We walked through a tiny doorway into a dark interior stairwell that smelled of urine. We climbed wobbly wooden stairs as steep as a ladder. On a tiny landing we took off our shoes and bent down to enter a small room, divided into even smaller spaces by pieces of cloth hung from the ceiling.

As my eyes adjusted to the dim light, I saw a closet-sized kitchen with a gas burner and a shelf, a slightly bigger space for a sitting room, and a third space not visible, where they slept. There was no bathroom. The air was still and heavy. It must have been suffocating during the hot season, with just one small window and no fan or cross breeze.

Riya's mother gestured to me to sit in a threadbare upholstered armchair, while they settled on the floor on a worn Tibetan carpet. We were joined by the oldest daughter, who emerged from behind the curtain. Riya introduced her sister Samjana, who at sixteen had finished the 10th grade. Samjana was even prettier than her sisters, with dark eyes outlined in a kohl-like makeup. As we greeted each other with *namastes*, I wondered what her prospects were for a job, or even marriage.

Samjana spoke in clear, well-pronounced English. She said with pride, "Our cast name is Timilsina; we are Brahmin." Everyone in Nepal seemed to speak matter-of-factly about their caste, though the system was officially outlawed. I wondered how a Brahmin family could be so poor. Clearly castes didn't correspond with economic prosperity in a country where most people lived on less than two dollars a day.

Riya then said, "We have a brother, Sabin. He's six. He doesn't live with us." Sabin was sent to live in a government hostel because they couldn't afford to take care of him.

I asked how long he had to stay at the hostel.

"Ten years," Samjana replied. The girls then related different versions of how Sabin cried each time they visited him, begging to come home. They seemed to accept this cruel separation as a fact-of-life.

As the girls prepared tea and brought in a small plate of cakes, I began to realize I was in the position to change their lives with my means, modest though they were. The UN discouraged personal acts of charity by its staff. But I started calculating what $50 a month could buy them —a year's rent, Riya's school fees and books, a larger home and more food to bring Sabin back from the orphanage.

I decided that at my next visit, I would propose helping Riya with her schooling. As a high-achieving student, she needed a chance to complete her education, which for girls in Nepal was not easy. In a country with one of the highest child marriage rates in the world, maybe Riya could be spared that dreary fate. Skeptical about the long-term efficacy of the work I was doing, I could at least make a difference for one child.

During the winter holiday break. I met Riya near the stupa where we had first met and we went to the apartment. I presented the family with a holiday gift, a large hand-carved wooden bowl filled with cakes, chocolates, and fruit. Ambika disappeared behind the curtain and emerged with a necklace of purple-colored glass stones, which she handed to me. Before I left, I took a thick envelope filled with rupees out of my purse and gave it to Ambika. I asked Riya to tell her mother it was for her school fees and other household needs. Ambika touched her heart with both hands and her eyes moistened.

By the Nepali New Year celebration of 2006, I hadn't seen the family in three months. It was a turbulent time. Mass demonstrations were met with all-day curfews imposed by the king, followed by a cut in mobile phone service to quash dissent. Riya and I still managed to meet in Durbar Square on New Year's Day.

Kathmandu was tinted in shades of red—crimson buntings were hung from doorways, women were wrapped in scarlet saris, and blood-red bracelets were displayed on racks in jewelry stalls. Kathmandu was determined to have its holiday despite the war.

Riya and I admired the decorations, ate sweets from street vendors, and exchanged news about our families. I put an envelope filled with rupees into her hand before we parted. This ritual took place every three or four months until I left Nepal.

The new year brought historic change. A cease fire was declared, and a peace accord signed by the prime minister and the Maoist leader. Prime Minister Koirala announced: "This has given a message to the international community and terrorists all over the world that no conflict can be resolved by guns. It can be done by dialogue."

Just before my job ended in December of 2008, elections were held to establish a constituent assembly to replace the parliament. To everyone's astonishment the Maoists received the highest vote total of all parties. Nepal was to become a federal democratic republic. The monarchy was abolished and the king was given fifteen days to vacate the palace.

On my last visit to the Timilsina's apartment, Ambika presented me with a gold filigreed pendant that looked like one of the necklaces Riya was peddling when I first saw her. Riya was in secondary school, maintaining her grades and high exam scores. I gave Ambika a last installment of rupees to cover several years of school fees. I doubted I would every return to Kathmandu or have the means to help Riya again.

Riya and I communicated intermittently during subsequent years. In 2009 an email message from her found me in Nairobi, where I was then working.

She urgently asked what course of study she should pursue for higher education. I asked her what she was passionate about, how could she contribute to Nepal's development? She never replied.

The following year I received an alarming message from her when I was working in Bangkok. The subject line contained the words: *My future is in ur hands.* Riya said she was in college but unable to pay her fees. I managed to get some money to her through a colleague in Bangkok who was travelling to Nepal.

An unexpected contract brought me back to Kathmandu in 2014. I sent Riya a message of my arrival but it went unanswered. I went to Durbar Square anyway to find news of her. I approached a middle-aged woman named Maya, a vendor who knew the Timilsinas. She was standing next to her table laden with faux Tibetan metal goods. I greeted her, asking if she remembered me and she nodded.

"I'm looking for Riya... have you seen her?"

"They're all gone, left the country,' Maya said. "Except for the mother. She's still here, but she's sick."

Alarmed, I asked where the girls were. She said she thought the two older ones were working in Europe, and she thought Riya was in Romania. I couldn't imagine what she was doing in Romania. I asked Maya if she would send my best wishes to Ambika and I quickly left the square.

* * *

It had been almost a year since I last heard from Riya and she was at a vulnerable age. Was she a victim of some Eastern European sex-trafficking ring? Or had she gone off to another country to work as a domestic servant or worse.

When I returned to the US, I emailed Riya to tell her I had been in Nepal and pressed her with questions about Romania. To my relief, Riya responded within several days. saying she was busy with her studies. She was living with a family taking care of children and studying the Bible in a program sponsored by a church. It seemed preposterous but I was convinced she wasn't ensnared in a sex ring.

A year later, on a spring morning in 2015, I woke to news of a 7.8 magnitude earthquake that struck Nepal. In Patan Durbar Square, old brick homes and centuries-old temples and stupas became huge mounds of rubble. I messaged Riya with great concern about the safety of her family and received a reply 10 days later.

Hi thank you so much for the mail. I am still in Romania. All my family members are fine but we lost our home and facing so many problems. I don't know where they will live and how they will survive we are in need of a helping hand to overcome this nightmare.

Only once before had Riya asked me for financial help. I was glad to be able to help her family now. I took a chance and called Riya's Skype number. I heard a distressed voice answer. Relieved to have reached her so easily, I listened as Riya explained, through her sobs, that her mother had no assistance, and that her sisters were overseas and couldn't help.

Riya and I devised a plan for me to wire funds to her mother. A week later, Riya messaged that her mother received the money and managed to find suitable housing in a secure building. Riya wrote:

Thank u so much. You have been helping me in every step of my life. I feel like that I am not alone. Thank you so much for being with me and for your kindness.

Then months of silence. One last email came, and I was again confused about Riya's whereabouts. She said she had completed her studies in Romania and was looking for work, maybe in Portugal. Months passed with no replies to my continued attempts to contact her. In the succeeding months, my apprehension about Riya receded from my immediate thoughts, as it had over the years of our friendship. But misgivings about her uncertain life and future continued to return in unexpected waves, a reminder of the danger and displacement that beset so many people fleeing instability or poverty or war, seeking better lives in unknown destinations.

* * *

After a year without communicating, Riya sent a message from Lisbon, where she had gone after Romania to find a job and qualify for a resident permit. Portugal has become a magnet for Nepalis seeking work permits and resident status in Europe, since the requirements were less stringent than in other European Union countries. Riya had joined the ranks of millions of migrants in the world, sending remittances home to help their families in countries unable to produce livelihoods to sustain them.

In late March of 2020, as the world rushed to contain the devastation of the coronavirus, I received an urgent email from Riya. She had seen reports of high infection and death tolls in the U.S. and wanted to make sure I was not sick. She urged me to take care. What a role reversal. The US had become the epicenter of the pandemic, and my young friend, whose uncertain path I'd always worried about, was now concerned about my welfare in the world's richest country.

I replied that I was fine, thanking her for her concern and assuring her that I was staying safe at home. I didn't tell Riya that when the pandemic reached American shores, it exposed the structural and political weaknesses that have made the US respond more like a developing country than the world's leading economy. The writer George Packer referred to the US as a "failed state." Perhaps we have joined the ranks of countries, like Nepal, that cannot take care of its most vulnerable.

* * *

 **Melinda Smith** has worked for the UN in Africa, the Middle East, Asia and the Pacific, places that inspire her writing. She was runner up in the Missouri Review's 2019 Editors' Prize in non-fiction. Her essay appears in the Spring 2020 issue. She is working on a novel.

Memoir/Biography Poetry   Silver Medal
Sylvia Ramos Cruz

TO SEE WHERE YOU'RE GOING, LOOK TO WHERE YOU'VE BEEN

Haibun for Historic New Mexico Women: Helene Haack Allen (1891-1978) ~ Louise Massey Mable (1902-1983) ~ Eve Ball (1890-1984)*

November 8, 2016. 240 years into this republic. 96 years after women won the vote by dint of hard work, sacrifice, grit. Another man, the 45th, becomes President. Totally unqualified. Beat superbly qualified woman—first to run as major party's candidate. Whatever pundits spout into airwaves, whatever some people tell their neighbors, my well-informed gut tells me she lost primarily because she is a she.

Three days later, my friend and I go looking for historic New Mexico women road markers. I need to mull the view outside the car window, still the turmoil in my head. I need to feel cool wind caress my face, soothe stinging slap of this immeasurable loss. I need to see women celebrated. If only on small plaques scattered along the state's byways.

The roads uncurls mile after mile, sometimes visible far into the montaña-layered horizon. Other times unseen until it springs up behind a stand of sun-licked cottonwoods. The ash, cloud-smudged sky complements mid-autumn dying landscape and my melancholy.

from Adam's rib

to the White House—

a reach too far

sorrows of the soul

mirrored in nature—

somber palette

life twists and turns

blind to what lies ahead

how do we go on?

We drive into Fort Sumner on NM-84 to find Helen Haack Allen (1891-1978). Philanthropist. Civic Leader. Businesswoman. Fought hard to keep Billy the Kid (scorned by the Mescalero as a horse thief) buried in the town. Wanted him to do his part. Bolster the historical and tourism base of the county. Her celebratory marker, down an unpaved road, easy to miss. Soaring nearby, curious juxtaposition—Fort Sumner State Monument and military graveyard; Bosque Redondo Memorial Museum, repository of Apache and Navajo memories. Linked forever on this homestead she and her husband donated.

Navajo architect, David Sloan, combines Navajo hogan and Apache tipi in the Museum's design. Reverent memorial to Mescalero Apache (N'de) and Navajo (Diné) peoples' internment at the garrison. The ones who survived the long walk. The ones who did not. The ones who crept out in the night—fled famine, pestilence, death. The ones who stayed to tend the flames, conceal their brothers' steps. The ones who would not settle alien lands. The ones who crossed the Rio Grande. Wept at Mount Taylor's sacred sight.

From one hall to another, the story marches in beauty. Gentle. Relentless. Vintage photographs Maps. Ledgers. Documents. Exquisite beaded and silver jewelry and clothes. Face to face murals of interminable chain of bedraggled, weary prisoners. Men, women, children. Trudging, falling, standing, lying still. Watched, across the narrow winding canyon, by blue-uniformed White Eyes. Sneering, vacant, hate-filled. Some look kind, perhaps ashamed. We emerge mute. See, painted above a doorway, the count-down, month by month, of captives held at the camp. Human misery whittled down to lines. Tangible joins ineffable.

fires dot night

shadows fill empty spaces

hide flying braves

homeward-bound Diné

wagons, horses, sheep, mules, goats

ten miles long

reservations

tribes no longer free to roam

turquoise tears

We drive to Roswell under a cloudless sky and the weight of that history. Spend the night. Rise ready for the day. Head west on NM-380. Look for marker honoring Louise Massey Mable (1902-1983). Original Rhinestone Cowgirl. Among the first female radio stars in the 1930s. Western songs sung en español e inglés. Landscape subdued. Grizzled-green rocky flat desert . Knobby mesquite. Alas! At mile post 313, no marcador for Louise. Instead, marker for dead Atlas Missile Silos site.

Disappointment doesn't linger. The drive along Rio Hondo past Riverside, Picacho, Tinnie in slant autumn light magical. Conical hills rearguard gold-patinated alamos. Shriveled leaves chatter like castanets in the wind. Black angus punctuate fields. Poplars rise sinewy from carpet of chartreuse grama. Shimmering mirage of wild broncos—brown-gray-pinto-chestnut—thunder headlong into flock of long-legged turkeys. Flurry of feathers, dust, gobbles.

Road between Lincoln and Capitan gravelly. We cruise mesmerized by the valley. Hunter-green elms line one side. On the other, plants and small trees have dropped anchor in the creviced wall of craggy hills. Hanging gardens! Oh, Babylon! Farther on, a tiny fenced campo santo sits lonely a few feet down from the road. Its ancient graves adorned with fresh coat of plastic flowers and miniature American flags. Where did they come from?

Just then, a roar behind us. Charcoal black pick-up crowds our Ford Escape into the almost non-existent shoulder as it passes. Through fog of toxic-diesel-fumes we spy a middle finger flicked. Irate eyes flashed. The huge Stars-and-Stripes lashed to its bumper snaps wildly as the truck swerves back onto our lane. Disappears like Beelzebub in an explosion of acrid smoke. Unearthly apparition. At first, we think we drove too slowly for them. Then realize "H for America" sticker on our rear windshield a more likely reason for their fury.

We stop. Unfurl our fists. Deep breathe. Slow our hearts. Then move on. Find marker for Eve Ball (1890-1984) in a gravel turn-out. Teacher, Author, Preservationist. Honest, Patient, Dedicated. Saved oral histories of Apache people—Warm Springs, Lipan, Mescalero, Chiricahua. Children of Geronimo, Cochise, Victorio and their warriors. Imagine! Men and women whose families and way of life had been disrupted, derailed, destroyed by the power of our government, entrusting their long-heard stories to one not their own. One they may have called "enemy" not long ago.

Atlas shoulders Earth
humans bear
one grain at a time

the road home
oxblood sky
in rearview

trust
each word
a compact

*   *   *

* Haibun is a prose poem narrative of a journey interspersed with one or more haiku.

 **Sylvia Ramos Cruz** is inspired to write by art, women's lives, and every-day injustices. Her award-winning prose, poetry and photographs appear in local and national publications. Ongoing projects focus on woman suffrage in NM, road markers celebrating historic NM women, and journaling during this pandemic.

Biography/Memoir   Bronze Medal
Robert Stuart

WHEELCHAIR LIBERTY

All of us were maimed, but we were young and vigorous, and we were still Marines. Between us, there was empathy, little sympathy, and no pity. But, camaraderie is ingrained in Marine Corps ethos, and it played a vital role in the recovery of the forty amputees in Ward 76B of the Oakland Naval Hospital.

No matter how bad off an amputee was, there was always someone in the ward in worse shape. If a one-legged man began to feel self-pity, another Marine, missing an arm and leg, would chide him about not appreciating his luck at surviving combat, and bolster his confidence by pointing to Corporal Davis, who was proudly practicing his stride on his artificial legs.

One morning, a group of patients huddled around the bed of a newly arrived Marine. He'd spent a night moaning from pain and screaming through nightmares. They talked to him in subdued tones: encouraging not sympathizing. I only caught snatches of the conversation and asked one of the men as he hobbled away on crutches, what they had said. "It's none of your business. Drop it," he said.

A sanctum existed among the patients, which had only two requirements for inclusion: be a Marine and be maimed in combat. Although I had the two-basic qualifications, my amputations were paltry compared to the other amputees. An enemy bullet had torn off most of my right hand and the little finger of my left. I felt like a goldbricker, who only qualified as an associate member. I wanted to earn my spurs and acceptance into that inner sanctum.

After a few weeks, the doctors reduced my bandages to elastic wraps, and I was ready to tag along with any patients who needed help on a jaunt into town. The first takers were Bill and Steven. A mine had blown off both of Bill's legs below the knees. Steven was also the victim of a mine, but both his legs were gone above the knees. Neither had gotten their artificial legs, so both were still in wheelchairs.

Don, an arm amputee who had been shot through the wrist, also decided to join the foray. At the field hospital in Vietnam, the doctors had tried to save his hand by reconnecting tendons and blood vessels and closing the wound. It became septic, but the doctors didn't detect the gangrene because the wound was sealed. When they discovered the infection, they amputated half his lower arm, trying to save his elbow joint. Even with the open wound that could be monitored and scraped clean, it wasn't enough. The gangrene spread to his elbow. They couldn't take any more risks. The doctors amputated his arm above the elbow leaving a short stump to be sure all putrefaction was removed.

While I was napping one afternoon, the three cajoled a regular visitor nicknamed Bulkhead—after the steel walls on a ship—into driving them into town. Bulkhead was a bald, pot-bellied, old guy who hung around the hospital visiting the patients in 76B and running errands. He often harangued us about being wimps compared to the Marines he had visited during the Korean War. He shamed us with tales of hoisting patients in body casts over the perimeter wall to escape the hospital for a night in town.

Bulkhead had two stipulations: someone more able-bodied would have to go along, and he would only drop the group off at a bar and then leave. They would have to get back to the hospital via a short taxi ride. The two, double-leg amputees wheeled high speed across the ward to my bed. As they came to a screeching stop, they explained the situation, and I agreed to go along. Steven charged back across the ward and told Bulkhead, "You got a deal. Frank's goin' with us."

All three put on their dress uniforms. Bill and Steven folded their trouser legs up from the bottoms of their stumps, and pinned them squarely. Don pinned his right sleeve up near the shoulder. All wore Purple Hearts and battle ribbons. They were proud of who they were, proud of their battle scars, and anxious for a romp in the Oakland bars. I wore civilian clothes. My uniforms were still somewhere in Southeast Asia.

Only I was authorized regular liberty—allowed to leave the hospital at will. The other three were not allowed to leave without specific permission verified by a liberty card. The amenable duty nurse busied herself with a task elsewhere as we prepared for our departure and wheeled out of the ward to Bulkhead's waiting station wagon. One at a time, I picked the two, double-leg amputees up from their chairs and placed them on the back seat. Don wedged himself between them. Lifting a man with no legs is easy, but the lightness and unnatural balance is eerie. *Fate had been so kind to me.* I folded the chairs and put them through the rear hatch behind the back seat. Bulkhead slid behind the steering wheel. I rode shotgun.

Darkness covered our loading and escape as our car rolled away from the building. Ahead, floodlights lit the gate area like an all-night gas station on a lonely road. The two-lane street split around the guard shack: one lane going in each direction. As we approached, Bulkhead asked if we all had liberty cards.

"Bulkhead, it's a little late for that question," I said. "Nobody's got a liberty card."

Bulkhead sputtered profanities for a few seconds, then reached down on the seat, picked up a porkpie hat, and jammed it low on his bald head. The hat concealed little of his face, but it transformed Bulkhead from an old man full of hot air into our cohort-in-crime.

The navy guard, wearing crisp whites, a Dixie-cup cap, and a duty belt complete with sidearm and polished nightstick, stepped out of the shack to check our liberty cards. Bulkhead stomped on the gas pedal. The engine of the old woody clanked and banged. Gray smoke belched from the exhaust pipe. The guard jumped back as we rumbled past. Through the rear window, I watched him give a nonchalant shrug as we raced around the corner. It wasn't the first time he had seen Marine patients run the gate. He knew we weren't going far, and we'd be back.

The four of us slid across the seats as the old wagon leaned through the sharp turn onto the highway, its tires squealing. The wagon leveled off and the four of us hooted praise for Bulkhead's gumption and driving skill. Bill reached over the seat, pulled the hat off Bulkhead's noggin, and patted his hairless dome.

He drove to a nearby lounge where we insisted he come inside so we could buy him a drink. A dozen round tables were scattered around the room, each with a small lamp in the center and surrounded by four well-padded lounge chairs. Dim, indirect lighting reflected off the ceiling illuminating an array of expensive liquor bottles on shelves behind the bar. The lounge was a dark place: walnut paneled walls and nut-brown carpeting. A few men dressed in dark suits and white-collar shirts sat on stools with padded backs at the bar sipping martinis. All the tables were empty, so there was no waitress. The ambience was elegant and relaxing. Loud and rowdy would have been more our style, but it was Bulkhead's choice and we wanted the party to begin.

I pulled two chairs away from one of the tables, and Steven and Bill maneuvered their wheelchairs into the vacated spots. The bartender came from behind the bar and took our order. Only Bulkhead and I were of legal drinking age, but the bartender didn't question our ages and served us a round of drinks. After Bulkhead gulped his down and bolted the place, I waved for another round. The bartender ambled over to our table. "Sorry," he said, "but this time, I gotta see IDs."

I fished mine out of my wallet, passed it across the table and tried to pull off a bluff to cover my cohorts. "Did you dumb shits leave your wallets at the hospital?"

"Yeah, no lumps," Steven answered.

I looked across to the bartender, "We don't put anything in the pockets of a dress uniform. They're tailored and wallets and cigarettes make lumps."

Steven played the sympathy card, normally a distasteful tactic, but we were desperate. "We usually stuff those things in our socks where they don't show, but we're a little short on shoes and socks."

The bartender was apologetic. "If it was up to me I'd serve you. Those guys at the bar are regulars and they're pissed because I served you, and they're pals with the owner."

A couple of white-collar assholes conniving to deprive us a drink. The situation enraged me, but my companions were content with moving on and finding a saloon with an ambience more suited to us.

The next bar was three blocks down the street. In the sixties, the sidewalks didn't have sloped curbs at the intersections for wheelchairs. When we came to a curb, I rocked Bill's wheelchair onto its back wheels and eased it onto the curb. An experienced wheelchair rider can rock his chair onto its back wheels and stay balanced in that position, even while wheeling backward or over obstacle such as curbs. Bill and Steven hadn't yet mastered those skills, but Steven announced, "I wanna try this by myself."

"I'll stand behind you," I said. "Give you a little boost if you need it."

"No, stand back. I wanna do it on my own."

There was no traffic, no other people in sight, and the intersection was dark except for a dim streetlight across the road. It was a good place for the try. Steven rocked onto his back wheels without a problem, but with no legs for a forward counter-balance, when he rolled into the curb, the chair flipped backwards, somersaulting him onto the pavement. Steven sprawled in the street as Bill, Don and I doubled over laughing so hard tears ran down our cheeks. Even Steven was laughing as he righted his chair and hauled himself into it. It was one of those things you laugh or cry about.

That episode instigated the wheelchair train. Steven's very short leg stumps did not protrude past the front of his chair, enabling him to get close enough to the back of Bill's chair to hold its handles. I was the caboose and pushed from the back of Steven's chair. We avoided curbs by running down the edge of the street with Don leading the way screaming warnings to us and the few passing cars.

The next bar was our kind of place. Small, tile floor, simple wooden tables and chairs, four-legged bar stools, and no mirrors. A slight odor of stale beer and sweat hung in the air. Ten or twelve patrons, including three women, all wearing jeans, work shirts, and hard hats, sat at the bar. We picked a table by a window and near the restroom, features of tactical importance. I went to the bar and bought a round of drinks.

The patrons began a friendly conversation with typical questions, "You guys from the Navy hospital? Were you in Vietnam? How they treating you?" Within minutes, a patron wearing a sleeveless t-shirt, a blurred tattoo of a hula dancer on his upper arm, sauntered up to our table with a round of drinks. Soon, another patron brought over a round of drinks. Then another patron, and another, and another until drinks and beer bottles covered our table. The party was on. As soon as we emptied a glass or beer bottle, somebody whisked it away. When there was room for another round, a group at the bar rolled dice for what they called the *privilege* of buying us the next round.

Within an hour, we were plastered and the conversations had reached party-level volume and bawdiness. Steven wanted to talk face-to-face and close-up with everybody at the bar. He wheeled over, and I lifted him onto an empty stool. He hoisted himself from the stool to the bar, and from there he scooted on his butt from end-to-end. None seemed bothered as they took their drinks and cigarettes off the bar when he scooted past. He was especially interested in chatting-up the ladies, none of whom were beauty contest winners. But, all were friendly, cheerful, and had the body parts to firmly round out the back side of their jeans and poke out the front of their t-shirts.

As the evening wore on, Steven got drunker, lost his balance easing back onto a barstool, and crashed to the floor. The shocked crowd went silent. The three of us were indifferent. We knew he could handle the situation. Steven wasn't hurt and pulled himself into his wheelchair. I lifted him from the chair, and plopped him back on the bar. Even so, the bartender was worried about Steven hurting himself, and restricted his gymnastics to the barstools.

About that time, we encountered a problem. The bathroom door was too narrow for the wheelchairs. When Steven or Bill needed to piss, I went into the bathroom and held the door open as the pisser rolled his chair up to the doorway. From there, I lifted him out of the chair, plopped him on the toilet, stepped out, and shut the door. Inside, the pisser wrestled his trousers down and peed from a sitting position. He hollered when finished, and I'd go in, wrap my arms under his armpits, and lift him off the toilet seat. We'd wobble around the tiny room bouncing off the walls like two drunks screwing in a phone booth until the pisser got his trousers up and zipped. Then I'd set him back on the toilet seat while I opened the door, lifted him again, and we'd push and wiggle through the doorway until I could plunk him back in the wheelchair.

The system worked okay for a while, but as we got drunker and my arms got tired, we needed a plan *B*. Also, I was spending more time around the bathroom helping people piss than drinking. Fortunately, Bill had anticipated pissing problems and had brought along a duck.

"Duck" was our nickname for the long-necked pitcher designed to lay on its side, used by bedridden, male patients for urinating. In those days, the duck was stainless steel and reusable as was the bedpan, which we tagged the "silver saddle."

The next time Bill had to empty his bladder, he rolled up to our table, slipped the duck under it and pissed in the duck. Then handed it to me and I carried it to the bathroom for dumping. Plan *B* had only one fault. Very few things make me vomit, but two of those things are piss and shit. I emptied the duck once and only gagged, but vomiting was inevitable. I couldn't continue; I was a failure as a piss dumper. Don was limited by his one arm. He was also snot-flying drunk and staggering so badly that he had to use his only arm to wave around for balance like a tight-rope walker.

Steven had a plan *C*. After his first piss in the duck, he removed the wing nuts holding the bottom of the window screen behind us and pushed the screen far enough away from the frame to stick the duck through and dump the piss.

After a few hours in the saloon, it was time to head back to the hospital. None of the patrons were sober enough to drive. So, the bartender called a taxi and the patrons started taking up a collection for our taxi fare. We turned down the money. Accepting it would have been an abuse of the generosity of that outstanding bunch of blue-collar workers.

The taxi driver was a good soul, but he wasn't willing to risk his license racing through the gate past the guard. He stopped around the corner from the gate, unloaded the chairs, and helped me get Steven and Bill into them. He refused our tip, thanked us for our sacrifices, and wished us luck.

The road to the gate was slightly downhill. Bill powered the wheels on the lead chair as Steven hung on in the second chair. I pushed from behind. We gained speed until I was bounding along, no longer pushing, just trying to hang on as the wheelchairs kept gaining momentum. Don sprinted ahead, his one arm pumping frantically, as the empty right sleeve, which had come loose, flapped behind him. Blaring repeatedly, "Make way, train coming through!"

We swerved through the sharp turn to the gate, Bill's inside wheel lifted off the ground. Steven grunted as he struggled to keep Bill upright. As he leaned to the inside, Bill was blaring, "Oh fuck, oh fuck." The movement tightened our turn slightly and the wheelchair train swung through the gate close to the navy guard. He casually stepped back, shrugged, and waved us past with a smirk, accustomed to drunk Marines chugging along in wheelchairs.

I have heard stories of civilians unduly treating Vietnam veterans contemptuously. I believe the frequency and intensity of such treatment has been highly exaggerated. Through the passing years, most Americans have treated us with respect and appreciation. The rare exceptions were usually in the academic and white-collar worlds.

*   *   *

Biography/Memoir Poetry   Bronze Medal
John Cornish

SPLITS

(Same Birthday)

We rush one long laugh-length down, climb puffing,
perch on the brink in a saucer sled,
snowfall coating us, the scent from your hair
more pungent than pine pitch or candle smoke.
We are born just inside Aquarius,
me 44, you infinity
upside right and the sum of your potent
razzle dazzle deep open eyes. Today
you are eight, too cool to care about it,
while I'm inspired by it, by our
balance in years, and by my halved life,
though I might mean something sad by decay,
since growing old splits youth into age.
But I rejoice in the scale of my life
as measured by yours, my heartbeat
quickened by the scope of our adventures
some day to be sung by your memory.
We launch, snow flying from our future
into our faces, sled spinning frontward
backward frontward bouncing bouncing, your arms

wrapped fast around my legs during our wild
rush down cold conductivity. We lurch
to a stop, my butt suffers, but
we both split the lumbering air
with our intimate and ageless laughter.

* * *

John Cornish
Retired college administrator and English
instructor, I am looking for critique partners to
exchange draft novels or several shorter works.
These days I write urban fantasy, but appreciate all
prose genres, including non-fiction. Poetry is
welcome too! jcornish643@gmail.com. Go
Dems!

SECTION TWO

ANIMAL STORIES AND POETRY

You'll find more than just a human's best friend in these stories.

Animal Stories   Gold Medal
Donald De Noon

WE'RE NOT TALKING
SESAME STREET HERE

For 14 years, I intentionally decided not to have a dog. I did not need or want all the responsibility: the feeding, bathing, grooming, walking, cleaning-up-after, and any other attendant duties. It was clear to me that having a dog would complicate my independent lifestyle in retirement.

But in June of 2003, while on a road trip through the Pacific Northwest, I began to rethink my decision about remaining pet-free. Several households I visited on that journey included dogs as family members. It was while I was with friends in Port Angeles, Washington, that a little bundle of fur hopped onto my lap to welcome me as a guest into her home. Her soulful eyes looked into mine. And, I swear, she winked at me.

She was the one who made me question my no-dog-policy.

After returning from my trip, I began to notice the bond between my next door neighbor Dan, and his dog Ernie. He's a really smart and playful dog. And I caught myself watching enviously as Dan and Ernie headed out each day on their walks. I started fantasizing what it would be like to have an intelligent, companionable dog like Ernie; one I could walk, romp and run with. Well, maybe not run.

On a Friday afternoon in July, I decided to visit the Westside Animal Shelter to check out the dog population. And what do you know? One appealing little guy caught my attention. He had a dark tan coat with white markings on his face and chest. When I placed my hand on the wire gate to his cage, he sniffed it and his happy tail wouldn't stop wagging. I spoke softly to him, "Hi there, fella." He responded by cocking his head to one side. He was adorable. I quickly wrote down the identification number displayed on his cage which I would present to one of the personnel. As I entered the reception area, I noticed a long line of people had formed waiting to talk to the only employee on duty. I decided not to wait, but to go home and enter a request on the shelter's website, instructing them to hold that adorable brown dog for me

I pulled into my driveway, stepped out of the car and went directly to Dan's house. Both he and Ernie met me on their porch and I started telling Dan about the dog. When I mentioned my plan to return to the shelter on Monday to complete the adoption, Dan indicated an interest to go with me. I told him the time I planned to leave and Dan said he'd be ready.

That evening I sat at my computer and logged onto the shelter's website to enter all pertinent data about the tan dog with white markings. I stated I would return to the shelter on Monday morning to sign papers, pay the fee and pick up *my* dog. Then I hit "send."

As we planned, Dan met me on Monday and we went to the shelter. Upon entering the building, I presented the ID number to the woman at the desk and said, "I'm here to adopt my dog." She checked the records to be sure the dog was still available. Then she looked at me and said, "I'm so sorry. That dog was put down over the weekend. We keep each pet only a limited time if they are not adopted."

I was stunned and suddenly felt sick as I thought about that adorable dog dying unnecessarily. I turned away and thought about leaving, but I didn't. Instead, I looked directly at the woman and spoke to her accusingly.

"But I went online to let you know I wanted that dog. I followed your rules for placing an online 'hold.' And you killed him anyway?"

"I'm very sorry, sir, the order for him to be put down was made before anyone had an opportunity to see your request." And then in a cheerier tone she added, "But we still have so many others. Why not take another tour of the kennel?"

I scowled at Dan. Dan scowled at the woman before turning back to me and saying, "I know you wanted that particular dog, but why don't we take a look at the others that are here now?" Reluctantly, I nodded. Dan led the way.

We passed cage after cage and kept on walking. Then Dan paused, dropped to his knees and stuck his fingers through the wire of a cage. The excited canine on the other side wiggled all over and sniffed Dan's fingers. Dan stroked the dog's nose and began talking to him. Then he put his face right next to the wire and the dog kissed him. Dan looked up at me and smiled.

"This is the one," he declared with confidence. "But, of course, it's your decision."

I knelt down just as Dan had done and the dog responded to me in an equally eager and affectionate way. Dan was right. It was, indeed, *the* one. I noted the information on the cage and returned to talk to the woman at the desk.

She carefully and kindly assisted me in filling out the required forms and gave me instructions to return the next day with a collar, a leash and payment for the adoption.

Tuesday I got up and made my way to the West Side Shelter. When asked, I told an employee holding a pen and pad the name I had chosen for my new four-pawed companion. He wrote the name down along with other information that would be entered onto a chip to be implanted under the skin on my dog's shoulder. I paid the bill and received paperwork indicating a neutered, two year-old Australian Cattle Dog Mix was now mine. And I realized I was his as well. A momentous day for both of us.

The attendant brought my dog to me. I put the collar around his neck and attached the leash. He did not resist. He eagerly tugged on his leash as we headed to the car. But after I opened the back door on the driver's side and encouraged him to jump in, it was as though his paws were glued to the ground. He was extremely nervous, so I reached down, patted him gently on the head and said as soothingly as I could, "Easy boy. Easy." He calmed a little, so I reached under him and lifted my skittish friend to place him on the back seat of the car. He continued to shake nervously as I closed the door.

All the way home, I spoke to him in a calm and steady voice trying to allay any fears he was experiencing.

I pulled the car into the driveway, turned off the engine, stepped out and opened the rear driver's side door. He immediately jumped out. No more shaking. I led him to the porch and, after opening the door, I removed his leash. He entered the living room and then proceeded to sniff his way throughout the house. He ended his tour in the kitchen where I placed a bowl of water on the floor. He lapped it up and splashed water all around. He was really thirsty.

Before stepping through the door which led to the back yard, I reattached the leash. And I accompanied him as he examined and sniffed the perimeter next to the fence. He stopped to take a pee and then we headed next door for his formal introduction to Dan and Ernie.

Dan knelt on one knee, drew the dog's face toward his and received a sloppy kiss. "See," Dan said, "He remembers me from the shelter." Ernie, on the other hand, wanting nothing to do with this new dog, turned and went back inside.

Dan stood, looked at me and asked, "Have you given him a name?"

"As a matter of fact, Dan, I have. Meet Bert."

Dan gave an approving nod which was accented by a broad grin.

They wouldn't be sleeping in the same bed like the friends on Sesame Street, but Bert and Ernie became next door neighbors on that special Tuesday in July.

* * *

As a Sixth Grade student in Indianapolis, **Don De Noon** was exposed to poetry. It became a lifelong infection. A college class titled The Novel helped Don find his voice writing prose. Years later, he's grateful to SouthWest Writers for providing competitions in which to demonstrate award winning skills.

Animal Poetry   **Gold Medal**
Jesse Ehrenberg

THE CAT AND I

I have seen the full moon
like a ghost
in the daytime,

and watched as it
traveled
across the sky,

and I could feel myself
turning
with the earth,

and wondered
at the
miracle of me

standing on this
planet,
in this universe

that we can only
pretend
to understand,

and I have turned,
and
looked around,

and seen the cat
sitting
in the yard,

her eyes
bright
with thought,

as she looked around,
and
reflected on her world,

and I can see no
difference
between us at all.

*   *   *

Jesse Ehrenberg started writing poetry as a teenager and has never seen a reason to stop. His poems have been published in multiple local anthologies. His book, *SURPRISE!*, won prizes in the New Mexico Press Women contest, and a Silver Award in the inaugural Margaret Randall Poetry Book Contest.

Animals
Patricia Walkow

Silver Medal

MARKED-DOWN DOG

I met Bing on the Internet. He was on sale. A mahogany-toned, one-year-old Belgian Tervuren, he lived in Ogallala, Nebraska. I lived in New Mexico.

My husband, Walter, and I had just lost our half-Belgian rescue dog, Cheyenne. After his death, the silence invaded our home with sinister tendrils of loss. We needed another dog, preferably a Belgian, but a dog who *needed* a new home.

Belgians aren't as popular in the United States as other breeds, so we started an online search. For five weeks, no Belgians were available, but our name was in some queue somewhere in the ether. At week six, Walter received an email about a young male—Bing—who needed a home.

"Why is he available?" I wondered.

The breeder easily answered my question: Bing was A head-shy show dog, growled at the judges, and was super protective when on his leash. She couldn't breed or show him.

"OK, he has issues," remarked my husband. "We'll work with him."

We offered to adopt him.

The comprehensive application required us to provide photos of our backyard and the dog's sleeping area inside the house. We provided references. Would the breeder run a criminal background check and credit report on us? Some questions required calculations: "How much do you think is reasonable to spend on yearly veterinary care?" and "What is the cost to feed and equip a dog each year?" and "Will you be carrying health insurance for the dog?" Interesting how my husband and I were asked all these questions, but it was the *dog* who had problems.

Three weeks after we submitted our application, Walter contacted the breeder and learned we were in the running for being awarded–yes, *awarded*—

was the actual word used—Bing. Not that he would be free, but his price was reduced because of his issues.

Two other parties were also interested in Bing, and the competition was on.

We sent regular communications indicating what a beautiful dog Bing was, based on the photos sent to us. We sent photographs of our previous dog, Cheyenne, accompanying us on vacation at Big Sur, walking in nearby parks, and eating at outdoor restaurants.

Still, there was no decision about who would get...I mean be awarded...Bing.

To clinch the deal, I sent the breeder reprints of my newspaper column, *Dog's Day Out*, which was published in our local newspaper. When Cheyenne and I visited different venues in the Los Angeles area "we" wrote about all the great things for dogs and their humans to do. The column apparently made an impression and we were—here's that word again—awarded young Bing. There was one stipulation. The dog must be neutered, so the shyness trait would not be passed on. The breeder would have him fixed before we picked him up, and the fact she would take care of it raised her esteem in my eyes.

* * *

Two days after Christmas, we drove 613 miles from Albuquerque to Ogallala. We spent the night in a local motel and drove to the breeder's spread the next morning. We were greeted by a posse of Belgian Tervurens of various sizes, ages, and colors. Bing's father looked like a bear; his mother was dainty. His brothers, sisters, aunts, uncles, and cousins welcomed us.

But not Bing. He stood apart, wary.

We entered the breeder's house accompanied by an entourage of dogs that rivaled the President's Secret Service detail in number, if not in serious, dour behavior. All tails were wagging, all lips smiling, except for Bing. With one whistle from the gal who bred them, each settled into their respective dog cage. Except for Bing. He clung to the breeder.

My husband and I gave each other a knowing look. "We can handle it," I reassured him.

The breeder gave us Bing's favorite toy. The other dogs followed us as we exited the house, and Bing's mother and father jumped into our car. Bing stood beside the car, refusing to get in.

I coaxed his parents out of the car, and Walter guided Bing inside. I felt guilty taking our new dog away from the security of his home and family.

Since I was driving, my husband turned in his seat and paid attention to our new pet. Although he was *our* dog, with all the attention my husband lavished on him, by the time we got to Denver he had become Walter's dog.

* * *

I didn't like "Bing" as a name, and the dog's American Kennel Club name was "Aktion Pak Behaving Badly," a moniker he later lived up to quite thoroughly by rummaging through garbage pails, bounding over walls, eating sneakers, and munching on sunglasses. But we didn't know all that, then. We just knew we had our new dog in the car with us. As I drove and enjoyed the beautiful images of sun and clouds casting rippling shadows on the vast expanses of rolling range land to the east, I asked, "What do you think of the name 'Ranger'?"

Walter nodded his head, "I like it."

From that moment, Bing became Ranger. He loved riding in the car, excelled at agility obstacle course competitions, and was game for anything—hiking, al fresco dining, doggie day care, dog parks, Halloween parades, hotel stays with his humans, and endless rounds of fetch. Yet, he remained a shy dog who felt safest with Walter.

Our Ranger died not long ago at fifteen-and-a-half and we cherish the memories of our marked-down Internet dog.

* * *

Patricia Walkow is an award-winning author and editor. She wrote an acclaimed biography, *The War Within, the Story of Josef.* She has contributed to many anthologies and edited several. Her editing work and short stories have been recognized for excellence. A member of the Corrales Writing Group and SouthWest Writers, her work appears regularly in print and online.

Animals Poetry   Silver Medal
Dodici Azpadu

COWS

Black cows pasture
far below the deck

heads down
grazing hours each day

then on the ground
hours more

chewing their cud
leisure comfort essential

milking on instinctive
schedule and socializing

with favorites in the herd
no mind for the deck watcher

layering their effortless
process with idle questions

juniper shrubs gnarled
wordless volcanic rocks

watching from sunset
behind the scene.

*   *   *

Dodici Azpadu has published poetry and novels throughout a long writing career. She has lived on both coasts and many places in between. She has made an art of falling between the cracks. Currently, she lives and teaches in New Mexico. Her website is www.dodici-azpadu.com

Animals
Paula Nixon

Bronze Medal

THE VISITOR

She showed up on a mid-July afternoon, all four feet of her stretched out in the shade up against the house. I had been expecting her for years, but not on the patio, her tail less than ten feet away from my back door.

I kept my distance, studied the row of dark brown butterfly-shaped markings that ran along the length of her tan, scaled back. Pretty, but she looked like a rattlesnake to me. I didn't know enough at the time to look at the shape of her head. Triangular, venomous; rounded, non-venomous. And I certainly didn't get close enough to check out her pupils—elliptical or round. But I did lean forward just a bit to check out her tail and didn't see any rattles. She never moved. I assumed she was aware of my presence, but couldn't tell for sure.

Since neither one of us seemed to feel threatened, I quietly opened the screen door and was surprised by the sound of my calm voice telling my husband, Dave, about the visitor. He and I took turns—one kept an eye on her and snapped photos while the other perused herpetological websites, trying to identify her species.

Like many people I harbor a serious fear of snakes that has nothing to do with any firsthand experience. But it runs deep. A few weeks before this snake showed up on my doorstep, I visited an outdoor exhibit of plant and animal life in the Mojave Desert. Although it was a 99-degree day in Las Vegas, I felt a chill as I hurried past the snakes in their glass enclosures. I didn't pause, not even a glance. As a kid I heard tales from Dad and his survey crew, who worked out in fields and along remote roads of western Kansas, about encounters with the limbless reptiles. Once or twice I found one of the crew's trophies—rattles cut off the tails of the dead creatures—on the dashboard of the company pickup. The half-serious joke at our dinner table was that ALL snakes were rattlesnakes.

Snakes have had a bad reputation from the beginning. Turn to the third chapter of Genesis and you'll find the too-smart-for-his-own-good serpent in the Garden of Eden chatting it up with Eve, telling her that nothing bad will happen if she eats from the tree of knowledge. Wrong. Even though Eve had been warned, the snake took the fall. God was unsparing: "Because thou hast done this, thou art cursed above all cattle, and above every beast of the field; upon thy belly shalt thou go, and dust shalt thou eat all the days of thy life."

And in the dust is where I always expected to run into a snake, not reclining at my back door. For more than twenty years I have lived on a wooded acre in the foothills of the Sangre de Cristo Mountains—lots of pine trees, rocks, and dirt—plenty of places for a snake to soak up the sun or snooze in the shade. Every time I walk up the gravel driveway to take out the trash or pick up the mail, I feel my toes curl in my open-toed sandals and wish I had remembered to put on sneakers.

Scientists are still trying to figure out if we are born with a fear of snakes or if it's learned. Humans and snakes have been evolving together for over forty million years, so it makes sense that we might have developed a natural wariness of this reptile since some of them can hurt or even kill us. Researchers have conducted studies with six-month-old babies, gauging the difference in their reactions to photos of flowers versus snakes by watching the pupils of their eyes. There is not universal agreement, but at the very least, it appears that humans have an elevated awareness of snakes from an early age.

This snake, relaxing on my patio, was my first encounter with one of the reptiles in the wild. I wondered what had attracted her to this specific shady spot. It was hot, 90 degrees, but not unusual for a July day in northern New Mexico. It had been a rainy month so far, twice as much as normal, but even with that extra inch of moisture the ground was dry. Maybe it was the color of the recently-stained concrete, a mottled brown, a hue similar to her own. And it was a quiet place, at least until she was discovered.

Forty-six species of snakes live in New Mexico; eight of them are venomous and seven of those are different types of rattlesnakes. The photos on the websites confused me: gopher snakes, hog-nosed snakes, rat snakes— all in varying shades of tan and brown with dark blotches. My snake didn't look exactly like any of those on NM Herpetological Society's website. I sent an email with a photo to the president of the Society and received a quick response, "Bull snake, harmless."

According to the field guide, bull snakes do look like rattlesnakes and, when threatened, puff themselves up and imitate the rattle by shaking their tails. Big snakes, they can grow up to seven feet long. Ours was a small one and at that, Dave estimated she was much shorter than my guess of four feet. More like two feet, maybe two and a half. After several minutes of our chatter and the repeated opening and closing of the screen door, the snake slithered along the wall to a spot behind a shallow pan filled with potting soil. But her tail gave her away and we followed.

Dave was the one who identified the snake as female, but didn't say why. It was a hunch; there was no way to know from where we observed her. Bull snakes have few predators—raptors and humans. Many don't survive crossing roads and highways, their large size a tradeoff for speed. Others die at the tip of a shovel, misidentified as the dangerous snakes they mimic in an effort to scare off those who would do them harm.

After she left and disappeared down the hill, I felt like I had passed a test, one of my own making. When the snake appeared I didn't panic, didn't call animal control, didn't rush to the garage for a spade.

I haven't seen her again. The seasons have changed several times and summer is once again approaching. Bull snakes can live ten years or longer in the wild, so it's likely she's still out in my untamed backyard, recently emerged from winter hibernation, hunting mice and gophers.

*   *   *

Paula Nixon is a freelance writer who lives in Northern New Mexico and writes about wildlife. See more of her work at paulanixon.com

SECTION THREE

SCIENCE FICTION/FANTASY

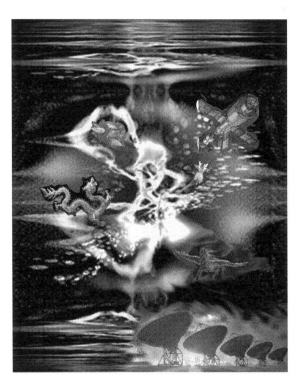

Prepare to be transported to startling futures and almost familiar planets. Great selections to expand your thinking.

Science Fiction/Fantasy   Gold Medal
John Cornish

MEEKER HAS RIGHTS

A body crash-landed in the back yard. Through his living room window Lyall saw the body bounce twice on the ground, flung by the cataclysmic winds. *What in this hell??!*

Severe storms surged infrequently up the Rio Grande Valley, the result of the confluence of surface heating and of moisture that high-pressure ridges pushed up from the Gulf of Mexico. The violent winds, powerful lightning strikes, and overlapping booms of thunder, often accompanied by deluges of rain, could last for hours. Although great innovations in the past decade had stopped the planet's march toward a total environmental catastrophe, the dreadful droughts and wild weather continued. Pandemics and other consequences of the human degradation of the planet had led to the deaths of millions and the extinction of all kinds of other life. A deep complex of guilt pervaded many souls.

Lyall had sat down to read just before the body bounced. He had been checking his electrical system. All houses in the Southwest had tall, seemingly spindly copper and aluminum poles, which captured and stored in batteries the electrical energy of lightning strikes. The power had gone out briefly after a huge strike, lights flickering dark, motivating Lyall to check the system. Lyall and Guadalupe, his wife, had turned on the lights only because the clouds of the storm masked Albuquerque, darkening the afternoon like a solar eclipse.

Staring out the window at the dark bulge on the ground, Lyall watched the rain pummel the body. A moment later, shocked, he realized it was Meeker!

Lyall had never learned Meeker's first name, but everyone, including Meeker himself, just called him Meeker, even his hundred and maybe one- or two-year-old mother, Diana.

On his daily walks with his dogs, Lyall had observed that Meeker, since about six months ago, liked to sit in his front yard. Meeker kept a large, weatherworn equipale chair near his lightning rod. He perched on the back of the equipale in a posture that reminded Lyall of a large raptor high on a branch of the dead cottonwoods along the Rio Grande River, now a mere trickle of its historic current.

Meeker would settle on the back of the chair, his feet flexible enough to clench the spine, the back of his wrists on his hips, and glare unblinkingly at passers-by while waving his elbows slightly, like wings ruffling for flight. He appeared ready to launch into the air to hunt, seize, and eviscerate.

Lyall knew that Meeker had moved into a shift-shaping. Lyall preferred the phrase, "shift-shaping," to mitigate in his mind commonly held views about shapeshifting as embodied in terms like "werewolf," "changeling," and "skinwalker." He knew that shift-shaping was not supernatural and not evil, and not caused by bites, scratches, or blood: it was no infection. He had developed a theory about why they happened. That theory also inspired his hard work to ensure, given his talents, that he did not become an object of curiosity, or of alarm.

In Lyall's experience, most shift-shapers ended up in some sort of facility, diagnosed with severe mental, behavioral, or physical disabilities, or a combination. Even with the physical changes considered, shift-shapers became to others something Lyall knew they were not: crazy. Shunned, so institutionalized, they suffered terribly. If not institutionalized, death occurred. A city bus crushed one young man shift-shaping into a Sulcata tortoise while he tried to cross a busy street at his plodding pace.

Lyall looked closely at Meeker crumpled in his back yard. What should he do? The storm was awful. If he ran out into it, Lyall, also an old man, worried about being injured as he staggered back with Meeker's weight in his arms. They could be struck by lightning. If a bolt hit the nearby, puddled ground, Lyall could be stunned, falling next to Meeker in the torrent. Yet he felt compelled to help.

Lyall theorized that shift-shapers represented something different than the desire for supernatural or otherworldly power. They represented a highly individualized calling to which those persons responded in order to return to something in the long tracings of evolution from the progenitor out of which all animals had been shaped—in biology called chordates: those animals who had vertebrate columns, gill slits, and post-anal tails. Even humans had versions of the latter two.

Lyall also theorized that shift-shapers responded to personal factors to become something other than human: devolution as intention. Meeker's case seemed to be personal.

One morning, but soon after Lyall had determined Meeker had started to shift-shape, Lyall paused in the street out in front of Meeker on his <u>equipale</u> perch. Instead of saying hello, Lyall volunteered to Meeker, "You don't have to make the change." Lyall didn't know Meeker well, so his pronouncement took some risk.

Meeker opened and then snapped shut his mouth a couple of times, glaring at Lyall, not speaking.

"What you're doing usually doesn't end well."

"God dammit, Meeker," Diana's voice raged from inside the house through an open window, "get your sorry ass in here and make me breakfast!"

Meeker cocked his head back a bit when his mother started screaming, and then, waggling his elbows, focused on Lyall. "I can do it if I want!" He sounded peevish.

Lyall realized, this time having taken a longer look at Meeker than in recent days, that the old man's silver hair had taken on a feathery appearance. Meeker swiveled his head back to look at the house behind him. His posture conveyed melancholy as he again looked back at Lyall.

"I'd try and stop you if I knew how!" declared Lyall, unexpectedly exasperated that Meeker simply dismissed his warning.

In some cases, Lyall had discovered, fear helped reverse the shift. Lyall had some success in stopping a couple of other shift-shapers by scaring them back to their humanity, though he did so very reluctantly. At the College where he worked, Lyall fired a bear banger near an instructor who was shift-shaping into a black bear. The explosion scared the near-bear almost literally out of his ursine wits and back into his human ones.

Otherwise, Lyall wished people would respect shift-shapers' rights, like they should respect all human rights—and all animals' rights. They should leave shift-shapers alone instead of trying for a "cure" or forcing incarceration of some kind.

Lyall's reluctance to scare shift-shapers involved experience and belief. All animals had a right to exist, to live and thrive as they each were capable. Lyall extended that value to those humans who shift-shaped. Since humans were also animals, it made sense that the human animal becoming, such as in Meeker's case, a raptor, would retain the rights that humans took for granted for themselves, but which humans usually failed to apply to other animals, causing great misery. It was the guaranteed suffering of shift-shapers, like most other animals, at the hands of humans that motivated Lyall, despite his reluctance, to try to scare shift-shapers back to humanity. At least humanness offered some protection, however mild.

To scare someone back to humanity, Lyall needed to know what might frighten the shift-shaper, either its human or animal component. In hindsight, the bear banger was obvious, but how could he scare Meeker out of becoming a bird of prey? He didn't know enough about Meeker or raptors to work out what to try. Meanwhile, Meeker seemed very afraid of his mother. Would that fear override any Lyall could produce? And what ill-will infected their relationship?

Outside, Meeker's rain-beaten form didn't allow a pause for that rumination. Meeker needed help.

Those who shift-shaped knew what was happening. That fact alone usually justified in the minds of others their opinions and diagnoses about shift-shapers. If someone indicated they wanted to become a horse, a black capped vireo, a mountain skink, or a tufted capuchin—the possibilities were endless—and demanded of others to leave them alone to shape, to those others the shift-shaper must be barmy or loony. More damning, the shift-shaper always ignored pleas to seek medical help or counseling—or whatever—to deal with the "problem," which to the shift-shaper didn't exist. Lyall considered their insistence to shift-shape an extraordinary framework for animal rights, something both he and 'Lupe deeply believed in, their belief amplified because of the mass die-offs caused by humanity's historical inability to control its own impulses.

"What are raptors afraid of?" asked Lyall of Reinaldo Cordova, an avian biologist at the College.

"What?" Reinaldo asked, a little startled at the question. He looked keenly at Lyall, trying to discern a motive for asking. Not seeing anything, Lyall's expression neutral, he asked, "Do you mean, 'What preys upon these great aerial hunters?'"

"OK." Raptors must fear what hunts them.

"Other raptors," smirked Reinaldo, the answer obvious.

"So, eagles prey on hawks is what you're saying."

"Yes, and larger hawks prey on smaller hawks. Smaller owls, such as long-eared owls, might kill bigger Cooper's hawks, if provoked for some reason, like the hawk threatening the owl's owlets. It's sometimes 'dog eat dog' out there!" Reinaldo smirked again, satisfied at his joke. Then he added, "Even if a mighty carnivore, like a grey wolf, wanted to catch a hawk for a snack, it's virtually impossible unless the hawk is very sick or injured and couldn't fly away, and was on the ground." He paused. "That might be something raptors fear, to answer your question—the ground—at least, ground that's not safe for whatever reason. For safe nesting, a cliff face or tall tree will suffice, or some other vertical slope or enclosed space that offers them and their nestlings protection from carnivores, including other raptors. The few, small animals that can climb to a raptor's nest for harmful purposes, to steal eggs or hatchlings, for example, raptors can take care of quite efficiently: Just a few well-placed pecks from their beaks or deep scratches from their talons would send the thieves quickly off! How would you like to be pecked or slashed on the face or head?"

Lyall felt stymied about how to try and stop Meeker from turning into a raptor. How could he capture a raptor to send after Meeker to scare him out of becoming a raptor, Lyall not knowing what kind of raptor Meeker wanted to become? Meeker was so much larger, anyway. Even an eagle or a condor would avoid Meeker like the pestilence he, as all humans, personified in these horrible times. And he couldn't take a carnivore, even a small one like a lynx or a bobcat, to threaten Meeker as if he were injured on the ground, like now. What if the wild cat attacked?

In the past two weeks as he walked by with his dogs, he heard Meeker's mother shouting at him more often, her voice loud and bold for a hundred-year-old: "What the hell's wrong with you?" "You're going batty!" "What sort of whack-job would ignore his mother, damn you!" Lyall feared Meeker would end up institutionalized, an aberrant human, probably leading to a miserable death at the hands of well-intentioned caretakers who thought they treated a demented human rather than a captive Golden Eagle or Northern Harrier.

Lyall otherwise was amazed at Diana's vitriolic cogency, given her age. He also now recognized that Meeker's shift-shaping reflected a desire to gain freedom from her, making the evolutionary factors in Lyall's theory about shift-shaping subject, in this case, to the personal ones.

A couple of neighbors stopped Lyall to discuss Meeker's "bizarre behavior" and "disheveled appearance." Lyall struggled in his response since he knew the truth, but he didn't want to say anything to endanger Meeker. Biases about mental disorders and against the subjective freedom of animals ran too deep: The mentally ill became pariahs; animals, according to custom and law, were property. What did humans do with property? So much became garbage. Humans became slaves. Then there were factory farms, holocausts of animal life.

Lyall would only say, "I'm sure his mother is aware," which was likely true.

To his beloved wife, 'Lupe, Lyall would bemoan, "It's not like Gregor Samsa turning into a cockroach. It's really much worse." Both Lyall and 'Lupe believed that any animal possessed intrinsic value equal to any human's, that animals must be treated as ends-in-themselves, never as a means to an end, such as food or property or object. Enough suffering happened accidentally, such as from a fall or through disease, so why should humans be agents of unnecessary suffering? They believed that humans, who had the wherewithal, should take on specific responsibilities about other animals, starting with closing factory farms, corporate ranches, and experimental institutions, and stopping involuntary medical, psychological, or physical incarceration and experimentation. For the latter, if humans wanted to volunteer, they had the right.

Lyall moved to the back door and grabbed the knob, ready to retrieve Meeker. He paused: What would happen with a human-ish raptor or a raptor-ish human inside? If the raptor in Meeker was dominant, lots of craziness could ensue.

Lyall's greatest worry about Meeker focused on abuse. If institutionalized, Meeker would end up in a psycho ward, or another form of imprisonment, a proprietary object, forced to submit to agencies outside of his control, and thus resulting in the one trait all animals shared, including humans: suffering. I suffer; therefore, I am, Lyall held. To hell with Descartes!

Meeker would suffer because those imprisoning him would not recognize his subjective, intentional state, and instead objectify it as mental, behavioral, or physical disorders. Joseph Merrick, the so-called Elephant Man, bore witness to such determinations made by others who, to a fault, used the superficial to judge and, thereby, to condemn the essence.

Lyall burst out the door into the rain, the smell of ozone strong in the air. He found Meeker alive, but clearly in distress. A lightning ground strike nearby might boil or scald the bird man since he lay in a pool of rainwater!

He pushed his arms under Meeker's shoulders and knees. Lyall maintained his balance in the wind and rain with some difficulty as he hefted Meeker only to discover that the old man weighed almost nothing. As light as a bird! He found himself clutching Meeker to his chest to keep the hands of the wind from snatching Meeker out of his arms.

Lyall forced his way to the back door, shouting for 'Lupe as he entered. "Oh my!" she said, dismayed at the sight of Meeker. "What happened? How did he end up in our back yard? How badly is he hurt?"

Describing what he saw through the window, Lyall lowered Meeker onto the couch, rainwater and small globs of mud sloughing off him. And water dripped off Lyall, sodden by the hard rains. He kneeled next to Meeker. His and 'Lupe's four dogs came around, curious. Lyall told them to "stay off," and they complied. Lyall had a special connection to dogs, like a dog whisperer.

Lyall looked back at 'Lupe, exchanging looks of dismay. They should call an ambulance. But how would they explain Meeker's appearance in their back yard, falling out of the sky? A question with a potentially perilous answer! A call now meant the ambulance wouldn't arrive until the lightning ended. How long would that take? Would Meeker last?

Meeker's eyes fluttered open, deep set on each side of his severely projected nose. Close up, Lyall saw that Meeker's nose had a rounded, hardened top and a decided downturn to its pointed tip and that his mouth, very small for a human, formed the crease where the bottom of the nose joined his face. "Ahh!" he moaned. He peered at Lyall. "Ahh, I was flying, *flying*!'

"What happened, Meeker? What do you mean, 'flying'?" But Lyall easily guessed at what Meeker meant.

"Flying," he repeated. "High up. Far away. Then the winds…rain came." He coughed, ratcheting his slight body. "Flying!" He smiled with his little mouth under his beak of a nose. Both joy and pain stippled Meeker's voice.

'Lupe said, "I'm going to call an ambulance," moving toward her com-pad.

"No!" Meeker managed to say strongly, and then less so, "no…no ambulance. I'm not right for an ambulance, for a hospital, for…. Lyall, you know."

'Lupe stopped, looking back at the scene.

Meeker peered again at Lyall, eyes intense. "Put me back outside. Help me. Let me be free! Help me, my wings!"

The winds howled, as strong as ever; the rain pounded down, the force of it on the roof easy to hear. Another bolt of lightning hit the rod out front, lights wavering.

"Help me," Meeker said again, his fingers inflexibly scrabbling at Lyall's arms and chest. "Help me to my freedom, my purpose!"

Lyall looked at 'Lupe. She nodded, her expression saying she would do whatever Lyall thought best. Long ago she had come to terms: She had wed an unusual man with a very old soul. His talents occasionally led to extraordinary situations. She could have called herself crazy at seeing shift-shapers, but she knew she wasn't crazy. They were real. She had <u>seen</u> them. And Lyall wasn't crazy. And he, too, was real. Much of what they did aimed at avoiding those who had the power, resources, and intolerance to interpret

Lyall's talents, his soul, the wrong way. Those inhumane sorts would put Lyall, and maybe even 'Lupe, into a straitjacket.

Meeker forced the situation by trying to sit up.

"You might have broken bones!" said Lyall urgently, trying to keep him down.

"If so, I don't feel them. Leave me be! If you won't help, I'll do what I need to do myself."

Lyall relented, standing up, and Meeker sat up. "Oooo! I feel dizzy!"

"Sit for a minute," said 'Lupe, "let the blood back in your brain."

All paused for a moment. The dogs understood their place in the situation, sitting quietly on the other side of the coffee table from Meeker, watching, curious.

Meeker tried to stand up.

Deciding from empathy, Lyall said, "I'll help you, Meeker. But let's go out front. It's more open than the back. You might get hung up in our dead cottonwoods out back. Lucky you weren't before."

"Good man," Meeker said, using Lyall for stability as he started an odd waddle-hobble toward the front door. "You're right," he gasped, "I might have a couple of broken ribs, a sprained ankle."

'Lupe and the four dogs watched Lyall and Meeker through the door screen as they made their way onto the street, the wind pushing the rain southeastward and away from the front entrance of the house, allowing them to leave the door open.

Lightning fractured the atmosphere, its light turning the world briefly into a diorama. Then the heavy rain turned the figures of Lyall and Meeker into dark, humanoid shapes. The winds grabbed rapaciously at the old man. Because Meeker had so little weight, his shift-shaping having converted his human bones to bird bones, human muscle to bird muscle, Lyall struggled to hang on to Meeker. No wonder he'd survived the fall into their back yard: Meeker wasn't heavy enough to suffer fatal hurt from nearly any fall.

Meeker put out his arms, and Lyall threw him by his waist up into the gales. Meeker soared, pushed violently to the southeast, Lyall watching him wrenched up and down and back and forth. A bolt of lightning flashed very close by, freezing Lyall in place briefly, it's nearly simultaneous thunder a crash like a million cymbals. Lyall crouched, hands clasped over ears. Then he scuttled back into the house.

'Lupe grabbed a towel for Lyall to dry off. He rubbed it around his head and neck, water once again dripping from his clothes onto the floor. "I can't see or hear well," he said. "Ugh!"

Then he said, "But you should know, Love, the bolt of lightning just after Meeker took off may have hit him. The bolt blinded me—I couldn't see clearly. If he was hit, he was killed."

"Oh, my!" said 'Lupe, shocked. The dogs sat diligently, a response to their humans' emotions, especially Lyall's.

"If not, he's still in great peril," continued Lyall. "I think he wanted to fly in the storm, knowing it would probably kill him. He didn't want to live his life as a human or a bird anymore. He saw the storm as a way to escape, to be free." *From his mother, and all she signified*, added Lyall, silently. "Otherwise, to be forced to remain human would have killed him as well, but probably with lasting suffering."

Lyall looked back through the front screen at the storm. Though he appeared calm, his heart raged, his blood its own deluge.

"Meeker has rights," he whispered fiercely. 'Lupe heard and understood. Then he went to change clothes and await that night's full moon, hoping the clouds would remain.

* * *

John Cornish
Retired college administrator and English instructor, I am looking for critique partners to exchange draft novels or several shorter works. These days I write urban fantasy, but appreciate all prose genres, including non-fiction. Poetry is welcome too! jcornish643@gmail.com. Go Dems!

Science Fiction/Fantasy   Silver Medal
Bob Montgomery

THE DALES OF ZIN

Zil4 stood before the dales he'd been told never to enter.

Only last redmoon, his Da had said, "When my Da was your age he ate seeds washed from there, and ever since, rain gives him trembles."

"But ho," Maa had added, "if you like disappearing, that`s the place."

What should I do?

A whole light-shift back, his pet dauje Sniffer had chased a slithe in there and hadn't returned. And his calls for Sniffer seemed to bounce off the tangle where he disappeared. *Why don't my shouts penetrate? Shouts go through greenery, don't they? Until they fall like a shot arrow?*

Nor could he hear any drumbarking. Daujes kacked out rhythms when they ran, rhythms that made you bob your head or tap your jogs. But now there was only looming quiet, heavy as thunder, full of imagined sounds that made him whip his seers about, seeing nothing but the innocent green of the sky-blotting dales.

Sniffy's in there. I have to go in.

#

The brush seemed friendly as he entered.

Too friendly. We've only just met!

Vegetation reached out as he passed, touching him no matter his side-steps or twists. Tiny antennas everywhere came out to wave, tasting his vibrations.

"Sniffy?" he softly called—his outbreath a startling whispergust that swayed nearby branches. "Sniffy!" he shouted—the loudness a raucous Black Flappinger, cawing upward, landing on the highest limb, where it peered around, shooting jaglight in six directions.

He heard a far, far away ticking response: *k'k, k'k, k'k kk kk!*

Sniffy!

A shooting star of warm relief striped his insides, glowing them gold.

#

"Shouldn't Zil4 now be home?" Zil3 asked.

"I was about to voice those very words," Salva said, worry flame-shaping her main mouth. A pulsing blue arced between their gazes, jolting them straight from the tent, Zil3's sonar in six far directions, Salva's in sixty-eight near ones.

Moving in tandem, they both heard their inwaves pounding the shores of their carapaces.

#

Zil4 suddenly stopped, and the yielding ground beneath turned hard as an arrowhead. *Maa and Da! They'll be shot from ease not knowing where I am!*

But he couldn't leave the dales now or shout so his parents could hear. The downslope itself was telling him this in a green, kind way.

Too kind?

#

"He's in the dales," Salva and Zil3 co-spoke, nerving circuits of dale lore into their probes.

The dales of Zin: friendly and green as growing season, snarly and dire as jungle night. Since ZinWar2, the dales had swallowed twelve younglings, and countless pets and vehicles. One dread night a whelphor-size beast thumped from the verdure and crushed many tents and bomb-making bots. But one fine day a spout of redwater shot from its center miles in the air, misting all around with a sixty-day giddiness, inspiring the Mist Day Remembrance dances. "The dales, the dales!" went the anthem,

> *"where all were once a loving look,*
> *where all at once this form we took,*
> *our beauty born and fears forsook,*
> *redmist writing our holy book:*
> *k'k, k'k, k'k kk kk!*
> *The dales of Zin, the dales of Zin!"*

Only Yau the Wise ever survived the dales, six days inside before coming out with a face too bright to look at. He never told what happened there, even during the Inquitorture that killed him. "The dales are the zoph *of the planet," was all he would say,* zoph *meaning both* revenge *and* promise.

#

The humming nest was tall as a Koian tree and wide as a buzzer mound. A home for what, Sniffer didn't know, but its woodsy weave and skurk-tunnel tang roused him like Zil4's nearing aroma after being unbreathed too long. His mounting glee kept heightening his leaps, but he could only glimpse, not gain the top crater rim, and his suction claws wouldn't stick on its sloping bark. Still, with each vaulting, more raw joy expanded his blood lines, inspirating higher takeoffs, until a ten-foot vertical leap stretched the wiry contraction tissue under his lower heart to the thinness of spinner web. The sudden pain came with an anthem command only daujes could hear: *tk'tk, tk'tk, tk'tk tk tk!*

In obedient response he arched his back, knowing his jumptime was now suspended—as he was, mid-air. He surrendered in trust to the fall, turning slightly to land on his riblature pad, thumping down hard, rushed by his ever-there ingod to air the zin sounds that lead to soundness: *k'k, k'k, k'k kk kk . . . .*

The sixty-eighth riff brought redolent love and relief—Zil! As soon as his masterfriend rubbed him *hello! good to see you, good good good, you're looking okay, I'm so glad so glad* he began feeling better and better. A double redmoon rose high in his chest, misting light on his aching heart.

#

Salva and Zil3 micro-eyed a sheen of their son's sweat at the edge of the northern dales. "Alarmazine content high," noted Salva, a zin-renowned analytica.

"He's in there, daujegonnit!" Zil3 growled. "How many times have we pounded that ban through his skullstone! I'll rip his daujegonne prober off and feed it to the skurks!"

Salva simply let his words relapse to the helpless air that formed them. "Should we or shouldn't we go in after him? That's the question." She x-rayed her inner sense of the dales for answer. "Hmm. I'm thinking *not."*

"Is that your deliverer talking or your self-protector?" Zil3 asked, his fierceness heartening to seeker's interest.

"My deliverer," she said, with a tinge of uncertainty.

"What's that leftover wonder?""He's not our tentmate forever, Z. The shadows of Between have been dark on him lately."

"His changing time? In the dales? Zinlings don't go there for that!"

"Yau did" she said, a sadness aging and wetting her far-off gaze.

Zil3 yelped, "You don't think—?!" then exhaled an alarmazine breath. "Good Yau!"

#

Under his ministering mid-palm, Zil4 felt Sniffer's contractors rebunch, stilling the underskin trembles. Zil's gladness over this healing mixed with something trembling his own insulation. *A new feeling—but not wetting my seers like it used to—curiosity taking over now halloo halloo!—heartbeats loud enough to dance to!* "Speak, you rising mood!" he sang out. "Dive into language!" He stretched full height to listen. Sniffer, too, huffed to hunting readiness, all noses like Zil was all ears.

You're a miracle creature, Zil4, came a slithery voice.

"Quiet, you!" barked Zil. "You belch words again, I'll feed you to Sniffer!"

Sniffer snorted a quatrachord in the rhythm of a pounding cave-vac, then hushed to attend the quiet Zil had enforced.

After a pause, the nest began humming. Zil leaned in, listened, then sang contrapuntally: "Shy one.

Respecter of all.

Why are you making me feel this way?"

And then he went still, like a storyteller waiting for his cue.

#

Inside the nest, countless Rememberers, each like a dust mote with zigabyte capacity, danced, joined and created—all thrumming in harmony and tonic dissonance with the music of the multiversal spheres. Ever-playful, they freshly homed on the youngling's request for connection. To research how best to respond in zin spacetime, they jigged through their infinite recall for the unique ID helix of this express singer *("Zil4" "Zil4" "Zil4")* as he/she/it had grown in undying life on innumerable planes and planets via ages and eons of the Creature Family. Instantaneously they swept across, swirled within, and downed memory drafts of more worlds than anyone could count in a lifetime, getting buzzed on Zil's holobio distillate:

> *sailing in lavender air on wings filled with eyes—*
> *trying to nurse putty laughlets in the folds of a sentient whirlwind—*
> *saving a world in a do-or-die match by bloodily running a bladeball ungrounded*
> *through the aliens' team—*
> *stretching a plank to fix a costly measuring error his carpenter foster-Da made—*
> *pulling legions of newborns from a vast burning hatchery—*
> *entwining with a multi-souled firerose vine named Efflora—*
> *shooting wake-up colors from an Anzer rain bow at a raging Gargantua who*
> *couldn't, for all her strength, wrest her attention from tired old thoughts—*
> *singing to the Whole World's people an improvised epic of the unsung heroines who*

brought them the jubilant years they all share—
playing tassel-tag during recess at Mount Holy Book—
crazy-stepping with a four-headed carrier crab, who only could move at right
angles—
thought-guessing games with Maa when she was his brother on Trelawn 12—
the deathblow from Zil3's romantic rival in the now-extinct wormhole Plenya—
funning with neighborhood imps in the xylophonic ice storms of Fined-EeNor—
the horror of the Little One massacre in the City of Jewels—
The Amisis Hive's lightening decay under Traumple the Me-er—
the desperate strain of Forgetter's Disease on three different desert worlds—
the dinner stories of Taxxer and his all-night desserts—
thirst in Hasari—
plague on Friaba—
the kindness of the poor on Mimmeze—
the courage of the Karans—
the unforgettable beauty of the murdered Ihainae—
incomprehensible loneliness on every inhabited moon—
the fires that brought him to water—
the water that brought him to fire . . .
the nest burst into vocal flame: *Come in for a swim.*

#

Sniffer scrambled from the blaze so fast his muzz outshot his legs, tumbling him fifteen loops before he syncopated into leaps and bounds toward the northern dales. He crashed through the archway where first he saw the slithe, right into a mesh of homey smells (hidewall, swept dust, cloth mites, meat smoke, Zilly spatter), halting at the jogbottoms of Zil4's parents.

Salva scooped him up and let him slather her headskin as his panting slowed. When he found himself no longer heaving with gratitude, he squirmed from her clutches and dropped to the zin, unsheathing his probes toward the archway, coughing out howls for Zil4 that boomed like a stoneslide. "But is he *alive,* Sniffer?" Zil3 shouted, cutting through the ruckus like a shoufhorn through thunderdrums. Sniffer promptly stilled, sussed the aftershocks of that bark from his master's master, and then kacked with an onrush of certainty: *k'k, k'k, k'k kk kk!*

"Thank Yau!" Salva bayed.

"He's not out of the dales yet," Zil4's Da said, trying mightily not to cry

#

The nest was as fiery inside as out, but all that burned were Zil4's thoughts. Whenever he tried to weigh what was happening, a scorching sound made the weight light, leaving him blank as a newborn. Recurring worry about

Maa and Da melted right in with the heat-wavy air. Jitters about Sniffer and how he was doing instantly cooked into nothing but warmth for his lifelong playmate.

And as his brainspew evanesced, the vast existence it had masked opened around him like breaking dawn to a waking sailor. This sense of a waterworld wondrously cooled him from the fire-nest radiation. He felt settled in some kind of ocean, breathing easily in water no more wet than the flames were hot. The spontaneous combustion of all his concerns had freed up a knowledge that his frets were nothing to fret about! That all was well on that front.

But not well on another front.

That's the new feeling news.

Something was wrong. A great danger zooming near.

Am I about to die?

No-o-o-o, rippled a voice, flowing through his psyche like a stream through a forest. *There's nothing now to fear.*

But something's wrong! What's so terribly wrong?

Zin is deeply wounded, came the reply, *and its creatures are suffering its blood loss.*

\#

From there the interchanges, like two friends eager to tell each other all, stirred up and swam in the waters of genius. The conversation both fattened Zil's compassion and improved his health. Talk of horrors and desperate needs educed solutions from the felt safety of their mutual trust. So filling was their savory communion, Zil soon forgot to think of food and drink. Untold hours piled up like gathering light from Zin's four suns rising to midday.

\#

"Is there food in the dales?" Maa, now home, wondered out loud. "A toxin-free stream or two?"

No one heard her. *Oh, right. Zil3's out jogging Sniffer.*

Then the warm tones of her best friend's voice: "Salva? It's Judama."

"Come in, Dama!" Salva hallooed. "In back! In the quietspace."

A rustle of robes crescendoing, and there was bejeweled Judama with her measuring seers, making Salva smile. Dama gracefully flopped on the red fur floor, her dangling gems tinkling like tiny wind chimes. "Zilly-boy braved the dales?"

Salva gave the zin-wide affirmative: a nod up, down, then across. "Sixteen meals ago."

"He's going the way of Yau," said Dama. "I always suspected he might. From the day he swam so far out to sea because of all the fighting over toys."

"And that way of moving he's always had!" clucked Salva. "Like his body's a poison sac he thinks wrong words will split."

Judama lanced her seers into Salva's matching gaze. Then nodded: up, down and across. "And now that sac's broke, like the waters igniting birth. But in his changing-time, it'll be elixir, not poison. Ah, my dear—" Seeing hot tears glittering in the windows of Salva's soul: "Come! Enfold!"As their loving limbs entwined and their breathing synced, Salva felt the worm of her worry transform into Zin's fabled Matriarch Moth.

#

On the sixth day, Zil3 jogged with Sniffer up the Prothenum Ledge, pushing his agile body hard to fight panic over his son and country. His voice in the Hall of Leaders was heard less and less these days, which was more and more vexing because the world's war-threats were mounting as fast as the greedy were looting the bare-survivors. The Grabber Sect had bought control of the worldwide ESP, and trumpeted "Get All You Can" as the prime directive so loud and long, it was yahooed enough to keep them in power. And the longer they were in power, the more they looted and the louder they shouted down voices like his.

How much clearer can it be that what they want to "get all of" is Zin itself? Even if it means savaging the bare-survivors with war, hunger, cold, rape and untreated disease.

Breathing hard, Zil3 reached the top of the Ledge, and gratefully leaned on its lone stunted tree. Sniffer kept moving, nosing around as if any second he'd find the Youth Root of Prothenum folklore—or a least a chompable skurk.

Zil3 was Prox for the Deliverer Sect, the great tide of female zinnians rising in resistance to the last Grabber coup. Salva and her friend Dama headed its Gathering Wing. Their Sect, though still short on official sway, was long on resolve and aura, galling the all-male Grabber heads to undo laws protecting women, while granting permits to beat, maim or kill them for unholy religious reasons.

Zil3 wept.

Sniffer loped over as soon as the first tears salted the Ledge's blond stubble. He lapped them all up in one taster swoop, then nuzzled hard into Zil3's neck. Soon the drenching of the dauje's upturned tri-nose made him sneeze: *CH'ch'cheechee CH CH! CH'ch'cheechee CH CH!*

Zil3 liked the rhythm so much, it sealed the leak in his seers.

#

Three light shifts passed in quiet sadness.

Zil3 reached over to rub Sniffer's muzz—but suddenly the dauje kacked

a double-time march to the Ledge's rim and howled *hallooooo!*
Then came a faraway trill, clear despite its faintness: "Sniffeeeee!"
A thrill shot through Zil3, and he was up and running, all tiredness gone as quickly as dread when a wandering child is found. Joining Sniffer, he saw in the twilit distance a tiny but exquisite zinnian woman, smiling with a light that hurt his eyes even across the great gulf.

He waved back, slow and long, nodding the whole time: up, down and across.

It was Zil4 in the new gender all zinnians acquire in the Holy Between of changing time. She was now a woman whose beauty as she neared burned with the brightest intelligence, shaking her father with an unnamed fear.

#

Her mother greeted her like a little sister she hadn't seen in ages.

"Look at you!"

"Please, Maa."

"Oh, give me a moment to let some gladness change my life!"

"Moment's over! Time for dale business. Soon as Judama gets here."

"Judama? I didn't invite—"

"Hello?" came her friend's voice and the xylophonic sound of her rushing approach.

Salva gasped to Zil4, "Did the dales give you prophetic foresight?!"

"Aunt Dama and I hallooed as I headed here. She was fixing a motor in the Square."

Judama riffled in, wiping grimed hands with an embroidered rag. "Look at you!" she blared, then fully caressed Zil's new shape. "Very smart, very strong," she said approvingly.

Zil4 smiled, and the women reflexively shielded their seers.

"Too blinding!" whimpered Judama, the first time she'd whimpered since her own changing time.

"Right," Zil said. "For now, then, let's get serious."

They all sat down like children obeying a father they adored.

Zil looked up, thinking a while. *Or is she listening?* Salva wondered. *She's so ...* breathtaking! *I could cry, but no, don't, she's about to talk.*

"Take our word for it," Zil began.

"Our word?" Salva and Dama co-chimed.

"Our word, my word, I'm talking truth, so hear it: the Deliverer Sect will soon have more than enough members to right the biggest wrongs in very good time."

"Easy to say," Judama blurted, "but we can't work any harder or with any more passion! We're losing ground every day, every hour!"

"Stop it, Judama," Zil said sharply.

"Zil4!" Salva scolded. "Your tone!"

"You too, mother," Zil said. "This isn't a birthday party, and I'm not some rude child spouting babble. Stop doing what Grabber men do, muzzling your intuition! There's a guide with us now, strong and good as our being here."

"What guide? Where?"

"A friend I made in the dales. We're inside each other. Can't you tell?"

"No!" Salva cried.

"I can," said Dama, with a riveted gaze.

"Of course I can, too," said Salva, "but what Yau went through, what his mother went through—"

"Clearing the way for this time," said Zil. "Once was enough for that kind of disgrace."

"Are you sure, Zil4?" Salva pleaded.

"I'm not Zil4 any more."

"Who, then?"

"Yau2."

#

The three Deliverers shared a look, then nodded.

Up and down to remember what's always still and present.

And across, looking forward to time's momento

*   *   *

 **Bob Montgomery** is a Pulitzer-nominated playwright and composer, as well as a longtime teacher of writing at Columbia University and The New School in New York City.

Science Fiction/Fantasy Bronze Medal
Kimberly Rose

DEPTH

The man did not let his tears fall, but Munin sat perched on a nearby tree and watched them glisten, turning the man's eyes to glass. Tears were a terrible way for Munin to determine if an emotion were anything he should covet, if the memories and thoughts and recent trauma a soul had endured were worth anything to him.

But Munin knew that the men, the Flame-Warriors in the red vehicles, never cried. They were strong and proud and wore their reflective-striped coats and heavy helmets like true warriors.

This man wore no coat and no helmet. He sat on the ground beside the large red truck and stared at things that Munin knew were neither important nor interesting—the cracks in the pavement and the green shoots of weeds growing up from them. He sat in silence, alone, as much as one can be alone and silent in the middle of a city with the constant bombardment of sounds and thoughts and the press of thousands of bodies living in close proximity around them.

And, of course, with Munin no more than thirty feet away.

A rustle of feathers and the sharp, metallic smell of another Odinkin alerted Munin to the arrival of his brother.

Hugin was identical to Munin in every way, except that Hugin's interest in the man was brief and dull, as it usually was when Munin took the time to observe.

"There are no deep thoughts within that man," Hugin said, speaking not with his mouth but with one large, mirror-like eye.

Munin considered it. The dull waves of thought radiating from the man— not that he was particularly dull, so much as dull is the nature of most thought waves of men—were not especially deep. But they were full and liquid and, as

79

they observed, congealing into the spongy stuff memory is made of. They weren't deep enough for Hugin, but for Munin they were sufficient.

"There is uncommon depth to the memory, brother. Something has stricken this Flame-Warrior to the center of his self." Munin replied in the same way Hugin had spoken.

Hugin rolled his eye away from Munin, then fixed it back where it was, silver gaze unwavering. "You fill your head with such nonsense. There is no reason to dredge his thought."

"Perhaps," Munin said. He hopped from the branch and spread his wings to glide downward onto the pavement before the man.

Hugin also took wing, but his carried him up and away.

It was for the better. Hugin's criticisms were old and tiresome, and Munin had more interesting things to ponder.

The man's gaze was unfocused and cloudy and glittering with emotion he would not show—not to anyone but Munin, and even then not knowingly.

Munin hopped into the man's line of sight and fixed his unblinking silver eye upon the unfocused gaze.

Within them was the answer Munin sought. It was rare to see a Flame-Warrior even slightly ruffled, let alone shaken so profoundly. The man's tears threatened to fall, and Munin could not fathom their existence, or why they were denied.

In the center of the man's unfocused eyes, Munin saw a room. A cramped and filthy room, the air thick with the miasma of illness. A lumpy bed took up a third of the space, and seven men crowded into the remaining area. Between them, an eighth man lay.

The room was too small for all eight, but the seven large Flame-Warriors filled it with efficient movements and the compactness of a common goal: one pressed on the eighth man's chest, while another squeezed a bag at his face, and a third pressed a needle into his arm.

Munin had seen the process before in the thoughts and memories of men, and with his own one eye on three occasions; the seven men were attempting to restore the eighth man to life, to restart a heart that had already given its spirit to the beautiful and terrible Hel.

The seven men continued their trial of resurrection, the memory in the man's eyes both a blur of movement and a crawl of intense focus. The better portion of an hour passed, within the memory, before the seven men stepped away from the eighth and admitted they could do no more to rob Hel of her gifts.

Deeper, within the image, superimposed over the memory of the eighth man's face, was another old man, just as frail and steeped in the sour smell of death. This one did not have a team of warriors attempting to save him. This one was laying in a bed, on a pillow, with the gaunt pallor clinging to his hollow cheeks. His chest rose shallowly, each breath coming farther and farther apart until they did not come again.

The superimposed old man had the same shape to his nose and ears as the man before Munin now.

Munin continued to stare at the man's eyes, drinking in the emotions and memories that swirled below the surface.

The man was not crying for the eighth man, nor was he crying for the superimposed man. His grief for the superimposed man had worn around the edges from years of being revisited at dark times, important times. It no longer ached as sharply, and the time for powerful mourning had passed. His grief for the eighth man had lasted only a short while—moments, after the defeat had been claimed and the seven men's attempts were abandoned. It was only in the moments when the man came face to face with the eighth man's family, all tear-red and seeking answers, explanations, promises.

Neither memory would have been enough to bring the silver tears to this man's eyes, Munin observed.

But the sight of the eighth man had conjured, like a witch bringing forth a Wight out of a newly turned grave, the long-buried image of the superimposed man. It had been so powerful, that when Munin watched the memory of the attempted resurrection again, he saw the superimposed man in place of the eighth man, and within the memory he saw the Flame-Warrior now before him falter and pause.

It wasn't a long enough pause to wrest defeat from the clutches of victory. But it was enough to make the man question what had happened, and enough to summon forth the tears that he still refused to loose.

Munin watched the memory many more times. Each time the superimposed man replaced the eighth man, and each time the Flame-Warrior questioned where the whole mission had gone wrong.

Munin turned the memories over, picked them apart and examined the pieces. Attached to the superimposed man were memories locked farther away, memories of childhood and baseball and one long lecture at the kitchen table on a cold autumn morning. Attached to the eighth man were memories of other eighth men and women, other wards of Hel whose bodies underwent the violent resurrection ritual to no avail.

They were heavy memories, substantive in a way that Munin had expected to find nesting away in the mind of a Flame-Warrior. They were big and strong men with memories to match.

That was what Hugin did not understand. Whatever depth he prized, he was missing an opportunity here.

Munin would not miss the opportunity, and he would not allow this Flame-Warrior to suffer the weight and sharp edges of this trick his own mind played.

Munin took the memory, the thoughts.

They would remain within the man, but as Munin felt the weight and sting of the memories pressing into his silvered eye, they shrunk behind the man's eyes.

Every detail remained as it had been when Munin first peered into the man's eyes, but the edges were dulled. The man would be able to poke at the memory with callused fingertips and not feel the pain, and he would not wake in the night to faces replacing others.

The man's gaze sharpened and focused on Munin. He blinked and his eyes were dry, and there was no sign of the depth of thought and memory and emotion that Munin knew was there, and which would always be there. It was an indefinable depth, something that he could not put words to no matter how many times Hugin ruffled his feathers about it.

Odinkin were for *thought*, Hugin maintained.

But Munin knew there was so much more to it than that.

This man's unusual combinations of grief would make for an interesting trinket to show the Allfather when Munin made his own final trip to Valhalla. Perhaps he would learn something from the man, or perhaps it would simply be another moment of memory to add to a vast store.

Regardless, the man was stirring again, and the eye contact was broken.

Munin fixed the man with one last stare and blinked his silver eye in parting. Then he spread his midnight wings and lifted himself into the air after his brother.

* * *

 **Kimberly Rose** received her BA in English from the University of New Mexico in 2017. She's had short stories and poems published in a few literary magazines and anthologies, and hopes to publish her first novel in the near future. She currently works as an EMT in Albuquerque, New Mexico.

SECTION FOUR

CULTURAL/HISTORICAL

These non-fiction stories explore women in WWII, the 1960's and several cultural icons.

Cultural/Historical   Gold Medal
Leonie Rosenstiel

SIDELIGHTS ON THE WACS DURING WORLD WAR II

President Roosevelt signed the first legislation creating the Women's Auxiliary Army Corps (WAAC) on May 14, 1942, five months and one week after the bombing of Pearl Harbor. Although the first WAAC graduating class had to be trained by male soldiers, simply because there were no female officers back then, later classes had their own female officers.

During 1943, graduation photos from Iowa's Third WAAC Training Center at Fort Des Moines, IA, show the relatively new commanding officer's name: Christienne Welsh. As a little girl, she used to say, she'd gone out to get ice cream, holding onto her grandfather's hand on one side and legendary lawman Wyatt Earp's hand on the other. Earp and her grandparents saw each other often.

On July 1, 1943, President Roosevelt signed new legislation, incorporating the WAAC into the regular Army, and changing the group's name to "Women's Army Corps" (WAC). This allowed women veterans, after signing up for a second time, with the new entity, the same perks as men.

The U.S. Forces had been using some 20,000 Australian civilians to work at various clerical jobs, but by the early months of 1944, as the offensive line moved further north in the Pacific, the brass on the ground realized that they needed more help, and not only in Australia itself. Then, too, the Australians had come to resent the American soldiers who, they complained, were "Overpaid, over sexed, and over here." They didn't like all the fraternizing between G.I.s and local women, either, something made both more likely and more frequent once Australian civilian women were employed as clerks by the U.S. forces.

As early as the end of 1943, U.S. officers within the Pacific Command had been talking about importing WACs from the States. Naturally, their discussions were not published and they wanted to believe that their plans were being kept carefully secret. Back then the general public was unaware that the area command was having trouble getting additional personnel from Stateside and that they were arguing with their superiors because they didn't want to take clerically-trained male troops out of combat.

Of course, they weren't going to tell the civilian population that the military was bickering! This entire matter remained classified then, but it isn't anymore. Anyone can now find accounts of these events posted on the internet.

Commanding General of the Allied Air Force and the Fifth Air Force, Lt. Gen. George C. Keaney, went personally to press his case at the War Department. They told him that they only had 800 enlisted WACs and 200 WAC officers "unallotted." (By that was meant, not already committed to other specific deployments.) The command protested this treatment by radio, complaining, "Proposed allotment totally inadequate for minimum theater requirements...Can use 10,000 or more Wacs [sic]...Theater Chief who should reach Washington today has data..."

Gen. Douglas MacArthur's Chief of Staff, Lt. Gen. Richard K. Sutherland, duly appeared on February 11, 1944, in the office of Col. Oveta Culp Hobby (wife of former Governor of Texas William P. Hobby), then Director of WACs, demanding 10,000 WACs. She refused. This thrust would be made by the Pacific Command, then parried by various bureaucrats using different excuses, several more times before Hobby eventually agreed to assign of about half that number.

After a few days, spent in training for "tropical" duty, the first group of WACs to be secretly assigned to Pacific duty felt confused. The souvenir booklet later created by the first WAC unit in New Guinea described their uncertainty this way, "Shots—PT—Inspection/Where are we going, INDIA?" [sic.]

WAC major, Hazel Miller from Racine, Wisconsin, supervised the trip and accompanied the troops. Capt. Edel V. Sattre (then the WAC adjutant at Ft. Ogelthrope, who, having later been promoted to Captain, would eventually be signing many WACs' discharge papers), assisted her. The troops—114 WAC officers and 526 enlisted women, along with an unspecified number of GIs—traveled on a converted cruise ship.

The Racine *Journal Times* article, published after the two "chaperones" (although they were certainly never called that, in the article) flew back, recounted an interview with Maj. Miller. "The GIs outnumbered the women on board and had to draw lots for attendance at the dances held in the ship's ballroom. There were six dances during the crossing, limited by the size of the ballroom to 75 women and 125 men. Some of the men…were offering scalper's prices [for their ticket, should they choose not to attend]…"

Some twenty-three WACs jumped right into their jobs as censors, vetting the letters sent back from on shipboard. According to the WACs' primary chaperone, a certain Chicago native, Pvt. Patricia D. Wilkus, sang to great acclaim on all occasions "at religious services on Sundays and at swing sessions on the after-deck in the evenings."

If the cruise included two Sundays, then it must have lasted for at least eight days. The article didn't mention stopping at any intermediate ports *en route*. According to Maj. Miller, the WACs disembarked, singing their corps song, "The WAC is a Soldier Too," and "Waltzing Matilda." Their task accomplished once the WACs reached Brisbane, Miller and Sattre returned to the States by air.

Frank Kluckhohn, one of the New York *Times'* major war correspondents, saw this event differently. Sydney, where the WACs first landed, his article gloated, was considered the Paris of the South Pacific, an R & R spot for armed forces, both American and Australian. "American fighters, anxious for a sight of girls from home—for many of them the first in two years—sought to 'make dates' as the girls got off the boats, despite an attempt by officials to minimize their arrival."

Had the authorities really taken measures to minimize attention? A bevy of American and Australian military dignitaries stood at the gangplank, to welcome the WACs. Also—and this was not directly mentioned, although it was alluded to by Kluckhohn in this particular article—the potential arrival of the WACs had been extremely controversial before they first landed, some suggesting that they were being imported as "comfort girls" for the officers. Finding out about this from other sources helped to explain Kluckhohn's generally leering and condescending tone.

Kluckhohn said that crowds lined the bus route, cheering the arriving WACs. He claimed the WACs were singing, "Give My Regards to Broadway" as they rode on. These WACs weren't the first American women in Sydney; they'd been preceded by nurses, so the *Times* was making a distinction between the "professional" nurses and the "typical American girls" who were WACs. The article seemed to consist of one insult or backhanded compliment after another.

After making it seem that the WACs were there to entertain the boys, Kluckhohn made an obligatory disclaimer that everyone knew they were there to work. (Wink. Wink. Particularly after the leering introduction.) The *Times* article reported that the WACs were wearing "rationed stockings," apparently a subject of great interest to Frank Kluckhohn, who is more generally known for refusing to bow to (instead shaking hands with) Emperor Hirohito after the Japanese surrender, thereby ignoring hundreds of years of protocol; he did, however, excuse his interest by claiming that the women in the area were greatly interested in the stockings.

A huge dance had been arranged at a major French Second Empire-style sandstone building, the Sydney Town Hall, but only for the enlisted people. The Officers Club took care of social arrangements for the officers. Kluckhohn said the feel of this event was materially different from the arrival of WACs in both North Africa and England, but it was difficult to follow his logic. Perhaps his piece was edited strangely. Tickets to the dance were gone within minutes. He made sure to say that the WACs had comfy barracks "with spring mattresses and an excellent dining hall where a fine dinner was served." Who showed him the mattresses? Did he attend the mess? Anyway, the evaluation of the food was strictly Kluckhohn's opinion. But then the man was a war correspondent, not a food critic.

Kluckhohn listed the names and ranks of all the WACs from the New York area. Reading this in another era, how shocking that not only a person's city of residence but also each personal address was published in the newspaper in articles like this! The concept of personal privacy simply didn't seem to exist.

Approximately half the WACs remained in Australia; the rest ended up in Port Moresby, New Guinea. The official military history described their arrival:

"Beginning on May 28 [1944], only two weeks after landing in Australia, 100 WAC censorship officers and 88 enlisted women left by air for Port Moresby. As perspiring WACs stepped from the first plane, clad in coveralls and wool-lined field coats, and carrying full field pack, they were met by an advance party with cameras and flashbulbs, intent on preserving the moment for recruiting purposes." (The "first ones" to debark in both places got a lot of press and photographic attention.)

Both American nurses and Red Cross women had been in Port Moresby for two years before the WACs arrived. Port Moresby had, the official history comments a bit dismissively, "long been regarded as a rear echelon" [i.e., not a combat zone]. This classification might have been used, for one thing, to negate the legal "parity" WACs had been given with male members of the armed forces, by law. Some legal niceties dictated the higher benefits that needed to be paid, should they be injured in a combat zone. Those would be lower if they were in a non-combat zone. Then too, the American government wanted to pacify those back home, to assure them that the WACs were in no danger.

*   *   *

A word about the seemingly oddity of the Army requiring the WACs to pack winter clothes. The best explanation—other than sheer insanity on the part of the Army brass—is that they hoped the instructions on what to pack would foil any enemy attempts figure out where the WACs were going. Forget about the fact that some of the WACs about to be assigned to Pacific duty had to attend a malaria awareness course, a dead giveaway that their destination was a hot, wet place. If you tell the women going to the Alps to pack summer gear and the women going to the tropics to pack winter gear (which was what the Army did), perhaps you'll confuse the enemy. They didn't confuse Tokyo Rose, however. She'd broadcast both the name of their ship and its destination before they ever reached Australia.

The Australians, who knew this region best, commanded all forces in the area, through an entity called New Guinea Force, from the group's formation in 1942 through its dissolution in 1944. They never said that New Guinea had been pacified. General MacArthur himself considered Port Moresby a strategic necessity. He demanded that it be held. Would he demand that an area be held unless he thought it was, or might be, under attack at any time? In fact, the Japanese forces on New Guinea didn't surrender until after Japan, itself, did. There seems to have been more risk in living there than standard U.S. military histories admit.

The presence of WACs created turmoil. Official WAC histories speak of both men and women being treated like captives of their own military services during this period. All the women's barracks were hidden behind barbed wire, guarded night and day, to protect the women from the male soldiers. They were—at least in theory—allowed no furloughs, no independent action. The military feared what it described as "incidents" unless they kept the sexes rigorously separated. The excuse was that the men hadn't seen an American woman, sometimes for as much as eighteen months.

The military, it seems, didn't trust its personnel. Soldiers fumed at so many military personnel being used to guard the women, because the supposed purpose of the WAC presence was to free male personnel to go into combat. If instead they were in camp, guarding women, the men reasoned, then they weren't in combat. The women, for their part, complained that they were being isolated and treated like children, a justified complaint. What was the alternative? Treat everyone like an adult and hope for the best, perhaps?

* * *

After about nine months of this treatment, the rate at which WACs were invalided out of the Pacific Theater skyrocketed. From 98 per thousand, it rose to 267 per thousand.

The WACs struggled as they learned to work in Port Moresby. New Guinea's climate was frankly tropical, which meant that it was hot and humid all the time. Air conditioning didn't exist there, then. It seemed to rain—not nice, polite drizzles, but rather torrential downpours—twice daily, at 10 AM and 4 PM. Some said you could set your watch by them. These storms turned the dirt roads into running canals. If you got caught out in one of them, with the rain pelting you, you'd feel as if you were about to drown. Small cuts turned into major infections, easily and quickly. The stunning coral beaches, with their sharp sand particles, readily created the small cuts that started this infective process.

The clothes that the WACs had been told to pack, by themselves, created additional hazards. They'd arrived in winter gear, which couldn't possibly have been more inappropriate for the climate. (Even if you'd breached security and told your relatives what you were packing, and the censors hadn't done their job and allowed these descriptions to stay in the text, no one would ever guess that the Army was sending you to a tropic isle.) The clothes they had been told to pack would have been far more appropriate to the Alps in winter.

According to the official WAC history, "Clothing requisitions posed a severe problem...The coveralls proved too hot for the climate and many women developed skin diseases...The theater commander insisted that the women wear trousers as a protection against malaria-carrying mosquitoes, but the khaki trousers worn by the [male] troops were scarce."

They wouldn't have been, except that "specially-trained" helpers in the major department stores instructed Stateside relatives and friends of the troops to send Army personnel in the South Seas only the best woolen garments. In addition to the issue of wool being much too hot for the tropical climate, an eclipse of clothes moths would devour them overnight, so that only meagre rags remained the next morning.

Even today, standard WAC histories complain that "khaki was scarce" in the South West Pacific during World War II.

"Most women," the official WAC history noted, "did not have enough clothing and shoes to allow laundered apparel the chance to dry before being worn again." The next claim made by this official history mystifies me:

"Pneumonia and bronchitis were aggravated by a shortage of dry foot gear." Really? How about taking the shoes off and allowing the feet to dry? Or, perhaps, using a towel. Exactly how do wet feet cause pneumonia?

"The malaria rate for women was disproportionately high because WAC's [sic] lacked the lightweight, yet protective clothing issued to the men…" the history continued.

Officers had additional problems. Their huts were close enough to the 4F barracks that they could hear the residents there—nurses, soldiers and WACs—screaming, moaning and crying at night. Some held there threatened to commit suicide if they weren't allowed out, which of course they weren't.

Perhaps no one will ever know how many personnel posted to areas with endemic malaria, and who ended up on 4-F status, and perhaps got dishonorable discharges into the bargain, were really reacting to the antimalarial Atabrine. Discontinuing the drug brought a court martial. Atabrine's three major, known side effects—diarrhea, skin discoloration, and psychosis—might have occurred relatively frequently. However, that's the modern literature on the drug. Officially, the government ceased its inquiries into Atabrine's side effects in 1943; they'd only interested themselves in acute reactions anyway.

Not only was this information not generally available, back then, but Atabrine was also a fairly new drug. How odd that a drug discovered in Germany during the 1930s might be causing such distress among American military personnel a few years later! Most New Guinea-based military personnel knew that it turned the skin yellow after about a week of use. Apparently, none of the military and nursing personnel in malaria-infested regions knew about the other major side effects, or if they did, they might not have been allowed to admit the truth.

The NIH now says about Atabrine, as it was then being administered:

"The scientists found that, at the current dosage, the Atabrine was soaked up in muscle fiber and the liver, causing uncomfortable side effects before it was able to build up in the blood. By changing the dosage-to a first-day big dose to saturate the tissues followed by small daily doses that would then go right to the blood-the Goldwater group [working at Goldwater Memorial Hospital during 1943] was able to save Atabrine, as well as millions of American troops abroad." Leo Barney Slater, in *War and Disease*, contends that neither the Army nor the Navy considered Atabrine's side effects to be worrisome at that point.

The word on the ground, however, was that these orders to use a dosage level adjusted downward after the initial high doses weren't followed in New Guinea.

*   *   *

One thing that the WACs in Port Moresby truly hated was that Stateside folks, wanting to be kind to them, were being advised by special personnel in department stores like Macy's not only to send them woolen clothing, but also to send them cans of SPAM. This "mystery meat" had a number of nicknames among the military personnel, ranging from "meatloaf without basic training" to "ham that didn't pass its physical." It was so difficult to deliver fresh meat that the Army eventually purchased over 150 million pounds of SPAM to feed overseas troops. Canned SPAM gifts from anyone other than Uncle Sam were received, and quickly discarded, with rancor and some well-placed, unkind words.

The troops were practically surviving on a diet of SPAM (perhaps alternating with chipped beef) as it was, and they certainly didn't want any additional cans of SPAM sent to them as "special presents" from loved ones at home. Sometimes they simply didn't send proper thank-you notes, because they couldn't find anything to say that would pass the censors. The women in this particular unit knew what they could get away with saying, because in this case, they were also the censors.

An enlisted WAC received, one day, what looked to be an oversized—in fact a huge—can of SPAM. Angry, she put in on a windowsill in the office, in direct sunlight, intending to punish the contents with the tropic rays. "Do you believe it?" she said to her colleagues. "Another can of this stuff!" While the can sat on its perch, members of the unit would pass it periodically, and throw an odd nasty remark or gesture at it.

The can stayed on the windowsill for months, as a joke, until the unit was about to leave for Biak. As they were packing up the office, the giftee decided, at last, to see what was left inside. After those humid, hundred-degree days, with no air conditioning, she was curious to see what the SPAM looked like. She opened the can, then gasped, "Can't be!" Inside was the moldy taffy, all melted into a gooey mass and fused together, that her benefactor-with-a-sense-of-humor had originally sent her. "Guess I owe him an apology."

Official histories claim that a total of only 150,000 WACs served, of whom 657 received citations. Something about these statistics doesn't match up with the facts, unless unit citations don't count. Major Peabody, the Army officer in charge of the Port Moresby censorship unit, recommended every WAC who'd served for six months or more for a Meritorious Service Unit

Plaque, writing, "I don't know what it is about women that makes them so sharp-eyed in reading letters, but the ones I have possess an uncanny knack for picking up hidden security breaches, such as tricky codes a soldier may devise to tell his wife where he is .... They are turning out more and better work than the male officers they released to the combat area."

About 20% of all WACs in the Pacific worked in the Port Moresby censorship unit, vetting material in some twenty-one different languages. One of the officers had studied music at Juilliard. She censored material in German, French, Italian, Russian and English. Another, who'd taught languages in high school before enlisting, spoke seven languages fluently and found ways to use all of them in this work. A third, Helen, the artist-daughter of Taos painter Ernest Blumenschein, had already acquired an international reputation before she enlisted. She censored mail in English and Spanish. Kluckhohn erred in calling these WACs typical American girls.

* * *

Léonie Rosenstiel, a SWW boardmember, has worked in many different genres, including biographies, record liner notes, translations from French and Spanish, and a college-level textbook for Schirmer Books, a division of Macmillan. She has won awards for her fiction and nonfiction from SouthWest Writers and New Mexico Press Women.

Cultural/Historical Poetry   Gold Medal
Nathan McKenzie

WE WERE

We were born once-
In this job losing,
Depression inducing
Time.

> We were lonely once-
> In this mind fucking,
> Mask wearing
> Time.

> > We stood together once-
> > In this news watching,
> > Health cost rising
> > Time.

> > > We were selfish once-
> > > In this world shattering,
> > > Stimulus pending
> > > Time.

> We fell in love once-
> In this social distancing,
> Government mandating
> Time.

> > We came into grace once-
> > In this curve flattening,
> > Testing and testing and testing
> > Time.

We fell away once-
In this ethical questioning,
Talking heads keep talking
Time.

                    We cried once-
                    In this business shuttering,
                    Security destroying
                    Time.

         We even died once-
         In this makeshift morgue mounting,
         Body count climbing
         Time.   We lived once-
                    In this time
                    And found that once
                    was all we needed

             To know who
             We Were.

              *   *   *

Nathan McKenzie has a Master's degree in Public administration. A member of Southwest Writers, he's featured in their last two publications. Currently he's working on two books, and needs a nap. He is thankful for all of the support and collegiality he has found as a part of Southwest Writers.

Cultural/Historical   Silver Medal
Gregory Walke

DREAMING OF YEW

One of the stranger things I did last year was to take a guided tour of ancient yew trees in South Wales, definitely far off the tourist track. Like many of the stranger things I do, this was instigated by my wife, Pat. Her love of trees and forests led her to search for a focus for our planned trip to the U.K. that was not centered on cathedrals, castles or any other architecture (I am an architect). Pat contacted a Tree Sister (don't ask, I can't explain) in southern New Mexico, where one would think—wrongly—that trees would be worshipped for their very rarity. Tree Sister put her in touch with a Tree Singer (again, don't ask) in England, who put her in contact with a woman in Wales who has devoted her life to the ancient yews.

This was the circuitous path by which I find myself standing beneath the spreading canopy of what is supposed to be the world's oldest tree, a giant yew (*taxus baccata*) in the village churchyard of Defynnog (pronounced Da-ven'-ock) in the Brecon Hills of South Wales I have subsequently been corrected by people who tell me that the bristlecone pines of the American southwest are older, or that the clonal colonies of Rocky Mountain aspens are actually older, or that this tree or that in the world is really the oldest. None of this matters much to me. I'm not out to establish a scientific fact. As with people, once you reach a certain age, there's no more prestige to being the oldest. Anyone who gets that far is already worthy of great respect and admiration.

This is also true for trees. Maybe even more so for trees because they are so casually seen as products for the capricious use of human beings. That a tree should live five or six thousand years without being turned into matchsticks or toilet paper is cause for celebration. You see, humans by and large do not consider trees to have any more significance than any other natural resource, beyond its utility to us. Certainly they aren't seen to have innate rights. And their importance to other things in the world-for example, the

96

micro-world of the forest floor or the oxygen-providing benefits of the rain forest-are rarely thought of at all.

Thus it feels remarkable to be standing beneath the twisted branches and dark green leaves of the Defynnog Yew, which has been scientifically aged by the British Forestry Research Institute at 5,600 years. Take a moment to let that sink in: 5,600 years! It has helped this particular tree that it's located in a thousand-year old churchyard, surrounded by graves. This has preserved it from the most recent and most rapacious of human centuries. Humans revere their own dead much more than they do any other living thing, so they are given pause when considering disturbing a grave. (This isn't always the case. A few miles away, a 4,000-year-old yew was cut down and many graves disturbed in order to widen a rural highway. Nothing can stand between humans and their need to get somewhere faster.)

This utilitarian attitude is not shared by Pat. When she had her DNA tested, she was unhappy to learn that her direct ancestors were not yews or redwoods or any other species of tree. Nonetheless, we are told by the scientists that 25% of human DNA is shared with trees, so that gives her some consolation, as it should give us all food for thought. So, as a sort of family reunion, we have arranged our trip to visit the old ones.

Our guide for this three-day tour is Janis Fry, a short, sturdy English woman with a halo of wild, curly blond hair who has lived in Wales for many years. She laughs a lot. I mean, really a lot. And her cheerfulness is infectious. Her years of study and research into the ancient yews has made her a recognized expert in a little-studied field. She mixes difficult-to-understand science with just-about-as-difficult-to-understand mythology and legends. But she explains all of this, whether we understand or not, in a happy and nonstop barrage of information as she whisks us from one lonely place to another along narrow single-track back roads bordered by tall hedgerows, with occasional glimpses of green meadows dotted with sheep and church steeples, a "green and pleasant land" indeed.

Our little group of four stands under the drooping branches. (We have been joined on the tour by an Australian woman who dreamed of yew trees and who concocts yew essences.) A couple of Boy Scout troops could fit in the space shaded by this very old being. Yews, Janis tells us, are considered the tree of life, a symbol of eternal renewal. This is because they *do* eternally renew themselves. After about 1500 years the youthful yew begins to hollow out-I know the feeling-and after a few centuries more, a new trunk begins to form within the hollow core, sometimes from below and sometimes from above. Another way the yew renews itself is that the long branches arc downward to touch the earth and at that point form new trunks. Such trunks gather in circles along the drip line around the mother trunk. Janis has done extensive testing to show that the DNA in the circling trunks is exactly the same as the mother trunk, proving to the scoffers that this is one tree, not a circle of individual, newer trees.

Our little group wanders from yew to yew up and down the valley of the Usk River. Inside the hollow mother trunk of another giant yew on our tour there are a small table and two chairs, placed there in the eighteenth century by the local curate, who delighted in taking his tea in the heart of another being. We take turns sitting there, too, drinking in the experience of a kind of restful communion with the long ago. My mind wanders to the past and to the stories we have collected about this and other ancient yews-to 1745, engraved on a shaded headstone, when David Williams was laid to rest in the bosom of this circle (as were many others), or to the 1600's, when a church's steeple fell in a storm, precariously near a yew already four thousand years older than the church itself, or to 1120, when the Normans first built the little square stone church at Defynnog. I think of the King of England, his entourage and all their horses who kept dry under a similar ancient yew tree during a sudden thunderstorm in the thirteenth century. I think of the all the ordinary lives sheltered by these symbols of resurrection and the host of ordinary dead now surrounding most of them.

Janis switches from scientific lingo to the mythological. It is her belief (and I feel convinced by her research and her ardor) that the "lost years" of Jesus of Nazareth's youth were spent in Wales. A thriving trade existed in Roman times between Palestine and Britain, both outposts of the Empire.

Wales was known for its tin mines, and Jesus's uncle, Joseph of Arimathea, a tin importer, was thought to be a frequent visitor. This history is doubted by people in Glastonbury in Somerset, who believe that Joseph and his nephew traveled *there* and not Wales. As they have quite a large financial stake in saying so, due to the enormous New Age center they have become, they have always had the advantage over the Wales theorists. Whatever the case, there is a strong belief, as William Blake wrote in what is now the de-facto English national anthem, "And did those feet in ancient time, walk upon England's mountains green?" Or Wales, perhaps?

Janis also tells us that the yew, a native of the Middle East, was the True Cross, upon which Jesus was crucified. This theory may be a tad sketchier, but she backs up the tale by telling us all about the reverence the ancient people had for the yew and its powers of renewal. As an aside, she points out a small yellowed branch on the side of one of the minor trunks of the yew. It looks for all the world like something that has a bad case of some disturbing tree disease. In America we would immediately spray it with pesticides or chop it off before it could contaminate the rest of the tree. However, Janis tells us, this is the famous "golden bough", of which tales are told and songs are sung all over the ancient and medieval worlds, the focus of many a hero's quest. And it is the natural, golden and everlasting off- spring of the yew, which in its long lifetime changes back and forth from male to female, another of its remarkable feats of sustainability.

Now Janis is speaking of King Arthur and his Round Table. "Camelot," she tells us, "was in South Wales, and the yew plays a significant role in the Arthurian legends-which are fact, not legends at all, but history". In this, again, she is contradicted by the economic forces in Glastonbury, but that doesn't faze her.

"But what of the Druids?" we ask. Ah yes, those pre-Roman cults of wood-loving priests and their mysterious religious rites. Druids were the religious and professional class of the Celtic world, stretching from Ireland into most of Western Europe. But the yews were ancient long before there were Celts or Druids. Celtic influences are still felt in the western British Isles and as far afield as France (especially in Brittany). They did center their worship around certain groves and trees, most notably the yew. And their religious sites were later chosen as the locations for Roman temples and Christian churches. This is how the yews ended up in churchyards, or rather, how the churchyards ended up beside the yews. Some churches we visited were set within a circle of yews, some older, some younger, but all of them older than the churches, which were themselves sometimes a thousand years old. (Churches were usually built to the south of the oldest yews, so that the tree spirits would protect the little buildings-an early example of covering your bases.)

"Ironically, all parts of the yew are toxic, especially the bark and the berries," Janis is telling our Australian companion.

"But can I safely use the oil in my essences?" she asks.

"In very small quantities—it's similar to belladonna in that respect," Janis responds. "Yew essence is thought to have the power to induce dreams." She explains the chemistry with some scientific details, and our companion in turn tells Janis about the dreams she has had under the influence of yew essence.

"Too much for me," I whisper to Pat. "All this history and science…"

*   *   *

I take a break, wandering through the churchyard and inspecting the very old tombstones (or maybe not so old in the larger scheme of things; I'm gaining a whole new conception of age). I wander into the little medieval stone church to look for Green Men. These carved wood or stone images, usually of a face surrounded by lush vegetation, are meant to invoke the spirits of the woods, of the forest, from a time long before (whether for protection or for whimsy it's hard to tell).

A few days before, Pat and I had wandered through Horner Woods in the far west of Somerset. None of the trees in that forest pre-dated Queen Victoria, but as we walked the forest in the crepuscular light of a summer evening, they seemed frightening and primeval in their twisted shapes and deep undergrowth. It was easy to understand how one could visualize a face in the hollows and knots of a tree. It would only be left to a primitive imagination whether the face was a demon or a god.

I imagine standing under the Defynnog Yew more than two thousand years ago, before the Romans or the Christians, a thousand years or more before the Battle of Hastings, and try to see what it was like to live here. The tree, of course, was more than three thousand years old even then, and probably looked very similar to the way it looks today. But beyond…beyond would be very different. What are now villages and green pastures would have been covered in dense, almost impenetrable forest, as was most of the British Isles. Yew trees would have been plentiful. There would be open glades here and there, small patches of farmed land, for agriculture had arrived in this area two thousand years or so earlier, when the Defynnog Yew was "only" a thousand years old. People lived rough lives in small hamlets with rude structures and never ventured very far from home. Danger lurked everywhere.

There are still today yew trees that were ancient long before the Celts or the Druids revered them. The trees were venerable when the Neolithic people built Stonehenge and Avebury on the Salisbury Plain far to the southeast of Wales. They were very, very old before any human recorded history. The yews were here first, and at least some of them have persevered.

As they age they cover more territory—they spread low and wide rather than grow tall. They are not the most magnificent of trees, not the most lush or most perfectly-formed—those accolades, as in people, usually go to the young. But there is beauty in the intertwined convolutions of the reddish bark and the graceful arc of the limbs reaching to touch the earth. And there are a presence, even a wisdom, and a solid peace in the gnarled and twisted arms of the ancient ones.

Of that we can dream.

*　*　*

A retired architect, **Greg Walke** is following one of his earliest interests, writing. He's completed one and a half mystery novels in a series, in addition to numerous short stories. He enjoys travel, history and research, all of which led to this story, his first attempt at non-fiction.

Cultural/Historical Poetry   Silver Medal
Jesse Ehrenberg

IN THE TIME OF THE GREAT PANDEMIC

Like Bedouins
lost in a sand storm,
we brave contamination
with faces covered,
to stand
vaguely recognizable,
outside a friend's house.
Where,
behind a picture window,
a family capers and jests
like monkeys in a zoo,
while we,
both audience and play,
wave and yell,
doing our own pantomime
for their amusement
(as well as for any neighbors,
who happen to be
looking out their windows
or driving by)

All of us,
now sharing
the same realization.
That though we may be
caged separately,
we're all still part of this
strange menagerie
we call
The Human Race.

*   *   *

Jesse Ehrenberg started writing poetry as a teenager and has never seen a reason to stop. His poems have been published in multiple local anthologies. His book, *SURPRISE!*, won prizes in the New Mexico Press Women contest, and a Silver Award in the inaugural Margaret Randall Poetry Book Contest.

Cultural/Historical   Bronze Medal
Jonathan Chisdes

IS 1960 EPIC *EXODUS* LOST IN TIME?

I recently started watching DVDs of the TV show *Mad Men*—they were a birthday gift from my wife. I'm very much enjoying this series about advertising executives in New York set in the year 1960. I'm only about a dozen episodes into it, so far, but I'm quite amazed at how historically specific the show is, highlighting events, social attitudes, and trends from 1960. It's a fascinating prism through which to judge contemporary society, seeing how far we've progressed, or haven't. For example, one of the major themes is how men in the workplace in 1960 treat women in the workplace—such blatant sexism appears shockingly outrageous to contemporary viewers.

I was particularly struck by one of the early episodes in which the advertising firm is approached by the Israeli Ministry of Tourism; as they discuss with the ad-men why and how American tourists in 1960 should visit the twelve-year-old country, they point out that there is a very popular book by Leon Uris, *Exodus*, which is being made into an epic motion picture and is about to be released.

I smiled because I fondly remember seeing that classic film a dozen years ago. However I hadn't really thought much about the world in which it was made and what it says about popular American attitudes toward Israel in 1960—and how different they are today. When I re-watched *Exodus* a few days ago, I realized how, just like *Mad Men*, the movie helps us judge how the perception of our world—and in this specific case, the conflicts of the Middle East—have changed in a half-century.

Made only twelve years after the birth of the State of Israel, *Exodus* is a historical epic in the tradition of those great 1950s films like *The Ten Commandments*, *Ben Hur*, and *Spartacus*, in which fictional characters interact with larger-than-life historical figures and witness the extraordinary events which changed the world. But unlike the other epics, *Exodus* deals with history which, to most of its audience, was contemporary events.

The film basically focuses on that brief period of Jewish history between the Holocaust and the founding of the State of Israel. We sometimes forget, a half century removed from this time, that one event did not automatically follow the other, like a snap of the finger. Instead it was an extremely complex political process, fraught with all kinds of obstacles. The birth of the State of Israel as a direct result of the Holocaust was no forgone conclusion; many men and women had to work very hard to make the dream into a reality.

* * *

For those who have not had the opportunity to see this classic, the film, based on the novel by Leon Uris, is divided into three parts. In the first, a group of Zionists led by Ari Ben Canaan (Paul Newman) stages a daring rescue of 600 "displaced persons" (i.e. Holocaust survivors) from a British camp in Cyprus aboard the ship *Exodus*. In the second, the *Exodus* passengers and leaders deal with the difficult issues of declaring Israeli independence from British rule and the politics behind the UN's vote for the partition of Palestine. All the while, conflicts between Jews increase as the non-violent Haganah has little tolerance for the terrorist-like actions of the Irgun which blows up the King David Hotel. In the third section, the Jews face difficult challenges as the Arabs, with whom they had hoped to live peacefully, threaten to destroy them in the prelude to the War for Independence.

Colorful characters clash with each other, family ties are strained, romance blossoms, and a fight for freedom ensues against a sweeping backdrop stunningly filmed on location in Israel and Cyprus. An Academy Award-winning score by Ernest Gold sets the romantic tone. A number of powerful scenes rend the heart: among them are when Holocaust survivor Dov Landau (Sal Mineo) is forced to recall the horrors of Auschwitz which he had blocked out; when the Christian-American nurse Kitty Fremont (Eva Marie Saint) saves the life of Ari, whom she loves; and when the *Exodus* unfurls the Israeli flag and "Hatikva" plays in the background.

"Zionist propaganda," as one recent critic called it? Certainly an unfair trivialization of the film. And yet, as a very insightful article by Jacob M. Victor of Harvard College points out, *Exodus* is quite politically incorrect by contemporary standards. Victor's article draws a stark contrast between the warm reception Exodus received in 1960, and how it would probably be torn to pieces by modern-day critics if it were made today.

In a number of ways, the film doesn't hold up over time. Like *Gone with the Wind*, it can be seen as an anachronistic relic telling only one very slanted side of history. But in many other ways—perhaps ways even more important—Victor demonstrates how the film does hold up. It hits many key themes that resonate so well with American audiences—in 1960 as well as today—most notably the identification with the underdog. In one scene, a clear connection is drawn between Israel's fight for Independence and America's Revolutionary War. There is so much that a contemporary American—especially a Jewish American—can identify with.

Exodus is essentially an idealistic film. As Victor concludes his essay, "The way that *Exodus* so unabashedly presents its idealistic stance may be jarring to our modern sensibilities, but that may be simply the result of our cynicism over the many years of conflict in the Middle East."

I think he's right. In the film's final sequence, Ari gives a eulogy in which he laments untimely, violent death, yet it's filled with hope that peace is not so far off. This speech is spoken at the very outbreak of the War for Independence and the implication is that if Israel can just manage to get through this one war, the Arab problem will be solved and the Jews and Arabs can share the land in peace.

In 1960, only twelve years after the events the film depicted, this didn't seem that far-fetched. It's unfortunate that a half-century later peace seems far more elusive now than it did then. But watching this movie, just like watching *Mad Men*, is like traveling back in time; one can absorb the more innocent feelings of the era. The good and the bad. And realize how far we've come…

And how far we haven't.

* * *

Work Cited: "Politics, Cinema, and the Middle East: Reconsidering Exodus" by Jacob M. Victor. New Society: Harvard College Student Middle East Journal. January 29, 2008.

After earning his MA in English, **Jonathan Chisdes** taught writing and literature at Seminole Community College. He has written film reviews, short stories, plays, poetry, commentary, personal essays, academic papers, and a novel. He has also acted in several films. Jonathan lives in Rio Rancho with his incredibly supportive wife, Natasha.

Cultural/Historical Poetry   Bronze Medal
Princess Miller

CHILDREN IN THE CAVE

There are some children in a cave
Saw it on TV
Many people trying to figure
How to get them out

There are some children in a cave
Thailand, international news
Commands movement
Demands response

There are some children in a cave
Seventeen days
Deep darkness, airless
Famished, fatigued

Trending news
Heroic moves

Children in the cave
Prayers
Action
Miraculous rescue

There *were* some children in the cave

And yet . .
I still hear voices

Children in caves

Caves of poverty
Gangs, fatherless
Drugs, aimless
Trafficking, homeless
Abuse . . .

There are children
. . . still in the cave
Waiting . . .

*   *   *

Princess A. Miller is the award-winning author of *God's Little Sunflower (When a Child Dies)*, a poetic memoir of her grief journey. She is published in *Upper Room* which is distributed in 33 languages and over 100 countries. She aims to leave a legacy of poetry that changes everything.
www.projectsunflower.net

SECTION FIVE

Mystery/Crime

Just what you would expect from such a category. See if you can figure out the heroes and villains before you turn the final page.

Mystery/Crime
Linda Triegel

Gold Medal

STRANGER IN TOWN

"Who's the stranger?" George said.

"If I knew that," I said, "he wouldn't be a stranger."

George ignored me. He usually does, for all he's my deputy and supposed to take orders from me.

We were sitting on the porch in front of the sheriff's office watching the stranger getting his suitcases down from the wagon that had brought him from the depot. The driver was helping, but the cowboys leaning on the rail in front of the hotel were just watching the show, grinning and poking each other's sides.

He was a sight to behold that was for sure. He wore a gray homburg, a kind of headgear nobody in Coyote Wells had ever seen—hell, I'd only seen it in a Sears Roebuck catalogue myself—and a three-piece suit that didn't come out of any catalogue. He wore glasses and had a red face, but whether that was his natural look or the result of all that baggage he was hefting, I didn't know. He was a big man, though, and didn't look flabby, so the cowboys kept their distance. Just in case.

"Are you going to check him out?" George said.

"He hasn't done anything yet."

George Garcia had a lot of curiosity for a Mexican. That's one reason I made him my deputy, though there was a lot of head-shaking in town at the time. He'd been my best friend since we were kids, so I got away with it. Back then, Coyote Wells was as lawless as they come. Some days we had a higher body count than Dodge or Tombstone, but the two of us survived. Which is why they made me sheriff, I guess. No one else left standing. No one else white.

"He's coming this way," George said. "Guess you won't have to do any work after all."

He was taller than he looked across the street. I stood up to check. He had an inch on me, and I'm no pip-squeak. He held out his hand. "Sheriff Cooper, I'm Richard Henry. Good to meet you." He had a deep voice and an Eastern-dude way of talking. Polite, though.

"Welcome to Coyote Wells, Mr. Henry," I said. "What brings you to town?"

"Well, sir, to be honest—I'm writing a book."

That shook me up some. Behind me, I could hear the front legs of George's chair hitting the porch floor.

"Yes, sir," Henry went on, as if I'd said something. "About the Old West. This Old West." He swept his arm out to take in the whole wide, dusty, wheel-rutted main street. I didn't see the Old West myself. At least not outside the barber shop, where Fred Lindstrom kept a supply of dime novels to amuse his customers.

"I hate to be the one to break it to you, Mr. Henry," I said. "But the Old West is long gone. If it was ever here. Hell, there's even talk of stringing a telephone wire to town. Pretty soon we'll be civilized."

Henry paid no attention to me. Sometimes I wonder if I'm invisible. He was squinting down at George, probably itching to ask what tribe he belonged to but didn't know how to say it politely. George was part Indian and occasionally made use of his looks to confuse strangers. Maybe Henry thought he didn't speak English.

"That's my deputy," I said, but didn't help him out any more than that.

"How!" George said and put his feet back up on the rail. He was wearing boots, Levis, and a black coat covering the revolver at his belt. Maybe the sparsity of paint and feathers confused Henry, so he didn't pursue that line of research.

"You any relation to the Henry family used to be ranchers in this area?" I asked. The Henrys were rustlers, not ranchers, thirty years back. Murderers too, except nobody ever had the guts to testify against them. But I wasn't going to insult a stranger's family until I knew he was one of them. Old Ike Henry still lorded it over his broken-down spread up in the hills, waited on by a gang of female relatives like some reprobate Mormon.

Henry noticed me again. His pale eyes lit up. "No, sir, no relation that I know of. But I did read about the Henrys back East and thought this would be as good a place to start my field work as any. Rustlers, weren't they? Were they killers too?"

George made a noise in back of me, and I steered Henry up onto the porch. "Why don't you come into the office, Mr. Henry, and I'll answer your questions. You don't want to be standing outside slinging words like 'killer' around where folks can hear you and get nervous."

"Oh, certainly. You're right, sheriff. I beg your pardon."

Ignorant dude.

* * *

Two days later, Richard Henry was dead.

George and I were just putting Asa Briggs into a cell for being drunk and disorderly, and it wasn't even noon yet. He was making a hell of a lot of noise, so I slammed the door on the cell block to hear myself think.

"Damn," I said to Nettie Green, the manager of the Grand Hotel, who'd come running across the street to tell me a maid had found Henry in the stable with a bullet hole in the middle of his back. The maid was still hysterical, Nettie said, but she'd gotten the gist out of the girl quick enough. Nettie was an ex-saloon dancer, still good-looking at forty, and could coax or threaten secrets out of anybody. Except maybe George.

"Sorry," I said to Nettie, but I was looking at George. We both looked at the cell block. Asa was still yelling and cussing back there.

"Go listen if he says anything interesting," I said to George. Asa Briggs was Ike Henry's son-in-law. George understood and slipped behind the door quietly so Asa wouldn't know he was there.

"Your maid see who killed him?" I asked Nettie.

Nettie shrugged. "Nobody in the stable when she got there but Mr. Henry."

"Body still in the stable?" Nettie nodded. "Okay, Nettie, thanks. I'll be right over. Keep any curious guests out of the way for a while."

When she'd gone, I went into the cell block, and George and I tried to interrogate Asa, but he was still too stinko to make much sense. He did say he'd been drinking that morning at the Sagebrush Hotel, so I sent George over to find out how long he'd been there. Then I crossed the street to the Grand to look at Henry's body.

"Damn," I said again when I got to the stable. I hate to see anybody killed, most of all a man in his prime—Henry couldn't have been more than thirty-five—and one who had seemed harmless. Maybe he wasn't, but that didn't matter anymore.

The body was lying on the straw outside one of the stalls. The horse inside was skittish and started backing up when I came in, her ears flicking. Not used to gunshots yet.

"Easy, girl," I said, soothing her as I contemplated the body. There was a neat hole right in the middle of the fancy coat, but no powder marks. Good shooting. I looked around but didn't see that the stable floor was disturbed by anyone but Henry. Rifle from a distance then. Still could have been anyone. Almost anyone.

There was a carrot on the floor next to the stall. Henry must have been going to feed the mare. I gave her the carrot and bent down to feel the body. Still warm, not stiff yet. Hadn't been dead long. I looked at my watch. He was killed maybe about ten o'clock. The world was awake long before that, and anybody could have seen the killer, but I doubted I'd find anyone who did. I covered Henry with a horse blanket and went over to the hotel to ask around anyway.

Nettie sent one of her clerks back to keep the curiosity seekers out of the stable until the mortuary wagon could get there, and I started talking to drivers and stable boys. Nobody had seen anything. Same old story.

George came into the Grand a little later. "Asa was drinking at the Sagebrush, like he said, pretty much all morning. He'd rented a room the night before because he'd had a fight with Addie and she threw him out of the house. Manager said he didn't go anywhere until he started getting rowdy and the manager called us to come round him up."

"Guess it wasn't him. Too bad."

"Here's something interesting. Ike Henry came by the Sagebrush last night to talk Asa into coming home. Wasn't real diplomatic about it, I guess, because they were pretty loud. A lot of the guests heard them, but no one saw Ike after he went stomping out around midnight except Jim over at the livery. Ike got his horse and lit out."

"Anybody see him after that?"

"Not in town. Want me to go out to the ranch and ask some questions?"

If there was anything Ike Henry hated more than the law, it was Mexicans. Sending a lawman named Garcia into that house was asking for another murder.

"No," I said. "If it comes to that, we'll get a posse." I kind of wished it would come to that. Lawmen before me had tried to stick something on Ike, but he was slippery. Without a witness, we couldn't arrest him, and even if there was a witness, he wouldn't testify.

The dude would have made a good witness, I thought. Too bad he couldn't witness to his own murder.

Nettie came in with a cup of coffee.

"Henry's room been cleaned?" I asked her.

"No, I thought you'd want to see it."

The three of us went up to Room 302. It looked like Henry had been there for years. Books were piled on the tables and shelves, and the desk was covered in paper—old newspapers and yellow writing pads filled with Henry's neat hand. I sat down at the desk while George searched the rest of the room. Nettie sat next to me, putting everything into a box when I'd done looking at it. She was quiet, which was nice, and she smelled like vanilla, which was nice too.

"He tell you anything about this book of his?" I asked her.

She shrugged. "Not really. He asked a lot of questions about Coyote Wells, history mostly, who started the town, were there any Indians around, any outlaws or rustlers."

"He was kind of fixated on rustlers."

"I thought so too. I told him about the Henrys—I guess it's natural he'd wonder about people with his same name—but there's been no rustling for years."

"Wasn't his real name," George said just then, and showed us a leather case with Henry's calling cards in it. The address on them was New York City. There were also some papers with foreign writing on them—German, Nettie thought—and a passport.

"Richard von Eisenberg," she read. "That must be his real name. Not Henry after all. Oh, my God!"

We both looked at Nettie. She'd gone white under her face powder.

She handed me a yellow newspaper clipping she'd found tucked into the passport. It was the *Wells Gazette* from twenty years ago reporting the murder of a deputy marshal, Ben Silver. Ike's brother Jake had been tried for it, but there wasn't any real evidence, and nobody would testify against Jake on account of Ike would get them killed. Jake got shot himself two years later in a saloon brawl. Justice without law.

I looked at Nettie. "What about it?"

"I told him about Ben's murder," she said. "I told him about Ike. He thought it would make a great chapter for his book. He wanted to meet Ike...."

"You think he went out there?"

"He didn't have to. He'd been asking around. Word would've got back to Ike."

She looked at me, scared and sorry. "I got him killed, Ray. I told him to stay away from Ike, but he just thought it was a great story. For his book. Fool didn't even own a gun."

She slumped back in her chair. "It wasn't your fault, Nettie," I said. "He thought the Old West was some kind of Bill Cody show, all pretend to entertain strangers. Even the bullets were pretend to him."

Except the one that killed him. And damn if it didn't look Ike Henry was going to get away with it again.

George had gone back to shuffling through papers. Suddenly he was quiet again, even for him. Nettie stopped sniffling and looked at him.

"What'd you find?" I said.

George handed me a packet of letters. I read them, then handed them to Nettie to read. We were all quiet for a while.

"Well, damn," I said. "Cheer up, Nettie. Looks like we might get Ike Henry after all."

* * *

The letters were all from Ben Silver's kin and people who'd lived in Coyote Wells and moved away afterwards. All eye-witness accounts of Ike Henry's part in killing Ben Silver from people who'd seen him in town that day, seen him running out the back of the sheriff's office after they heard gunshots, or seen him hightailing it for home. No telling where the dude had gotten hold of them, or how he'd found out where all those people were, but he hadn't come to town unarmed after all. And I was betting that the bullet we dug out of Henry would be from the same gun that killed Ben Silver.

It was a real pleasure going out to the Henry place with a warrant for Ike's arrest. Never saw a man so surprised—or mad as a hornet when I told him what we had on him. After the hearing found the evidence good enough to convict him, the marshal took Ike off to the territorial jail, and George and I went over to the Grand to stand Nettie a drink.

"You suppose Henry knew more about Coyote Wells than he let on?" George said.

"We'll never know," I said. It didn't matter now, but George wouldn't let this sleeping dog lie.

"Maybe he was related to the Henrys back in wherever they came from. Everybody out here comes from someplace else."

"Except you," I said.

Nettie smiled. "Maybe George should write a book."

"Might just do that," George said.

I raised my glass. "Here's to the Old West," I said. "Rest in Peace."

* * *

Linda Triegel grew up in Connecticut and moved around a lot before settling in Albuquerque. She started writing after college and eventually published 12 romances under her pen name, Elisabeth Kidd, as well as short stories and travel articles. Her first cozy mystery, writing as Elly Kirsten, is *Civil Blood.*

Mystery/Crime
David Knop

Silver Medal

PAYBACK

Chapter 1

Al-Fadee, the Redeemer, lay dead over blood-clotted sand.

I'd seen this Polish stud last year at the Scottsdale Arabian Horseshow and the Missing Livestock Report described this horse to a tee–Champaign and white pinto markings in a tobiano pattern like big commas over the neck and chest.

I usually paid little attention to the online livestock theft notices, but my pueblo, the Cochiti Pueblo, halfway between Albuquerque and Santa Fe, exercised concurrent jurisdiction with the BLM over this place, *Kasha-Katuwe,* also known as Tent Rocks, a set of unique pumice formations southwest of the pueblo. When some picnickers complained of the smell, I drove down to the site with my own horse in tow. I needed the diversion. Divorce papers were slapped in my hand two Mondays ago.

The carcass decayed at the base of a precipice. Bands of gray volcanic tuff and beige-pink rock layered along the cliff face. Canyons and arroyos cut the cliffs in many places while water and wind had scooped holes and contoured slot canyons into smooth semi-circles.

Al-Fadee had been dead for at least three days, a period proven by flies buzzing by the thousands and the mass of wriggling maggots. I gagged as I circled the carcass to get upwind. White ribs protruded from his torn hide like an open picket gate. Coyotes or dogs. The Arabian's bloated legs stuck out straight and stiff. Pink cavities stared from the eye sockets. The stud's mane and tail fluttered in the wind, then straightened as a dust devil twisted by, throwing grit in my eyes and topping the carcass with sand.

A bullet between the eyes had finished off the stud point blank. Burnt hair surrounded the wound. Who could kill a horse up close like that?

Holding my breath, I pulled out my pocketknife, an eight-in-one do everything-but-feed-the-horses model and dug around the back of the horse's throat. I sliced through soft tissue and scraped along bone until I got lucky. The bullet, slightly distorted, had distinct land-and-groove marks. It looked like a .357, but I wouldn't know for sure until the lab examined it.

I stepped back for air, checked the pale, volcanic tuff cliffs to make sure I was alone. Phallic rock formations ninety feet high offered unlimited hiding places. A shiver mixed with sweat ran down my spine. Hell, even Crowd Killer danced and snorted where I'd tied him. I pocketed my knife and rubbed his nose. He settled down while we walked. While I talked to him he started munching brush.

Crowd Killer alerted again when a pebble scraped somewhere. The sound of a boot? I scanned the cliffs for sign of an intruder. My horse was skittish as hell, and maybe I acted jumpy, but that didn't explain the hair raised on my forearms.

Watching and listening exposed nothing, so I turned my eyes to the ground. A steady wind and a medium rain last night had muted critical characteristics of tire and boot prints. Tracks in the sand showed two assholes had driven a trailer to this spot, unloaded the Arab, led him to the base of the cliff, then shot him point blank in the head.

Tent Rocks was only one of many good places to hide a carcass. *Al-Fadee* came from a ranch north of Santa Fe. Why here? They had to trailer the carcass forty miles to this place and that didn't make sense.

A flash of light jacked my heart. I scanned the cliffs. Twenty years on this job netted plenty of enemies and a healthy dose of paranoia. No matter, I didn't see a damn thing except a hawk perched high on the cliffs.

The FBI, BLM, and sheriff needed notification and my cellphone showed no bars, so I strung yellow tape quickly and made ready to leave. The cliffs flashed again, but this time I caught the source at the top. I played dumb and mounted up. Crowd Killer made his usual protest by twisting away as I legged up. I trotted toward my truck and trailer like I was going home. Once Crowd Killer was loaded, I would track down that son-of-a-bitch watching from the edge of the cliff. Paranoia pays.

I loaded Crowd Killer into his trailer, hopped into my Jeep, a red and white '53 custom, and drove toward Cochiti Pueblo down Route 92 two miles until out of sight of the cliffs. I pulled into a ravine and hoofed back toward the place where I'd noticed the flash. I doubted the watcher was still there, but I needed to see his sign. Marks on the ground often speak loudly.

As I slogged uphill, I hugged ravines and vegetation, visions of *Al-Fadee* in life passed before me. Fifteen hands high and over nine hundred pounds. Muscular beauty. Flowing mane. A prancer in the Scottsdale Horse Show arena who had owned the crowd and knew it.

On high ground, I stayed off the skyline, but moved slowly. I needed to work out more. An overlook above the carcass showed footprints and scuffing where someone had crouched. I'd suspected the snoop was a cop wannabe who'd picked the missing horse off the Internet and got his kicks by watching the scene. But no; tracks created a path that showed the man had enough savvy to stay out of my sight. He was gone.

Shadows lengthened, and I didn't want to chance a broken leg in rough country after sunset. Seeking out an armed person at night didn't appeal, either. I trotted down the ridgeline to my Jeep.

The carcass would be there in the morning. And if the snoop was there, I would nail him.

Chapter 2

Next day, I called the FBI Albuquerque Field Office. My usual contact was on assignment, so I talked to an agent who was new and not enthusiastic about investigating a livestock killing. "I'll get right on it," he said, after consulting with his boss.

I took that as a euphemism for later. Much later.

Then I called the Sandoval County Sheriff's Office in Bernalillo, Deputy Robert Bowditch, an old friend. More often than not, the sheriff would jump in on livestock cases.

"Got a dead horse at Tent Rocks. FBI's not enthusiastic, how about you?"

"You mean that missing stud Arab from north of Santa Fe, what, Rancho Camino de Rincon?"

"The same."

He said, "Weird dumpsite. Why drive a horse all that way just to shoot it? Plenty of places for that up north. Why here?"

"Nothing comes to mind. Doesn't even make sense to steal a horse like that. Can't show it. Can't breed it. Can't even sell the sperm without papers. An Arabian without registration is worth zip."

"That all you got?" he asked.

"Questions is all I got."

"I'll let you know if I hear anything, but FBI and BLM is up each other's ass more often than not. Sorry, I'm not jumping into that hornet's nest. Enjoy." Bowditch hung up, no doubt going somewhere to protect and serve.

The Bureau of Land Management's Rio Puerco Field Office in Albuquerque had jurisdiction over wild mustangs, so I called. Special Agent Raphael Torres seemed interested until I gave details.

"This horse is wild or stray?" he asked.

"No."

"Not my problem," said Torres.

"Okay, I'll bury it."

"Not at Tent Rocks, you won't."

"You said it wasn't your problem."

"It is if you bury it in my national monument."

Great. I reported a crime and nobody came.

I hung up, punched in Rancho Camino de Rincon's number. The ranch foreman, Tyler Richman, answered.

"Found your horse," I told him when and where.

Richman exhaled. "You're gonna tell me *Al-Fadee* is dead."

"You knew?"

"Second one this month. A filly, *Mahbouba*. Found her up in Colorado a week ago. Shot in the head. Horrible thing."

"What you want me to do with the carcass?"

"You got a trailer?" he asked.

An image of the stinking remains flashed in my mind. "Carcass is in bad shape."

"Mr. Romero, the owner had great affection for that horse and wants him buried at the ranch. Believe me, he doesn't take no for an answer. You will be well compensated for your time and any damages."

"I'll get back to you." I hung up.

On the far wall of my office I'd hung a framed photo of me in my dress blues thirty years and that many pounds ago. For whatever reason, it grabbed my attention. Next to it used to hang our wedding picture. A rectangle of unfaded paint emphasized its absence. Costancia had taken the photo with her, a gesture that meant she didn't think the whole marriage a disaster. There were good days, for sure, and we'd raised a fine son.

A picture of Costancia hung to the left of the bare spot. She was nineteen then with long, thick hair, black, and radiant. Her smile delighted everyone she'd ever met. Her voice calmed. Her eyes captivated. She had tried to make it work for twenty-five years. So did I, but eventually I fucked it up by putting more effort into my work than into our relationship. I pushed the divorce decree to a far corner of my desk and hoped they'd disappear. Regret closed my throat and tightened my chest, so I directed my attention to circumstances I might be able to do something about, dead horses.

Who in hell would kill a beauty like *Al-Fadee*? Not rustlers because those outlaws have connections and the Arabian would be in Mexico right now. And people who knew horse flesh wouldn't kill a pedigreed stud that might bring over a few hundred grand. Kidnap for ransom? The owner would have received demands of silence and threats. There would be no missing livestock reports.

Animals have souls, and their killing with no need pisses me off. An old man, had to be one hundred, told me something that stuck. "When our ancestors moved from hunting to farming, they lost respect for animals. To justify how man treated animals, they had to play down their intelligence and deny them a soul."

The word Why had always been my matador's red cape, and now it enflamed my sense of justice and stoked an urge for retribution. Still, my bones warned of stepping unnecessarily into trouble, a habit of mine that cost me my marriage.

The next day I motored to Tent Rocks, this time with my Winchester lever-action. My ever-present paranoia had sounded the survivor's mantra: he that is forewarned best be armed. I usually carried my Ruger Blackhawk .30 carbine revolver, but it would be ineffective against a threat from the top of the cliffs, if it came to that.

The dead stallion lay as I'd left him. Coyote had visited during the night and buzzards sat on the cliffs watching me. Nothing else had changed. Neck hairs under my braid tingled so I scoped the bluffs. My instincts warned of a riflescope, its crosshairs made pin pricks in my skin.

Maybe this time it was just suspicion screwing with my head, but I worked for every bit of mistrust I possessed and kept my rifle close.

I had work to do and couldn't spend all day staring at the scenery. I love horses, always have, but I admit I was a little excited to use the new winch I'd installed last month. I flipped my braid over my shoulder and ran the cable through the trailer, then around the horse's chest. God, it stunk.

When I winched the whole mess onto the trailer, a hind leg snagged on the gate and tore off. I threw the leg onboard, thinking I should've kicked myself in the ass with it. This was once a beautiful animal. The image of the magnificent Arabian, minus a leg, lying jammed inside a small trailer instead of running through green pastures burned in my gut. My arms weighed heavy as I imagined *Al-Fadee* at full gallop trailing banners of long, radiant hair. The animal's killers had to be twisted and sick.

I headed north on Interstate 25. Ten miles south of Santa Fe, a hot sun shimmered the highway and surrounding grasslands of La Bajada Mesa, a juniper-studded flat top where wagon tracks of 17th century travelers are etched into volcanic rock. Interstate 25, a modern overlay of the *El Camino Real de Tierra Adento*, the Royal Road of the Interior, obscured the past of the original road, the principal trade route between Santa Fe and Mexico City for nearly three hundred years.

I reveled in the history of this mesa as I motored up its slopes. La Bajada nurtured my people long before the Spanish came. Pre-contact footpaths, stone piles, and agricultural grids bear witness to settlers as early as 12,000 years ago. The anthropologists are wrong about the origins, though. My people are not new arrivals, we have been here forever. I am not merely *from* this place; I am *of* it.

My awe of this country's past was deflated by the fact that in my trailer I hauled a carcass of a murdered animal descendant from a line of horses 5,000 years old. History enjoys little respect in the modern world.

The dead horse had drawn an audience yesterday. How'd the man on the cliff even know the stallion was there? The smell? Maybe, if he was a buzzard. No, he had to have a stake in the crime: stake enough to be following me right now.

A truck five hundred yards behind spiked my heart rate. I watched him for twenty minutes in the rearview. It must have been amateur hour because when I slowed, he slowed. When I sped up, so did he. I shook him loose at the Cerillos exit with a quick off and on.

North of Santa Fe, up US 84 past Pojoaque and south of Nambe, I turned on to a road shaded by gnarled cottonwoods and announced by a timber arch that framed the Sangre de Cristo Range. At the end of the pasture-lined road, I spotted a two-hundred-year-old stucco hacienda built in traditional pueblo style. The one-story beauty featured roof support *vigas* twelve inches in diameter. I knew the inside without even seeing it: lots of fancy tile, fountains and skull-cracking door frames built for shorter people who lived two centuries ago.

Ranch Foreman Tyler Richman greeted me under the shade of a cottonwood canopy over a century old. A breeze rustled the leaves. I appreciated the opportunity to cool down. The day was a scorcher.

Richmond looked forty, skinny horseman in his Wranglers and white, long-sleeve, snap button. A sweat ring soaked through his Stetson. Beat up boots and a lame gait confirmed my opinion. Anyone who's ever broken horses ended up broken, too. Richmond had the used-up expression of the over-stressed on his thin, tanned face.

I told Richmond what I'd observed at the crime scene including the suspicious gawker.

Richmond said, "The weirdo gets his kicks watching crime scenes?"

Without more evidence, any theory would do. "Drives a seventy-two Chevy C-10. Blue, patched and primed. Beat to shit. Not smart enough to trail undetected. Couldn't read the plate numbers, but it looked Colorado, ya' know, red and white. Veteran's plate, maybe."

Richmond nodded.

"How does something like this happen?" I asked.

Richmond dropped his eyebrows. "What do you mean by that?"

I'd stepped in it a little deeper than I wanted to. I had to sympathize with the guy because his job was threatened. "I mean, how do two expensive horses get stolen within a week?"

His eyes told me I'd pushed a button. "Where you get off, Romero? You find one horse and you're in my face with it? What the fuck?"

"Just asking questions."

"How 'bout minding your own fucking business." Richmond spit the words, upped the volume.

I was surprised by his reaction, but I matched him for volume. "I just drove a rotting carcass forty miles and made it my business," my face in his. His breath quickened, and I braced for a fist.

A man in a dark suit ran out of the home's front door, yelling, "Hey, hey. Knock it off." The man pushed his way between us. Richmond backed away. So did I, when I spotted a piece under his jacket.

Richmond said, "Some cop wannabe from rez Nowhere."

"I brought up his horse at his request. Who are you?" I asked.

"Name's Palafox. I've been hired to investigate the thefts. You two hotheads cool off." He swiveled his head between the two of us acting like he wanted to take us both on at once. A set of biceps pulling at his coat sleeves hinted he had the muscle to do it. His chin said, Try me. "You Romero from Cochiti?" Palafox had a calm way of speaking.

"Right," I said.

"I'm sorry for the misunderstanding, Mister Romero, but Tyler's been under a lot of pressure as of late. Tyler, you got work to do?"

Richmond turned to go but not before throwing a nasty eye-lock. He and I would knock heads again.

"Tell me what you know about this incident, Mr. Romero."

Again, I described what little I'd found at the scene, the stalker, and the vehicle he drove.

"We have a perplexing situation here." Palafox paused. "*Al-Fadee* was out of *Bask*, the sire of 196 national champions. Stud fees for him range around ten grand plus. Stud like that would sell for three-fifty grand or more, easy. Theft of an expensive Arab I get, but kill one? Got any ideas?" He asked the question deadpan, but I suspected Palafox was fishing. I get it. Too often the finder is the killer.

"You need to think about the fact you got two valuable horses killed in a week and Richmond is more than touchy about the subject," I let it go at that. "This is your case."

Palafox nodded, gave me a you-know-something smile. "Send us an invoice for the hauling," he said, as a ranch hand drove a front-end loader up and took *Al-Fadee* behind a barn.

A stench that overpowered the rotting cheese and feces stink of the remains flooded my nose. Insurance fraud with Richmond as prime suspect? The question raised my blood pressure, and curiosity all at once.

The dead animal haunted me as I drove south on Interstate 25. Part of me hoped to spot the Chevy pickup that had tailed me earlier, if for no other reason than to relieve the tedium of driving. No such luck. Monotony stuck with me until I sighted home.

Adrenaline replaced boredom when I spotted a beat-to-shit Chevy parked in my driveway. The man leaning against it hung an AK-47 from his shoulder.

David E. Knop is a retired Marine officer with twenty years of service. Dave's thrillers have been honored by Killer Nashville, New Mexico-Arizona Book Awards, Public Safety Writers of America, Military Writers Society of America, the Amazon Breakthrough Novel Contest, and the Eric Hoffer Book Award.

Mystery/Crime
Sherene Gross

Bronze Medal

DEADLY ENVY

Sparks shoot from the bottom of the '62 Plymouth Belvedere as the undercarriage bottoms on the concrete drive.

Ezra takes a deep breath as he leans against a support pole on the front porch. The butt of his cigarette dangles between his fingers. He eyes the front of the car for damage. Mary slams the brake causing the auto to lunge and halt a little too close to the house. He inhales smoke and another breath to steady his nerves.

God knows, Ezra tried to teach her to drive. Hours and hours in parking lots. They drove around the block while neighbors retreated into the safety of their homes. The final straw occurred during a tense moment, almost side-swiping a Wonder Bread truck on the highway. He handed her the keys and commenced praying. She'd managed not to kill anyone or receive a ticket. A matter of time. Her driving flat-out sucked.

He took an extended draw on the extra-mild, king-size Cavalier cigarette and reclined against the whitewashed post, shaking his head. The cigarette smoke floated in the breeze above the fresh-cut lawn. He spent most of the day digging weeds in the flowerbeds, hand-watering the yard, and tending to the vegetable garden.

She tumbled from the driver's side before saving herself from a face plant by grabbing the swinging open door. Her bouffant hairdo teased a Texas mile-high and dyed almost black, shifted into a replica of the leaning tower of Pisa. Ezra planned to take her to Italy, but in reality, a higher priority became a paid mortgage. And hospital bills continued to pile up on the dining room table.

"Late client?" Ezra said. His falling embers flamed on the top step leading to the front door. He snuffed the glowing ashes under his polished penny loafers.

"Elenore Rothwell. She died. Murdered behind the shop," Mary sputtered between breaths. She palmed her teased ebony-dyed hair, pressed the wrinkles of her white-starched uniform, and gathered her usual self-commanding dignity. She slammed the car door behind her with more force than necessary.

Ezra rocked to his feet and pushed against the porch post. He hurried to Mary, enveloping her in the fold of his arms. Arms in recent months that faced growing rejection.

"Dead? Are you sure? Oh, my Mary. Were you scared? You must be out of your mind. Please tell me you didn't witness her dying," Ezra said.

Mary patted his shoulder and stepped back. Her breaths evened while he waited for her to say more.

"No. No. I found the body in the alley when I hauled out the trash—scared the crap out of me. I ran inside and locked the back door. I'm not sure how long it took for me to pull myself together enough to call the police. The cops arrived darn quick and asked lots of questions, but I cleaned up the shop to stay busy until they arrived. Except…"

"Except what?"

"The scarf. The damn Hermès silk scarf. She wore it into the shop. The blasted scarf was missing from her neck. I forgot to tell the police."

"The one you've mentioned she bought in Paris?"

"She'd taken to wearing it every week to the shop, reminding me each time where she bought it. How much something so precious could cost. She repeated, laughing each time that an expensive Hermès would drain my pocketbook. Insinuating I'd never have the cash for such a precious item." Mary scoffed. "Eleanore remained oblivious to my pain or enjoyed salting my wound. I cared less about a damn scarf. My babies are dead."

Tears poured over her bottom eyelids and streaked her cheeks. Mary used the back of both hands to wipe them away, streaking her red lipstick in the process. She became a caricature of herself.

"The scarf is unimportant. I wouldn't bring up trivial details. The police will ask more questions. Why torture yourself reliving events? You fretted over that scarf too much. Any idea how long she lay on the ground?" Ezra wrapped his arm around her. She trembled against his chest.

"I didn't go into the alley all day, but she had an appointment with me right after lunch. Tuesdays, she has lunch at the Women's Club and a standing appointment with me to fix her hair afterward. We finished her hair at about 2:30. She left through the front door. Not sure how she ended up in the alley. Maybe she parked on the street by a meter? The parking lot by the shop emptied before I left. I assume the police found her car. They didn't ask me."

"So, a day like any other until the unthinkable happened? Do you know if anyone saw anything?" He squeezed her tighter.

"The other hairdressers left for the day. Little 'ole me—working after everyone left, as usual. The police waited for some medical guy to show up to pronounce her a goner. Deader than those squirrels, you keep shooting by the trash bins. The ambulance driver loaded her in the granny getter. I guess he drove her to the morgue."

"This is unbelievable. Why didn't you call me? Have the cops arrested a suspect?" The gravity of events settled and rippled in his gut.

Mary stepped back from his arms, sticking her hands in the pockets of her beautician-white uniform. Ezra spotted blood on the front of her dress.

"Oh, Mary. There's blood on your uniform. Is the spot hers—Elenore's?"

"They said I shouldn't touch the body, but I had to double-check to see if the witch had an ounce of oxygen left in her. I found her fresh-cut and curl caked with dried blood. All my work for nothing." Mary's eyes closed for a moment.

Did she consider being in danger a possibility for the first time? "Oh, baby, what if you charged out the door while someone offed her? And why resort to killing a woman? Her husband might be involved in shady business dealings, and the mob sent a message." Ezra shivered in the heat of the late afternoon.

"Mr. Rothwell is the most honest man, I know. Reliable. And generous. He helped me go to the bank for the loan. He was never a problem. It was always Eleanore." A grin traveled across her face at the revelation, and Ezra caught her upturned lips, unable to mask her relief.

"Mary! I understand your hatred towards her, but this isn't a time to celebrate. You don't want to raise suspicions." Ezra lit another cigarette and took a quick draw. He straightened the glasses on his nose and rearranged his thoughts. He wanted to drill for more information.

But without prompt, she unloaded her words. "Seeing her body—sprawled this way and that. Her neck marked up like a failing students' research paper. Well, I knew Elenore wouldn't torture me again. You know how I've struggled with her nastiness. Now, I don't say a word. The ghastly witch is out of my life. It's a miracle."

Mary's bitterness wasn't healthy. The miscarriage of not one, but two babies, was too much for his wife. The twins' death and the pressure of becoming the breadwinner forced Mary's emotions to bounce like an untethered ball across a busy street.

He felt the pressure too, and animosity. The boss fired him, and another guy on the spot after one of them forgot to close the gas line resulting in three houses exploding and people dying? A Saturday no less with a backyard bar-be-que taking place for an octogenarian. Ezra knew it was the other guy's fault, but how could he prove it?

Or was their problem his sagging gut and the pressure to make another baby? Couldn't he be to blame for Mary's unhappiness? Not a chance. She absorbed their ups and downs. If not for Eleanore's demands and belittlements, their marriage would bloom come spring. He blamed Eleanore.

Mary's lips, thick and pouty, blurred his mind and jumbled his thinking.

His Mary taped injured sparrow wings, delivered casseroles to ill neighbors. She put extra change in the parking meter for the next person.

Perhaps without Elenore's goading, his Mary would return to her old self. Mary's recent sour disposition was Elenore's fault. Elenore's superiority complex became Mary's undoing.

Mary unstuck the words fermenting in her throat. "You remember what she said about the babies. Her dead body sprawled in an unladylike position won't keep me up at night."

"Yes. Yes, of course, I didn't condone Eleanore's behavior. But Mary. Be careful. The words you speak to the police matter. Let's thank God you're unharmed."

"God. Where did God hideout when we lost the boys? At least he showed up today…" Ezra sensed a rush of blood course his veins.

"I am thinking of your emotional state. Every day. Every hour. Every minute. You may be in shock. Why didn't I insist you stay home longer after your pregnancy? I'm worried about you, dear."

"Not pregnancy. Births. Funerals. Work helped. Work is my friend. And we need the money. You can't protect me from the pain. I can't keep you from yours. But Elenore twisted our loss into something unimportant."

"I understand she had a poisoned mouth. A nasty streak flowed in that woman, but did she deserve to die?" Ezra smoothed the thinning hair on his head before replacing his cap.

"Not for me to say, but someone wanted her dead. Elenore riled hate in the saints."

"People screw up. They all need forgiveness."

"Maybe… The cops asked if I knew who would want to harm Mrs. Rothwell. I spoke the truth—the whole state of Texas. You know I'm right. The other beauticians talked. Their customers talked. We had more than an inkling of what people thought about her."

He ignored the comment. "Did you touch Elenore Rothwell's body?"

Mary glanced at the grass. She removed her hand from the bloody pocket as if there was a wildfire inside. "I put two fingers on her neck to check for a pulse—as if she had one. I want out of these clothes and Elenore out of my mind, if possible. Are sandwiches all right with you tonight? It's getting late, and I forgot to stop at the store."

"Sure. If you can stomach eating."

* * *

The screen door banged behind her. Ezra lit another cigarette, took one drag, and set the remainder smoldering on the arm of the glider before opening the screen. He followed Mary, across the living room carpet, and stepped into the hallway by their bedroom.

Mary entered the bedroom with her chin on her chest. She raised her head and opened the jewelry box sitting on her dresser. Without haste, she pulled the dangling earrings off her ears and placed them inside. After staring into the dresser mirror for an extended moment, she began to unbutton her beautician uniform.

When the bloody dress fell to the floor, Ezra backed from the doorway. He crept to the front of the house, opened the screen, and stepped outside.

Squeak.

Damn. Ezra reminded himself to find the can of oil in the garage before dark. He picked up the smoldering cig, took a lingering drag, and dropped the glowing butt on the concrete. He pulled a fresh one from the package in his shirt pocket and frowned as he observed a pair of those damn squirrels rummage through tossed-out scraps in the trash can across the street.

Squeak.

"What happened to your one-a-day limit?" Mary asked, leaning her head between the screen and the door frame.

"Today calls for three."

"Sandwiches ready in five minutes. Mayo or mustard?"

"The usual. Be right there." Ezra eyeballed the squirrels frisking around the edge of the bin. Their frantic tails whipped across their backs.

The sun rose the next morning, like always at this time of year—blazing. Ezra picked up the damp, rubber-banded newspaper from the stoop and went inside. He poured coffee in Mary's favorite cup. A few minutes later, she emerged from the bedroom wearing a fresh-starched white uniform.

"Not planning to work today, are you?"

"I'm booked solid. We need the money."

"It doesn't look good."

Mary stirred two teaspoons from the sugar bowl into her cup.

Making his point, Ezra slid the "A" section of the newspaper to her side of the breakfast table. The headline screamed what he wanted to at her.

LOCAL SOCIALITE MURDERED

She picked up the coffee cup. She swallowed hard enough that Ezra heard. She picked up the paper and scanned A1.

"Sketchy reporting. Not one mention of who reported the murder."

"Hmmm." How did he respond or remind her who got credit for finding the body of someone they disliked didn't matter when you considered what made for true happiness? Appearances were paramount, but not for the reasons Mary envisioned. The cash flow at the beauty shop took a backseat to the murder.

"How about I cook eggs this morning. Fried, okay?" Not waiting for an answer, he turned to the stove and lit the gas burner. He located butter, eggs, and bacon in the fridge. Better keep his hands busy and his mind on flipping eggs without breaking the yolks. He wanted to shake her.

"Well, her hair's nice in this picture, but of course, she's wearing the ostentatious scarf. Probably the latest picture Mr. Rothwell found in an album, or the newspaper pulled it from their files. What do you think?" Mary turned the front of the newspaper towards Ezra as he sat a plate of eggs and bacon in front of her, forcing him to take a second look at the picture of Eleanore Rothwell.

"You did a nice job on her hair. No wonder she insisted on you fixing it."

A pleased smile replaced her twisted scowl. She put down the newspaper and picked up a fork beside the plate and began to eat.

The gravel in their driveway crunched like popping corn on the stove. Someone drove into the driveway. Ezra and Mary traded glances. The vehicle shifted into park, and the motor rumbled to quiet.

Mary's fork hovered above her eggs. A piece of bacon stalled between her lips. Ezra stood and walked to the window. He lifted the ruffled curtain, took a deep breath, and turned to Mary.

"It's the police. I hope your story is straight. Try to muster a few tears."

Mary choked down the bacon, swallowed a sip of coffee, and smoothed the front of her uniform, but didn't move from her chair. She nodded at Ezra.

The doorbell chimed.

Without urgency, he stepped through the kitchen door and into the living room. He twisted the knob on the front door and opened.

"Hello, officers. I can't say I'm surprised you're here, given the circumstances."

"I'm Officer Callahan. And this is my partner Officer Wilcox. Sorry to bother you this early in the morning, but you understand, these are unusual times." The officers shook Ezra's hand.

"Of course. Of course. I'd be more upset if you didn't. Finding a killer is no easy task."

"And a woman of Mrs. Rothwell's standing in the community has elevated the investigation several notches," Callahan said. "Can we come in for a few minutes? We have some questions for your wife."

Ezra stepped from the door and waved them in. "Please sit down. I'll find Mary."

Mary stepped into the living room. She wore a printed housecoat. She emerged with her hair disheveled. Ezra pushed his surprise down, hoping the cops didn't detect his flinch. *Well. Well, Mary. I didn't give you enough credit.*

"Please excuse my appearance. I had a rough night trying to sleep. I hope you appreciate the stress I'm under, officers."

The uniformed men shook their heads. Callahan took the lead. "Understandable. No lady should ever witness what you saw. We wondered if you had a few minutes to answer a few lingering questions?"

"I want to do whatever I can to find the killer and bring Eleanore's murderer to justice. Would either of you like a cup of coffee?"

Both officers shook their heads. Their place on the floral sofa under the front picture window framed the cops' faces.

"What would you like to know?" Mary took a seat in an oversized chair and rearranged the housecoat around her legs.

"Mary? Would you like me to stay?" Ezra placed his hand on her shoulder, and she looked up to meet his eyes.

"No, dear. I'm fine. You said earlier you had errands this morning. Don't let us put you behind."

"Officers," Ezra shook the officers' hands again. "hope your day improves." Ezra cleared the doorway between the living room and kitchen but kept on walking until he reached the door to the garage.

Inside the garage, he slipped a loose Cavalier from his pocket. He put it in his mouth and flicked the silver lighter pulled from his right side pants pocket. Ezra took several long draws of the tobacco and stared at the ceiling of the garage before setting the smoldering cigarette with the end dangling on a shelf by old paint cans.

Morning sunlight and desert heat hit him when he lifted the overhead door. He picked up the metal trash can and walked across the street to stack his receptacle next to the neighbors' for trash pick-up day.

He passed the police car in the driveway and returned to the garage to finish his cigarette.

Chattering began across the street. Ezra recognized the sound, and his blood pressure shot sky-high. He stepped to the driveway. *Those damn squirrels were at it again.*

The family of three bushy-tailed creatures jumped from can to can, tree to tree, upending the waste covered moments before. Their blather reached a high pitch when one squirrel's head peeked out of Ezra's trash can with a brightly-covered silk scarf clutched in its mouth. The squirrel crossed a neighbor's lawn and climbed a tree with the fluttering fabric from a Paris boutique clenched in its mouth.

Ezra recognized the silk scarf. He'd pushed it to the bottom of the can in a rush.

* * *

Sherene Gross is a former journalism teacher and higher education publishing rep. She writes domestic suspense novels and short stories covering the romance, mystery, and thriller genres. A transplanted Texan, she currently lives in Alto, New Mexico with her husband and a very spoiled dog.

SECTION SIX

ROMANCE

A touch of moonlight, painful doubts and whispers in the dark…you will find all these and more in our Romance category.

Romance   **Gold Medal**
Mary Candace Mize

SZOFI

"Mother, Istvan and I want to get married." Gabriella's large blue eyes pleaded. She looked so childlike with her turned-up nose and her golden-red curls.

Zsofi felt the blood drain from her face. The moment she'd dreaded for years had finally arrived. "You're too young."

"Mother, he's a good man. You know he is. He'll treat me well."

"He's just a boy, and you're still a child. There's a lot you still don't know about life."

Gabriela's eyes filled with fire. Determination replaced her look of innocence. "You can't tell me anything bad about him. You have no reason at all. You just want me to be miserable."

Zsofi pictured Istvan. His face still reflected the optimism of youth, not yet sculpted by hard times and disappointments. Around Gabriela, he radiated kindness. She couldn't imagine his ever being cruel. He laughed often and spoke in a friendly manner. The neighborhood troublemakers he grew up with had given up on him long ago. He didn't like brandy, and he preferred to spend his time with his dog or playing his mouth harp. He would certainly come home at night. Probably he was the best match in the village, possibly the only one, and yet …. "I'm sorry, Gabriela, I can't give you my blessing."

"But why, Mother? What's wrong with him? He loves me. You know he does."

"Istvan can't provide for you."

"He's no poorer than anyone else. In fact his plot is larger than ours, and he works hard. There's something you're not telling me."

When Zsofi turned and stared out the window, Gabriela grabbed her arm. "You're not being fair. What do you have against him?"

Zsofi took a deep breath. "Gabriela, there's a curse on this village."

"Oh Mother, how can you be so old fashioned?" Her hands locked in front of her. "Istvan says men are dying because they have no money, and they can't sell their brandy. They've lost their pride, and without pride a man can't live."

"Gabriela, if men dropped dead from lack of pride, we'd all be gone long ago. No, there's a curse on this village, a curse that's now being fulfilled."

"Something to do with that Shaman, isn't it? Everything goes back to him. Istvan says he's been turned into a legend to scare people."

"In the past few years, the people who died were related to his hanging. Now the curse has fallen upon the sons of his murderers. Istvan's father Eduard tied up the Shaman and dragged him through the streets. He died in the war along with a number of others involved. I'm afraid the wrath will fall on Istvan and your children."

Gabriella stamped her foot. "But Istvan didn't do anything. Why should we be punished for what his father did? It's not fair!"

"What's fair doesn't matter. Children often pay for their father's sins. Another man lent Peter his whip to beat the shaman, and two years ago he fell out of a wagon onto his head and died. His son is dead now also."

"But I can't refuse to marry Istvan because he might die someday."

"Well, you can't have my blessing. Nothing will change that."

Gabriela gazed beyond her mother. "There is one thing you could do."

"What's that?"

"The Midwife is the Shaman's daughter. Ask her to bless our marriage."

"Are you crazy? What if she says no? That'll draw the attention of the gods onto Istvan. He'll only be in greater danger."

"It's a risk I'm willing to take. I can't stop loving him just because something might happen, someday. I refuse to live in fear."

Zsofi's heart pounded, and heat rose through her body as she looked into her daughter's pleading eyes. "All right, Gabriela, it's dangerous to interfere with the work of the gods, but if you're so determined, I'll try."

Gabriela stepped forward and kissed her on the cheek. "Thank you, Mother." She left the house looking relieved as if the matter were resolved.

Zsofi's stomach sank, and she doubled over as a wave of nausea threatened. Her daughter's trust was too heavy a burden to bear.

* * *

Gabriela was too young to remember the day the Shaman died, but Zsofi relived it in fiery nightmares that sent her leaping from her bed, screaming her children's names.

A flash lit the ceiling, and its light lingered even after the thunder clap, filling the room with a reddish half-light. Zsofi shivered. *The Devil must be here.* . She heard his footsteps, crackling like twigs underfoot on forest paths.

"Mama, look." Kati tugged at Zsofi's knee and broke her paralyzing reverie. The thatched roof was ablaze.

Clutching Gabriela in one arm, she lifted Kati to her hip and struggled outside, stumbling under their combined weight. She made her way toward the barn, tensing at the anguished cries of the animals. She ran blindly not knowing where to go, only certain she had to leave this place of death. Rain stung her face with its fury and blinded her to all landmarks. Through a momentary break in the torrent, she stumbled up to a cottage and beat on the door. Her friend, Marika , opened it and pulled Zsofi inside.

She lifted Gabriela out of Zsofi's arms. "What happened?"

Zsofi sank to the floor. "Everything's gone, our house, the barn. All our animals are dead. What's to become of us? Where's my husband? We need him."

Marika pulled her to her feet, put an arm around her, and led her to a stool. "Don't think about that now. You're alive. Your babies are safe. That's all that matters. You can stay here. There's plenty of straw in the loft."

Zsofi carried Kati up and returned for Gabriela. Kati fell asleep as soon as she lay down. Gabriela's sucking calmed her mother, and after the baby's eyes closed, Zsofi lay beside her in the straw and stared at the ceiling as though she could see her future on its rough surface.

* * *

The door opened, and Zsofi heard a choking sound like someone being strangled. She crawled over and peered down. The young midwife, Ilka, drenched from the storm, broke from Marika's grasp and spun around the room as if to erase the horror of seeing her father murdered. Her eyes had the look of a wild animal as they seemed to glow from an inner source of rage and terror. Sometimes she bounced against the walls, her arms protecting her head.

Ilka swung her head free. "A curse upon this village and all the men who killed my father and upon their sons and their sons until his death is avenged." Her voice held the force of thunder. Zsofi shuddered. The girl, Ilka, fell to the floor and lay still.

* * *

Now, years later, Zsofi's feet dragged as if her boots were made of rocks. When she approached the Midwife's house to ask her blessing on Gabriela and Istvan's marriage, her stomach roiled. Prickly fear rose as she knocked on the door.

"Come in,"

She pushed her way inside. The Midwife stood with her back to her. The Midwife turned. "What can I do for you?"

Zsofi felt the chill of failure before it became reality. "I've come to ask a favor."

"A favor? From me?"

She moved closer. "My daughter Gabriela is a good girl. She's kind to people, and she's helpful at home."

"So? What about it?"

"She wants to marry Istvan."

A shadow crossed the Midwife's face. "Have you forgotten who his father was?"

Zsofi felt her insides quiver. "He doesn't even remember him. Haven't we suffered enough?"

"You're right." The voice softened. "Most women suffer enough. So what does that have to do with me?"

"I told her no."

"So why are you bothering *me* about it?"

"I will allow it on one condition."

"What's that?"

"She must receive your blessing."

"My blessing? Ha." The Midwife raised her hands, leaned back, and shuddered with mirth. "You must be joking.

"All we need is your blessing. No one need know about it."

The Midwife's brows moved closer together. Her stormy look frightened Zsofi. "The gods have spoken. You know what happened to the men who murdered my father and some of their sons as well. Istvan's father tied him up and dragged him to the crossroads. I can't go against the will of the gods. Leave me alone. You should consider yourself lucky."

"Lucky? Why?"

She glared at Zsofi. "You had daughters."

* * *

Zsofi found Istvan and Gabriela together when she returned. Gabriela jumped from the bench, thrusting her embroidery toward Istvan. "Oh, Mama,

Istvan says if we need to escape the curse, he can buy a tinker's wagon, and we can travel around for awhile before we come back and settle down. Istvan loves to fix things. Mother, say it's all right."

Zsofi glared at Istvan. "You're putting too many ideas into the child's head."

"What happened? What did the Midwife say?" Gabriela asked. "Did she give her blessing?"

"No."

"Do you?"

"I can't either."

Istvan stood. "Mrs. Toth, Gabriela is no longer a child. We love each other. I want to take care of her and give her sons."

Zsofi shuddered. "Don't speak of sons."

Istvan's head jerked. "What? I'd be happy with daughters, too. We would like your blessing."

Zsofi shook her head. "That's impossible."

Istvan straightened his broad shoulders. "I don't want to seem rude, but some people are marrying without their parents' blessing these days."

"Then my curse will join that of the gods."

Gabriela clutched her mother's arms. "No, you can't mean that."

Zsofi pushed her away and pointed her finger at Istvan. "I'm warning you. I will try to help, but if you take any action on your own, both of you will live to regret it. Now, Istvan, get out of here. You can't see my daughter anymore."

He backed away. "I'm leaving, but I'll be back. I'm not giving Gabriela up so easily."

From the doorway Zsofi watched Gabriela follow Istvan down the hill. They embraced for a long time, making Zsofi so uncomfortable she returned inside.

* * *

The next day, Gabriela refused to eat. Zsofi was concerned, but belief she was protecting her daughter overrode her fears. Even a dog will fast for a few days when its master goes away. She pretended to ignore her daughter's obstinacy and concentrated on outdoor tasks so she wouldn't see Gabriela's sorrow. She'll get over it, she assured herself.

After a few weeks, her concern changed to panic. Gabriela picked at her food, and she'd lost so much weight Zsofi feared she wouldn't recover. Torn between sympathy and rage, Zsofi's helplessness flowed over her in waves of despair.

* * *

One morning, after Gabriela staggered out to their new barn, Zsofi shouted her name. When she received no answer, she stalked over, ready to holler at her daughter. Gabriela lay sprawled in the mule's stall.

"You're going to bed, young lady, and you are going to eat, do you understand? We'll have no more of your starving yourself."

Gabriela allowed Zsofi to pull her to her feet. The two staggered toward the house where Gabriela collapsed onto her bed. Zsofi brought her a boiled potato and watched her try to eat it.

"Gabriela, I can't let you marry Istvan unless the curse is lifted. It's for your own good. Otherwise you could lose your husband, and even worse, your children. If you have sons, they will die."

Without a word, Gabriela turned her face toward the wall, leaving the potato half-consumed.

* * *

Zsofi walked along the path toward the edge of town where she stopped at an old, but tidy, white-washed house belonging to the Matchmaker.

"Come in, come in. Haven't seen you in ages. What brings you here?" Erzsi's long teeth were stained and had a dark stripe at the top, so they appeared suspended in her mouth, but her eyes were friendly. "Tell me, is everything going well in your family?"

"It's Gabi. She refuses to eat, and she fainted this morning."

"Whatever is the trouble? I thought she's the one you never had to worry about. Has she quarreled with Istvan?"

"No, that's not the problem. She wants to marry him, and I don't want her to."

"Why not?"

Zsofi combined a slow shrug with a squirm. "I want you to find a match for her. You have connections, maybe someone outside the village.

"I can check. My sister could ask around in her town. And there's a young man who sometimes thatches roofs. There's always a call for that. But he lives at the manor. She'd hate it there, and you'd hardly ever see her.

"That's all right. She needs to be away from Istvan anyway."

"What's wrong with Istvan anyway? He seems a nice enough lad."

Zsofi hissed as she sucked air between her clenched teeth. "It's just . . . I don't want to talk about it."

"Oh, I understand perfectly." Erzsi's eyes shone, as enlightened comprehension flooded her face. Heat rose in Zsofi like lightning crossing a pond. "The way you've let her run free with Istvan all these years, you were just begging for trouble. She pregnant, isn't she?"

Zsofi's face burned. "No, nothing like that."

"I'll see what I can do, but . . . ." She jutted her chin forward and pursed her lips. "You realize we'll have to treat her as damaged goods, her having been with Istvan so long."

* * *

A week later Erzsi walked down the road accompanied by a stocky young man with curly red hair. Zsofi greeted them and ushered them into the house. The young man seated himself at the table before being asked, bit into an apple from the bowl, and swung around to talk to the women. When Gabi came in, he surveyed her from head to toe, and a grin spread across his face. "Not bad."

Gabi fired back a look of total contempt.

"You're a pretty thing." His grimy hand reached over and pinched her cheek.

Gabriela slapped his hand away. "Don't touch me. You pig!" She stood, glared at him and at her mother and stomped out the door.

"I like them fiery," the boy said. "They're so much fun to tame."

Zsofi examined the young man before her – his red hair framing a freckled, open face. She smiled as she recalled the old wives' tale. *Someone must have thrown a lot of liver at his mother while she was pregnant to get that many freckles.*

"Well, what do you think?" the matchmaker asked.

"We could be married in a couple of months," the boy said. "My relatives are coming here for my cousin's wedding."

Zsofi stared at him, trying to look past his eyes into the future. His eyes fluttered self-consciously from the intensity of her gaze, and he spat into his hand and rubbed it on his pants.

"No, I don't think so." She turned toward Erzsi. Somehow she knew Gabriela would never adjust. She might as well move Gabi away from Hungary as send her there. "Don't you have anyone from a town near here?"

"Well, I do have another one. I can bring him next week. His parents own a shop. I hope you realize I go to considerable trouble to find eligible people."

"I'll pay you when there is a match."

* * *

The following Saturday the sun shone so brightly Zsofi felt the day held promise. Through the curtains she saw Erzsi and a young man approach. His clothing — a jacket of a fine cut, certainly looked more like something an innkeeper would wear than the other villagers. His brown hair was tidy, and he had a lighter complexion even than Gabi. *They'll have pretty children.* She felt they were sure to get Gabi's reddish gold hair.

The knock came discretely, as if Erzsi herself were impressed with the young man and was trying to act in a genteel manner.

Zsofi opened the door and took a deep breath. "Come in. I'm pleased to meet you." *To marry my daughter to a shopkeeper would be such an accomplishment.*

He touched his hand to his lips and cleared his throat with an almost inaudible "Hum hum." He extended his hand. "Mrs. Toth."

"Let me call Gabriella. Make yourselves at home." She guided them to chairs. "I won't be a minute." She rushed out the door, shouted "Gabriela" twice, and waited until Gabi stuck her head out of the goat shed. "Come. And you better be nice."

Gabi entered almost shyly. To Zsofi's surprise, gone was the rage and contempt of the previous week's encounter. Maybe she'll go along when she sees how decent this man seems. Or is she up to something? What if she and Istvan are planning to run away?

Gabi extended her hand.

The young man squeezed it lightly. His deep-set eyes filled with admiration. Raising his hand to his mouth, he coughed.

"Let me tell you a bit about my shop."

Zsofi beamed. He's shy, more Gabi's style than that bragging manor worker.

"Why don't you two go outside? You can tell Gabi about how you live, and she can show you around."

The young man rose, touched his chest, and followed Gabi out the door. Zsofi thought of Gabi and Kati when they were small and what hopes she held for them. But she'd never dreamed of a shopkeeper.

"Well, Zsofi, what do you think? You can't deny I've done well by you this time. A young man, good family, good connections, some money, and his own business. Really you couldn't ask for more."

"At least Gabi's acting friendly. I don't quite trust her, but it appears to be a good sign. I know she wants children."

Zsofi had just set out the tea things when Gabi burst into the room, her blue eyes wild, her golden-red curls flying. She stomped her feet. "I won't marry him no matter how rich he is. I won't."

"And I won't have this defiance." Zsofi's fists struck her hips. "You will do as you are told, young lady."

"He's got consumption, Mother. He's coughing up blood. He says he's had it for months. He's dying. You want me to die, too?"

"Oh, Gabi, what am I doing to you? There's got to be an answer." Zsofi opened her arms and hugged her rigid child. "I'm so sorry. Of course you don't have to marry him. All I want is for you to be happy."

Gabi's jaw scarcely moved. "There is an answer. I want to marry Istvan." Zsofi had never heard her daughter's voice so deep, her words so deliberate.

Zsofi glared at Erzsi. "Did you know about the consumption?"

Gabi, say goodbye to the young man. Be polite, but don't get too close." She flew outside, beaming.

Zsofi turned to Erzsi. "How could you? You could have killed my child."

A blood vessel on Erzsi's forehead throbbed. Her look turned icy. "I'm trying my best for you. What on earth do you have against Istvan anyway? They adore each other."

"Well, I suppose you deserve to know. I just don't want people thinking I'm a superstitious old fool."

"Superstitious? In this town? Are you crazy?"

"Well, it's the curse."

"What curse?"

"The one the Midwife made when her father died. I was there when she said it, and now it's coming true."

"So? What does that have to do with Istvan?"

"His father brought the rope."

"His father? What are you talking about?"

"Eduard tied him up," Zsofi spoke louder, her anger heating her upper body.

"Aah." A look of understanding flooded Erzsi's face, widening and brightening her eyes. "So that's it." She smiled, throwing her head back with a tinge of superiority that made Zsofi want to pummel her. "That's what this is all about."

She paused to extend her superior knowledge and condescension to the last possible moment. Her large brown teeth seemed to overwhelm her narrow face. "But my dear Zsofi, Eduard wasn't Istvan's father. I made the match myself after his mother got pregnant. Someone's nephew came for a wedding and had a few more festivities than he bargained for." She hugged herself and cackled. "He was long gone before the Shaman died. You have nothing to fear on that score."

A surge of relief and happiness flowed through Zsofi, tingling her scalp and raising the hair on her arms. She flew to Erzsi to hug her, almost knocking over a chair and leaving the woman gasping and grabbing the table for balance.

When the chair came to rest, a crafty smirk spread across Erzsi's weathered face. "You owe me some money."

"What? How's that?"

Erzsi thrust her chin into the air. "After all, I made the match."

Zsofi smiled. "You will be paid."

* * *

 **Mary Candace Mize,** author of *THE FLYPAPER WITCH MURDERS*, grew up in Albuquerque, graduated from Brandeis University, and traveled to 81 countries, including 17 in Africa, and worked on the Amazon River. She taught elementary classes in Australia, Italy and Pakistan, as well as in the Albuquerque Public Schools.

Romance   Silver Medal
Barb Simmons

THE WAR WITHIN

Chapter One

Former Marine Raider, Gunnery Sergeant Mike Ramos pushed up into his last 225 pound bench press, then lowered the bar to the rack with a solid clank. He sat up and stretched his neck and shoulders, relishing the after-burn.

There she was. He could always count on seeing her on Thursdays. Tall, fit and defined, but not overly so. Still had curves in all the right places. Stunning long red hair, like fire. Made him ache to weave his hands through that hair and pull her mouth to his, hard.

He growled low in the back of his throat. He hadn't been laid since he'd gotten blown up in Kandahar. That was a year ago. He'd always considered himself a decent fuck, but now—who knew?

He grabbed his water bottle from the floor and hoisted himself up onto his good leg and his damn prosthetic. He hadn't minded a wheelchair initially, but quickly tired of looking his buddies in the balls. The fake leg was tricky and he was still working to master its use. At the worst times he'd lose his balance and look like a total fool. He lurched over to the water fountain and refilled his bottle. While standing there he was aware of someone walking up behind him in line for water. With his bottle full, he sidled sideways a step to give the person a chance at the water, only to lose his balance and fall back into the poor bastard. Feminine arms came around him, defined and strong. *Oh, Christ! Her arms.* He recognized the distinctive bracelets at her slim wrists. She held him fast for only a moment, giving his balance right back to him. He turned to face her. "Thanks," he murmured, feeling so damn embarrassed. His anger and frustration with himself must have shown up in his face, looking like the pissed off Hulk.

Her genuine smile faded. "Not a problem," she said, then filled her pink metal bottle. She walked away without giving him another look. *Well, shit*, he thought watching her disappear into the women's locker room. *Fucking well done, Ramos.*

*   *   *

Viv walked into the locker room, sweaty from cardio and irritated with that guy. What was with him giving her the stink eye? What an asshole. She should have let him drop.

Nope! No, way. By the looks of his military tats and missing leg, he'd given a lot for his country. She gave him tons of respect for that.

But, any time she encountered a veteran with an intimidating energy, she steered clear. Pulled her right back to her grandpa. He'd been to Vietnam and according to her mom he'd never been the same. All Viv remembered was the abuse and cruelty he hurled at her grandma and she took his shit. Drove her crazy mad, even as a little kid. Back then she swore up and down, she'd never let herself get into that situation. Ever.

She closed her locker with a little too much force and startled the woman next to her. "Ooh, sorry," she said, grabbing her gym bag.

Viv came around the corner out of the locker room checking her iwatch and almost walked right into the guy.

Dear God! At least 6'3" and all definition, bulk muscle. But, not overdone. She bet there was a stunning eight-pack under that black tank. Viv had to swallow hard. What was happening to her?

He put out his hand to her for a shake. "Mike Ramos."

She didn't take his hand right away, she watched him while she made him wait. He didn't flinch or retract his hand one bit. His intense green gaze remained tightly fixed on hers.

When she joined her hand with his, the tiny hairs on her forearm stood. Exhilarating warmth traveled up her arm.

"Vivian March," she whispered in awe of what had just transpired. She eased her hand away from their clasp.

He crossed his amazing arms over his amazing chest. "Vivian, let's get coffee."

Viv was stuck to the spot. She didn't know what to say. She had to admit to herself that there was an unquestionable pull, but he was all wrong, totally wrong—an angry Vet. Hands off.

"I, ah..."

He didn't move. Didn't withdraw.

"You're not right for me." So awkward.

"What?" His left brow rose. "Because I'm brown?"

"No," she said with vehemence.

"The missing leg?" he asked raising the knee of his prosthetic.

"Hell, no!"

"Too many tattoos?"

"Oh, no," she said, in a voice smokier than she'd intended.

He reached up and moved a stray tress off of her forehead. "It's coffee, Vivian, not a marriage proposal."

"Ok, Ok. Where are we going?"

He held open the door to the gym, and she stepped through. "To my place of course, I've got my own Espresso machine."

She pivoted and nabbed him with her disapproving gaze, only to find him grinning.

"Kidding! To that coffee shop." He pointed at the cafe across the street.

Smart ass, she thought. But, he'd made her smile. He totally got points for that.

As they crossed the street they stopped a couple times, to avoid cars. Then stepped up on to the curb to the side entrance of the coffee shop. He seemed to struggle a bit with his prosthetic. She wondered how recently he'd been injured.

When they were between the two sets of dark gray glass doors, Mike stopped and pulled her to him. Standing toe to toe, she could feel the heat of his body as he drew closer.

The hand holding hers disengaged and with sure fingertips, caressed up her arm leaving tiny chills in its wake. All movement came to a stop when he palmed her cheek. Then looking into her eyes, he lowered his mouth to hers, slowly. Giving her the chance to stop him. But God help her, she didn't.

The touch of his lips, hot and soft, soothed and excited at the same time. And just when her mouth began to course with a luscious heat, he pulled back.

"There, now we don't have to think about when or how that first kiss is going to happen—it's done," he said with a mischievous grin.

"What? OK." *That sounded lame.* Things were moving too fast. At the same time she couldn't help imagining what he looked like completely nude, sans prosthetic and all. How far down did those amazing tats reach?

She followed him up to the barista. He ordered a plain black coffee. When he moved aside to give her the chance to order, she stepped up to the counter and ordered her regular—almond milk latte with hazelnut.

As they walked over to the far side of the counter, to wait for their drinks, Mike kept his hand at her lower back. She had mixed feelings about that. His proprietary gesture kind of bugged, but at the same time the warmth of his hand was...nice.

An older man who just claimed his coffee stopped and raised his hand to shake her companion's. "Thank you for your service."

She felt Mike's hand drop from her lower back and his body tensed beside her. He took the guys hand for a shake and nodded, but didn't say anything.

She led them to a booth and she sat before he did, giving her an opportunity to see his face. His expression was tight and he looked miserable. She reached for his hand. "What's wrong," she asked.

"Nothing," he said. "Drink your coffee." He looked down into his, dismissing her.

Oh, no. Not going to happen. She leaned toward him, keeping a firm hold on his hand. "I don't really know what's going on here." She made a movement with her free hand, pointing at him and then back at herself. "But, I won't be shut out or dismissed. So if you want whatever *this* is to continue, *don't* do that again."

He sat back, disengaging their connection. His expression went though several rapid changes. First scary irritated, then morphed into contemplative, ending with his eyebrows pulled down to pure curiosity. "OK. But, I'm not talking about my deployment."

"Fine. Don't want to hear about it," she responded, taking a sip of her coffee. The creamy and sweet hazelnut flavor flowed across her tongue. "What *do* you want to talk about?"

That wicked grin covered his tempting full mouth again. "I want to talk about how I'm going to get you in the sack."

She laughed at that. "Slow down, Ramos. But you can start with being straight with me, and not being an asshole."

"Sounds easy."

"Not as easy as you may think." She looked at her watch. "And all that will have to wait for another time. I've got a commitment."

He sat back and studied her, suspicion in his eyes.

"What?" she asked, putting the stir-stick in her mouth and sucking on it on purpose.

"You're not looking for a wedding and kids any time soon, are you?"

"Not in my plans at the moment." But they were definitely in her plans, for sure.

"Good." Mike looked up at her face. "Let's go then."

"'Kay." She finished her coffee and slid out of the booth seat, securing her gym bag over her shoulder.

He felt awkward disengaging from the booth with his damn fake leg, but he managed it without too much fumbling.

They walked back to the gym parking lot. As they passed his car, he leaned over to remove a flyer someone had left under the wipers.

"You're the one with the black Charger?" she asked with excitement. "What year is it, 68 or 69?"

'69. You know cars?"

"A little. My brother restores classics." She smiled real big at him. Made his heart thump. "Can I get in?"

"Sure." He tossed her the keys. She looked like a kid in a toy store. He loved that.

Vivian scrambled into the driver seat, and he went around and got in next to her. Her enthusiasm was contagious.

"Start her up."

She looked over at him, her eyes lit with excitement. "Really?
"Sure."

Carefully putting the key in the ignition, she turned her over. The car's finely tuned engine roared to life, then settled into a seductive rumble. She leaned her head back, and look of delight on her face was amazing.

This was more than wonderful. Vivian was smoking hot, she knew her way around the gym, she knew cars, and didn't take his shit. He sure hoped she knew her way around a man's body—his body, just fine, too.

He turned to look at her face and she was staring at him. He grasped her elbow with care tugging, pulling her toward him. Her throat pulsed from swallowing. She slid across the bench seat, until their thighs touched.

Bringing his palm up to her cheek he held her there as he sought her mouth. He sipped at the side of her lips, and then covered her mouth with his.

His mouth watered at the contact. Spurring him forward to breech her lips with his tongue and explore the soft, warm recesses of her mouth. Her arms twined around his neck as her tongue sparred with his. She gave as good as she got. *Holy Christ!*

* * *

Chapter Two

Time always moved slowly for Vivian when dreaming.

She stepped through the dark toward a dimly lit hallway. Her pace slow, as though moving through water. She approached the doorway and glanced through, then swallowed with the thrill of anticipation.

Mike stood at the end of a softly lit corridor. His hand extended, palm upward. A faint halo of light surrounded him as though back-lit by a photographer. He stood gloriously naked, and in her dream he still had both legs. His amazing quads stood out in sharp relief.

His stellar tat reached from his shoulder and spread over the left side of his chest, curving and swirling down over the left side of his eight-pack, and covering the majority of his left quad.

Impatience scratched at her as she made her way to him. She couldn't move fast enough. Her urgency to get to him bordered on frantic.

When she finally reached him, they came together with a soft crush of warm flesh, arms winding around each other. He reached between them, covering her breast with his palm, shaping and molding.

He pulled back from their luscious kiss to lean down and take her entire aureola into his hot mouth. The powerful pull of his mouth prompted Vivian to lean back a little, giving him better access. She gasped with pleasure as the heat from his contact ripped a devastating connection between her breast and her throbbing core.

Mike reached down and around, grabbing her by her cheeks and hoisted her up against him. She twined her arms around his neck.

"Wrap your legs around me, Viv," he directed in a low rasp. She did it without thinking, opening her hot, wet center against his erection, shivering with anticipation.

Mike pulled back and entered with one hard thrust. She cried out with the searing pleasure of his intrusion. Then he backed her up against the wall of the corridor and began thrusting in and out of her, hard and fast. The sensation of growing inner tension grabbed her and held on tight as unbelievable pleasure spiraled throughout her body.

"Come for me, Vivian," he ordered, pushing deeper still. Vivian shattered around him. Her delicious rhythmic pulsing wrenched Mike's orgasm from him and he groaned her name.

A relentless and annoying high pitched beeping sound penetrated her orgasmic glow. Viv opened her eyes and stared wide-eyed at the ceiling. The wonderful orgasm from her dream faded away, as the drone from her damn alarm pulled her into the here and now.

She sat up too fast to smack the clock and got a mild case of the spins, then took some slow, deep breaths to clear her head.

Dear, God. She hadn't had a sex dream in forever, couldn't even remember *ever* having one as hot as the one that had been interrupted by her alarm just now.

Mike was inserting himself in her thoughts way too much these days. Well, if she were honest with herself, those thoughts started the first time she'd ever seen him at the gym, and that was weeks ago.

Whew! Viv was *so* glad she made up that faux commitment yesterday. If she hadn't left when she did, she could have ended up in the back seat of Mike's Charger with her shorts down around her ankles.

She rolled her legs off the side of the bed and stretched, enjoying the awareness of her still happy girl-parts. She rose and padded into the bathroom, stopping in front of the sink and mirror. Her naturally curly red hair sported its customary morning witch do, after a restless night. Viv laughed out loud at the spectacle.

Though she kind of liked the drama of the look, it was not good for the gym. She grabbed a bottle of product from the vanity tray and commenced the process of bringing her curls into submission.

What was it about the guy that had any sense of propriety sailing right out the bedroom window? *More than crazy*, she thought. He was just plain amazing. She sighed when her excitement was quelled by the angry Vet business.

After three twelves of floor nursing on her Ortho floor at the hospital, she was on divine day two of her four days off. The first day off after a particularly grueling shift was to rally her strength. Day two was just plain golden. *Gratitude.*

Wanting to get to the gym before it got too busy, she threw together a smoothie and scrambled up some egg-whites. Her favorite Wonder Woman travel mug full of hazelnut coffee with almond milk stood on the little red table by the front door, all ready to go with her.

When done with breakfast she found herself spending more time than usual picking a workout outfit. Finally, she decided on her black and pink leggings and black sleeveless, ruched top. That particular combo made her butt look smaller and her boobs look bigger.

Viv smiled to herself thinking, perfect way to head on into leg day.

* * *

Mike pulled up to the gym, bringing the Charger right up to the last handicapped spot out front. Just as he was about to pull in to the space a van with the same placard as his pulled up, vying for the very same spot. He looked over to the driver. The guy's expression was ripe with disappointment. Raising his hand, Mike motioned to the other driver as he put the Charger into reverse, offering him the space.

The incident pretty much settled the inner debate he'd been having with himself about even using the reserved spaces at all. He was perfectly capable of parking in a regular spot and walking the distance to the gym.

After parking and locking up, he weaved through the other cars making his way to the entrance.

Waiting there, was the guy from the van, relaxing in his wheelchair. While shielding his eyes from the morning sun, he watched as Mike approached.

The guy looked to be somewhere in his 60s, but in amazing shape in spite of the fact that he was a double amputee with not a whole lot of leg left from hip down. He wore bike shorts with the legs folded under. His chest and arms were big, with stout definition.

When he stepped up, the older man reached out his hand for a shake. "Thanks, man. Really appreciate that. When I came here yesterday I had to turn around and go home. Not a damn space with the ability to unload to be had," he said on a deep exhale of frustration.

Mike took his hand and gave it a quick shake. "No problem," said Mike, noting the faded Marine Corps tat on the guy's left shoulder.

"Mike Sala," he said, introducing himself.

"Trevor Drury."

Then there was that uncanny silent communication between them, the kind that happened with Marines.

With open palms, Trevor motioned to his stumps, "Vietnam."

Mike lifted the knee of his fake leg. "Afghanistan."

"What do you do now?" he asked the older man.

"Well, for about thirty years now, I've worked for the government, for the Division of Voc Rehab, helping Vets find jobs.

"Worthy calling."

"Yeah, it was." Then he grinned. "But I'm retiring."

"What are you going to do next?"

"Compete in bodybuilding."

"No shit, really? You can do that with no legs?"

"That's what they tell me. Signed up for my first competition in August." He smiled broad and confident, rolling his chair forward a little, lifting the front two wheels off the ground maintaining a perfectly balanced wheelie.

"Fucking cool, man!" Mike's respect for the guy brightened his own mood. "I guess you're just about to start prep."

"Yep."

Mike stepped over to the front door and opened it wide. Still on two wheels Trevor swiveled and rolled on into the gym.

*   *   *

While Mike and Trevor worked out at one of the Smith-Racks at the far end of the free weight area, he kept a watchful but distant eye on Vivian. She was doing squats on the rack she occupied five stations down.

Slow and controlled, excellent form. He loved the look of her in exertion. Beautiful, defined quads. *Yowsa!*

Ah, oh. Three young, self imagined bad-asses had stopped behind her rack, pretending to talk. Their gazes often angling down—at her ass.

Fury blew through him at the thought of their disrespect. Not that he'd never checked out a woman's ass before, but goddammit this was Vivian!

Mike watched her as she continued her exercises. She looked behind her, well aware of the three stooges. He could feel his body tense as he became more provoked.

"Mike," Trevor spoke from behind him. "Is that your woman?"

"I'm working on it," he responded in a tight voice.

Trevor rolled up beside him. "Stand down, Marine."

Finishing her last set, she secured the bar to the rack and came to her full beautiful height. She stepped over to the "boys," towering over them. Putting her hands on her hips, she leaned over and spoke. He didn't know what she said, but whatever it was the three of them appeared to shrink before his eye.

As they skulked away down toward the treadmills, she stood watching their departure, arms crossed over her chest, looking like a damn Valkyrie ready to send those fuckers to the underworld.

What a woman!

* * *

Barb Simmons (Belle Sloane) is an award winning writer of edgy romantic fiction. This piece is the beginning of the first in a new series of Wounded Warrior romances.

Romance   **Bronze Medal**
George McFall

ONE GOOD TRICK

"Uuuuh!" Red-faced, Charlene's last trick of the night grunted and gripped the iron bedstead with both hands. Charlene lay still, caressing the back of his neck till the tremors passed. Then she sighed—a sigh meant to convey pure contentment.

Charlene knew that deep down her customers wanted to believe they were good in bed, even those who pretended not to care. Her sigh provided validation. It was part of the service.

"Whooee, Charlene." He rolled onto his back, then peered tentatively out of the corner of his eye. "How was it for you?"

"Great," she lied. Though she did appreciate it when they asked. The question advanced him to "preferred customer" status, meaning Deputy John Sutherland would get preference over a john of lesser status in the event of a scheduling conflict. It did not, however, entitle him to a discount.

Charlene rose, plucked a robe from a hook on the wall, discretely counted the bills on the dresser, then slipped them into her pocket.

"You're not just saying that are you?"

"No, honey, it was great and I do appreciate that you asked."

Deputy John beamed. He swung his legs over the side of the bed and looked for his pants. "How about next Saturday night?" She asked. "You'll get first dibs."

He frowned. "There's a hanging that night and I got to set things up and make sure it all goes right."

Charlene's eyes widened. "A hanging? Who's getting hung?"

"Lee Gray. Governor denied him a stay and he's going out a week from tonight at ten o'clock sharp. I can get you in if you want to watch."

"Lee Gray," Charlene whispered.

Against all odds Charlene was a romantic. Every man she'd ever known had disappointed her in one way or another, yet she held fast to the belief that somewhere out there her ideal man awaited her. She'd followed Lee Gray's exploits in the newspapers. There was even a dime novel about him. The dashing bandit of the New Mexico Territory. Men feared him; women adored him. He pulled his jobs where least expected then melted away into the Sacramento Mountains near his native Tularosa.

Charlene remembered his picture in the newspaper after the jury convicted him of a double murder. He'd made off with the Chino Mine payroll, leaving two guards dead and another a one-armed cripple.

He'd looked into the camera like he hadn't a care in the world. Charlene felt his gaze bore right into her. He had gypsy black eyes, wavy black hair, a strong chin and flaring nostrils. But what sealed the deal was the twinkle in his eye—like he had a secret and it tickled him pink. She'd have sworn that the photograph winked at her. She was in love.

They'd never have caught him except one of his men got careless—spending some of the loot and letting himself be trailed back to the hideout. They never found the rest of the money and Lee Gray wouldn't say where he'd stashed it.

They held the trial in Hillsboro. He lied through his teeth on the witness stand, saying he'd had nothing to do with the robbery or the shooting of the three guards, two of whom were family men and the third little more than a boy—just nineteen, without a left arm thanks to a bullet from Lee Gray's gun.

It was a good thing for the prosecution that they didn't let women serve on juries. No woman would've voted to convict Lee Gray after hearing him testify. But the jury was all men and they had different notions when it came to men like Lee Gray. They deliberated less than an hour. Guilty on all counts. Judge Fountain sentenced Lee Gray to hang, the execution to take place in Silver City.

"Promise me you'll let me know the minute he gets here," Charlene said to Deputy John. Two days later they met in the parlor of Millie's sporting house.

"He's here," said Deputy John.

"Wait for me. I'll just be a minute."

She put on her favorite dress. High-necked and long-sleeved, it reached to the floor.

Charlene knew there was more to sex appeal than showing a little skin. If they wanted to see the goods they could pay the price. The dress did have a barely-noticeable slit that occasionally revealed a slender calf, delicate ankle and dainty foot but it covered more flesh than most women's dresses. Its form-fitting nature showed Charlene's hips and breasts to their full advantage, covered though they were.

Charlene had made her way to Silver City through a half-dozen mining camps and boom towns. Her Puritan forebears would've blanched at her choice of profession but they would've applauded her work ethic. The top producer wherever she worked, she moved her customers in and out quickly yet they never felt hurried. Not beautiful, she was pretty in a way that grew on you. A working girl who's too beautiful can be off-putting but Charlene made men feel comfortable and comforted. Other girls were prettier or better endowed in other ways, but Charlene always attracted more customers—more repeat customers—and that attracted her employers.

She made a lot money for those employers, and set aside a lot of money for herself. She planned to buy her own house and hire a string of girls to service the customers, saving her own favors for those special clients who could afford the premium prices she intended to charge.

Now she had her nest egg—almost seven thousand dollars—kept in a strong box in her room. Charlene didn't trust banks.

She trusted Pato.

Pato, the Duck, so named because in his youth he'd worked as a hod-carrier in Juarez and El Paso. He mixed the "mud," the mortar the brick layers used bind the bricks together. He spent so much time standing in puddles of water his co-workers said he must have webbed feet.

Pato was Millie's bouncer. Charlene told him about her nest egg after he'd bounced a customer who'd gotten rough with her. Pato threw the man out, which should've ended things but the customer rounded up five friends and came back to teach Pato a lesson, with a bonus lesson thrown in for Charlene.

But Pato's skills as a hod-carrier were surpassed by his skill with a six-shooter. After he wounded three and put the others to flight, they conceded the only lesson learned was that one should not mess with Pato and, by implication, one should not mess with Charlene.

That night Charlene told Pato about her plans. He would be the chief bouncer at her new house and if a day should ever come when he could no longer handle the drunks or the would-be toughs, she would hire a team of bouncers to do the dirty work while he supervised.

*   *   *

From that day forward Pato took even better care of Charlene.

"I want you to arrange for me to meet Lee Gray," Charlene told Deputy John. Deputy John frowned. "No visitors" was the sheriff's strict order.

When he told this to Charlene she asked, "How much?"

"How much what?"

Charlene sighed. She liked Deputy John but sometimes he could be a bit dim. "How much money do you want to let me in to visit Lee Gray?"

"Oh," said Deputy John. "I wouldn't know what to ask."

"How much do you make a month?"

"Forty dollars."

"I'll give you forty dollars if you get me into the jail for an hour." That night Charlene realized her dream.

"What's this?" Lee Gray said as Deputy John opened the door and ushered Charlene into the narrow corridor in front of the cell.

"You got a visitor."

Lee Gray sat up on his cot. His eyes met Charlene's for the first time. He was more splendid than she imagined. He was the most beautiful human she'd ever seen.

Lee Gray stood. Charlene reached out to touch the bars.

"You got to stay back, Charlene."

"John honey why don't you step outside. I promise I'll stay back but I have something to say to this gentleman in private."

"He might grab hold of you and try to use you as a hostage."

• Lee Gray's appreciative eye traveled up and down Charlene's figure. "I promise I won't try anything like that, Deputy," he said.

Deputy John had to admit that Lee Gray's smile was ingratiating and that it engendered trust.

"If you try anything like that I'll kill you where you stand."

It was Pato. He never let Charlene too far out of his sight. He stepped into the hallway, his long-barreled six-shooter pointed at Lee Gray's head.

"You can trust me," Lee Gray smiled lifting his hands shoulder high, palms outward.

Pato's expression didn't change. He didn't find Lee Gray's smile to be ingratiating. "It's okay boys," Charlene said. "Just step out behind the door and give us a few minutes."

Pato looked at Charlene, then led the way out the door leaving her alone with Lee Gray. "Well, this is sure something," Lee Gray said. "Who are you anyway?"

"I'm Charlene. I work over at Millie's. You know..." She trailed off, suddenly reluctant to say what she did for a living.

"Oh," he cleared his throat. "I know Millie's. Nice place. Worked there long?"

"A year or so," Charlene said. Then she summoned her resolve.

"I'm in love with you and I want us to get married."

Lee Gray's eyes widened.

"How can you be in love with me? We never even met."

"I've read all about you. How you rode with Butch Cassidy and how you robbed the Santa Fe near Lamy and got away with five thousand dollars. I read about that Chino robbery, too, and how you killed those guards and left one a cripple."

"I felt bad about that boy. His hard luck I guess."

"You're as famous as Billy the Kid or Jesse James. I know all about you."

"I guess you do, but how do you suppose we're going to get married? In case you forgot, your friend Deputy John Sutherland is fixing to hang me come Saturday."

"I've got a plan to get you out of here before then," she said.

"I'd like to hear it."

"Well, John took forty dollars to let me in here tonight. He'll take a hundred to help me break you out. I know it."

"But . . ."

"Just listen," she said. "Pato's going to throw you a rope up to that outside window." She pointed to a window about six feet above the cot.

"Wait, is Pato that fellow who said he'd blow my head off if I touched you?"

"That's him."

"Go on," said Lee Gray.

"He'll tie a gun onto the rope and you can pull it up. Then when John comes to bring you your supper you can get the drop on him."

Lee Gray thought about it. "Might work."

"Just one thing, though."

"What's that?"

"You don't hurt him—John I mean."

"What would it matter? They've already got me for two murders. They can only hang me once."

* * *

Lee Gray wasn't as kindly disposed as Charlene toward the man who was supposed to spring the trap and send him to eternity.

"You'll have no call to hurt John. Remember he'll be in on it. The gun's just for show, so nobody will suspect he helped you. Pato and I will be out back with a horse for you and we can hightail it while everyone's asleep."

"Then what?"

"Pato's cousin has a place up by Pinos Altos. We can lay low there for a few days then we head off to Tucson. That's where I'm going to buy my own house and go into business."

"You've got money?"

"Seven thousand. We'll be set up pretty as you please. I'll hire girls to do the heavy lifting and I might not even have to turn tricks, except maybe for special customers once in a while and maybe at first to build up a reputation.

"You won't mind if I turn a few tricks now and then will you? It'll just be business and I won't come with anyone but you."

"I guess I won't mind," Lee Gray said.

This was a lot to take in. An hour ago all he could think about was how that rope around his neck was going to feel, and now he was looking at a future. And a wife—nice looking with money to boot.

"I've got something to add to the plan," he said."I've got ten thousand— that Chino Mine payroll. Why don't the two of us go after it and then we'll have seventeen thousand to stake us? We could go to Mexico. The money'd go a lot farther down there and we wouldn't have to worry about the law coming after us."

"What about Pato?"

"I don't think Pato cares too much for me."

"Oh, he's just looking out for me. As long as we're together Pato's the least of your worries."

"He could go on ahead. Get things ready while we pick up the loot."

Charlene thought. "Hmmm. He could take my nest egg and buy us a house. He knows a good deal when he sees one."

"You'd trust him with your money?"

"More'n I'd trust you."

"I think we ought to keep most of it with us," he said. "I might have to pay some people off when we get where we're going. I'd feel better knowing we had the money with us."

"Can't you pay them out of the payroll money?"

"They'll likely want payment in advance, and I won't be able to get to that money right away."

"Alight," Charlene said. "I'll talk to Pato".

"Now," she winked, "I'll go to work on Deputy John."

* * *

Two days later Charlene and Lee Gray rode northwest out of Pinos Altos into the Gila country. Pato'd reported that the sheriff was leading a posse into

Lee Gray's old stomping grounds in the Sacramentos. They'd be going in opposite directions.

She wore a man's shirt and trousers and a pair of riding boots. Charlene's strong box, minus a thousand dollars, was tucked into her saddle bags. They'd agreed to send Pato to Nogales with the thousand to set up shop on the Mexican side. Lee Gray could tell Pato wasn't happy about the arrangement.

Their trail took them past several abandoned mining operations. At one point as they picked their way around some unstable rock Lee Gray's horse triggered a slide that almost carried them both away.

After another half day's ride they stopped at an abandoned mine high among the pines. Three wooden buildings whose windows lacked glass and whose roofs sagged to the point of collapse flanked the entrance to a tunnel sloping downward into the mountain.

"What's this?" Charlene asked.

"This is where I hid the loot," Lee Gray said. "Slung it down a ventilation shaft, hung on a rope. All we have to do is pull it up."

"Where are the people you said you had to pay off?"

"No sign of em," he said. "They musta took off."

"You don't think they took the payroll money do you?"

"No, I can see the rope tied off right where I left it. I'll show you."

He led her to a deep pit about four feet across, half surrounded by a broken-down rail fence. Charlene looked over but saw only blackness below.

"Where's the money?"

Lee Gray pointed to a tripod, an iron frame with a pulley suspended from the high point.

A rope tied to a fence rail looped over the pulley and disappeared into the pit. "All we got to do is pull it up."

He took hold of one end and began pulling the rope through the pulley hand over hand. Soon a leather satchel appeared, "Chino Copper Company" stamped on its side in gold letters.

Lee Gray set the satchel down and opened it. Charlene smiled at the packets of greenbacks, neatly wrapped. Her nest egg had nearly tripled.

She looked into Lee Gray's eyes. What she saw looking back at her was not what she expected—not a look of love.

"Well honey," he said. "This is where I'll be leaving you."

"What?"

"I'll be going my own way from here. You'll have to stay behind."

"Stay behind?"

He cocked his head, indicating the ventilation shaft. "Don't worry, it'll be over quick."

"Wait! You're going to kill me?"

"I'm sorry honey."

"But they'll come after you for another murder."

"I figure it'll be months, maybe years before they find you, if they ever do. And like I said, they can only hang me once."

She backed away.

"But I'm offering you the good life. We can settle down. You won't always be on the dodge. We'll be rich and—well, you'll have me."

"Don't you know you can't change a man's nature? Being on the dodge, taking what I want, going where I want when I want—that *is* the good life."

"Don't you like making love to me?"

"Oh my yes. But we have to live with the consequences of our choices. Anyway there's other whores. Let's get this over with. I got to get moving. Don't make me have to chase after you."

"Wait!" Charlene was thinking fast. "Won't you give me a last wish?"

"If the wish is that I don't kill you, forget it. Otherwise I might entertain the idea."

"Make love to me one last time."

"Don't imagine a little nookie is gonna make me change my mind."

"You're the only man I ever really loved. At least let me go out on a high note." She unbuttoned her shirt and dropped it to the ground. "You like looking at me, don't you?"

"Yes, I do." He surveyed her appreciatively, then nodded. "Alright, I'll let you turn your last trick. But this ground looks a mite uncomfortable."

"We can get the bedrolls."

"No time for that. Stand here and brace yourself against this rail."

Charlene removed her boots and trousers. Lee Gray stepped toward her. "Wait! Let me put my boots back on, there's goat-heads all over."

"Alright, hurry up."

Charlene jammed her feet into the boots and walked to the railing. She put her hands against it and bent her back, extending her derriere. "Since this is my last, I've got nothing to hold back for. I promise this will be the best either of us ever had."

Lee Gray liked the sound of that. He unbuttoned his fly and approached her from behind. "Let me, honey." Charlene reached back to guide him in.

She took control, moving her hips in slow circles she clinched and unclenched her pelvic muscles rhythmically. His head began to swim.

He closed his eyes. He heard Charlene moan softly and felt the mountain breeze caress his face. He heard the cocking of Pato's pistol and felt the cold gun barrel behind his ear.

"God," Charlene said, "I thought you'd never get here. What kept you?"

"Rockslide." Pato kept the muzzle against Lee Gray's head as he removed Lee Gray's own revolver from its holster. "Lost your trail. Took me an hour to find it again."

"Your timing's pretty good. I don't know if I could've kept him going much longer," Charlene said.

"Can I do up my pants?" Lee Gray asked.

"No," said Charlene.

She dressed then picked up the satchel.

"Well honey," she smiled, "this is where I leave you. I'll be going my own way from here. You'll have to stay behind."

"Stay behind?"

She indicated the pit.

"Now Charlene," Lee Gray's mouth was suddenly dry, "there's no need for that. You've got the money. Just ride away."

Charlene shook her head. "And look over my shoulder the rest of my life? Uh-uh. But don't worry, it'll be over quick."

"You don't want a murder hanging over you."

"I figure it'll be months, maybe years before they find you, if they ever do."

Pato's gun pressed into Lee Gray's back, directing him toward the ventilation shaft. "Wait, I let you have a last wish."

"And look how that worked out," said Pato.

Charlene looked into Lee Gray's gypsy black eyes and watched the breeze whiffling his wavy black hair.

"Come on now honey," he smiled and she saw the twinkle in his eye.

He saw her expression soften.

"I hope this teaches you not to waste opportunities," she said. "Good ones don't come along every day."

She shook the satchel and the greenbacks thumped against the leather.

"Come on Pato, time to go."

With that Charlene shoved the only man she'd ever loved into the pit.

*   *   *

George McFall is a former lawyer, hod carrier, carpenter, classical radio DJ, drug store clerk and building materials salesman among other things. Currently a husband, father, grandfather, friend, he wanted to be a writer when he grew up. Still working on that one

SECTION SEVEN

SOCIAL CONSCIOUSNESS

This category echoes thoughts and feelings from the turmoil of today and from ages past.

Social Consciousness Gold Medal
Mary Therese Ellingwood

THE URN

I stood in the back, far behind the last row of the open-air theater. Far enough away that I would not disturb anyone, but close enough to the path leading to the pyre that those leaving would pass me and notice my offerings. I had spent all morning climbing the countryside in search of wildflowers and had a beautiful selection with me, lying loosely in the bag at my side. The wildflowers were of all colors, but their blossoms were much smaller than those sold at the main street shop in the village. As I looked at the crowd gathered, many of them already had purchased the full blossoms and held them proudly in their lap as they listened to the Speaker.

Soon it would be time for the Reading of Prayers. It was a time for both grieving and celebration as individuals received acknowledgment from the deceased.

In our small village, the custom was to purchase or be gifted an urn on the day one was brought to the village as an adult. The urn was often placed in a dominant area of the house–perhaps at the front entrance or on an indoor altar. I knew not, exactly, where such urns were placed as I did not have a home for myself. I slept in the wilds, with my flowers for company. But I knew the custom well enough. Attending as many Days of Passing as I had, I picked up on the rituals quickly.

During life, the urns were used as a Prayer holder. The owner would place a name on a slip of paper when they prayed and place it in the urn. Sometimes the Prayers would have a thought or specific intention written on the back, but often it would just be a name. The Prayer itself an intimate secret between the person and their god. Then, when the person died, the Prayers would be drawn one by one from the urn and read aloud to the village. There were three piles created: the names of those who had left the world, those not present in the assembly, and those present. As each name was called, the person present would be granted a moment to share a word of thanks for the newly deceased. Sometimes they would share a story of encounter and other times they would give a small blessing in hopes to aid the Passing–the Journey of the newly deceased into the afterlife.

Once the urn was empty of all Prayers the Speaker would say the last rite. The villagers assembled would walk to the pyre, where the body was laid to rest, and offer their flowers to the departed. The flowers represented the beauty held in death. For flowers themselves would die once picked, but their petals would fade with time and during that time, appreciation for their beauty could be given. The plucked flower also represented newbirth. For each stem that was taken from the plant made room for a new stem to bud and take its place. Such was the method by which the village celebrated the Passing of a soul giving way to new life on earth while Journeying to the next stage.

Once the villagers all placed their flowers, the Speaker would place the Prayer notes atop the body and the pyre would be ignited. When all had turned to ash, the ashes were gathered and mixed and placed back in the very urn that had previously held the Prayers.

When the villagers offered their flowers, I would be ready to sell my wildflowers to anyone who had not brought one. It was considered bad taste to not offer a flower, especially if one received a Prayer from the deceased. There were not many, but I could spy some villagers sitting on the curved tiers of the theatre whose laps were empty. My morning efforts would not be for naught.

Standing in the back, it was a strain to hear the Speaker, but I noticed the reverent silence that indicated the Speaker had finished his tale of the life of the deceased. In my mind wanderings I had not caught the name of the departed. No matter. I was an outcast from society and while none knew my name, I in turn never learned the names of others. It was a man who had died. That I knew. And judging by the large crowd that over-flowed the theater and forced some to stand, he was a prominent man of the village. I wondered if he was the one who owned the vineyard on the hill. A bountiful expanse of land that drew many villagers and foreign merchants alike. Many wildflowers grew along its edge and I often picked blossoms there. Once I had tried to sell my flowers to those passing through the entrance to the estate but was rushed away by servants and threatened with arrest should I be caught selling on private land again. The vineyard master was a tyrant indeed. Though I knew it was wicked to think it, I secretly hoped it was his Passing I attended now, selling my wildflowers to those unprepared attendants. The thought of the irony in the act brought a smile to my lips.

The Reading of Prayers was beginning. Given the number in attendance it would be a long ceremony and my knees were starting to cramp already at the thought of standing through hours of name reading and acknowledgements. I glanced around to ensure no one was looking my direction and then squatted down beside my flowerbag to await the end of the Reading of Prayers.

"Callian," came the first name as the Speaker opened the urn and pulled out the first Prayer. A man in the back raised to his feet and said, "May his Journey be swift."

"Thuma."

A woman stood. "A gentle soul, may his Journey end in the same riches he gave in life."

"Justine."

There was a pause. Then the village record keeper came to stand next to the Speaker and announced in a loud voice, "Justine made the Passing three months ago. May her soul look down in favor and guide his Journey."

"Callian."

Having already said his piece, this time the man in the back merely nodded in acknowledgement and the reading continued. To receive more than one Prayer was a blessing indeed.

The piles grew of those in attendance and those who had already made the Passing. The pile of those not in attendance was small, however, with just a few names. Truly, I thought, most of the village must be here except those on sacred duty in the temples or guarding the village walls.

Some told stories as their names were called: "I met him in business and gained much from his mentorship. May his Journey profit him more than life." ... "He was like a second father to me. May his Journey be made easy knowing his legacy will go on." ... "Last solstice he helped me gather my bounty for market as my sons had taken ill and could not work the fields with me...despite his age, he was able-bodied and strong in his efforts. May his soul gain the strength that has now left his body and thus ease his Journey." ... "Many moons he would sit up with me in philosophical conversation. May this time be rewarded back to him and hasten his Journey toward the spoils of Afterlife."

The wonderful stories of this man who had Passed gave me pause. Surely this was not the vineyard owner who did all these wonderful things. The tales told made me wish I had known such a generous and kindly spirit as this man surely was. I thought back on my own life. No one wrote Prayers for me and I did not write Prayers for any other. I had no urn of my own and no home in which to place it. My few prayers were spent on myself and while some might call that selfish, I knew it was all I had to offer to the gods who had given me such misfortune in life. Perhaps that was why my station had never changed. Did the gods grant favor to those who only prayed for themselves?

Suddenly I was brought back to the present by a noticeable shift in the air. The evening had grown heavy and those gathered were shifting uncomfortably in their seats, looking from side to side. I glanced at the stage and saw the village record keeper consulting in a whisper with the Speaker who still held a Prayer slip in his hand. There was great confusion about something. The Speaker seemed to waver the slip over the non-attendance pile and the departed pile, unsure what to do. I wondered at what the slip must say to have even the record keeper at pause. Was it not a name at all but perhaps a general prayer? Was it a curse of some sort? I had heard rumor of a deceased person placing a curse within their urn as a way to avenge a wrong done in life, though I had never witnessed such an evil. A curse written in a Prayer urn was a powerful condemnation indeed.

The crowd began to murmur to one another. I paid rapt attention now, having missed the reading of the slip initially, lost in my thoughts. Perhaps he would read it aloud again or I could learn of its contents from the whispers dancing on the air around me. I concentrated hard on the secret words being said but could not grasp them anymore than I could grasp the breeze on which the incoherent murmurs drifted.

Finally, the village record keeper stamped his staff on the stage. A booming sound echoed around the theater and silenced the voices.

"We will try again. If no acknowledgement is given it will be placed unanswered as our village records hold no memory of the name."

I waited and held my breath. For a Prayer slip to be placed unanswered meant it would be sent on the waves of the sea away from the village and forgotten. If the person whose name it was existed, they in turn would be forgotten for they neither gave an acknowledgement nor were known by the village itself and therefore unrecognized as a citizen.

The Speaker held the slip back up and read the name once more.

"Ayana."

I let out a small gasp that none around me heard, but at the same time I stood. For it was my name that had been called. I could not remember the sound of it on another's lips for ages and though I recognized it, it felt foreign.

But being in the back and hidden from the assembly, none noticed me standing and I watched in horror as the Speaker went to place the slip in a separate, fourth pile. Before he could let go the paper, I moved forward into the light of the evening lit torches. I felt eyes shift toward me, looking at me with recognition for the first time. The Speaker paused, the record keeper was pensive as if trying to remember who I was, for it was his job and he had failed. Then he gave a slight nod at the Speaker who straightened back up with the Prayer slip in hand and beckoned me with open palm to give my acknowledgment.

I felt guilty and strange. I still did not know the name of the deceased. I had no family in the village and no one fit to call friend save for the strangers that stopped to purchase a wildflower from me on the cobblestone streets. Though their friendship had always been fleeting in the passing of coin in exchange for flower and I had never learned even one name.

Those around me waited and I could not think what to say. My mind raced, trying to pluck out a memory which would reveal the man who had thought of me enough to write a Prayer. In this mental search, I lost the words of the general acknowledgement given for a Passing Prayer and stood silent as a stone.

Then my mind started to relive memories which I had locked away as meaningless in my life of misery, but now recognized them for all the kindness shown to me: a smile from one who walked by; a woman who purchased a wildflower although she already held a beautiful arrangement from the flower shop; a man who insisted I take a small extra coin for finding a certain wildflower upon request; a girl who brightened when I made a flower wreath for her hair; another man who offered a loaf of bread for a fresh bouquet each week; a kind stranger who offered the bag to me that I have used for my flower gathering since.

Suddenly, I realized how much goodness and blessing had been bestowed on me despite my poor existence. I took another step, so to stand in the middle of the tiered benches and gave my acknowledgement for this stranger of Passing.

"He was a man of compassion and great sympathy for those in need of kindness. May his Journey be filled with the blessings that he left behind to those in need here on earth."

There were several nods and smiles at my words.

* * *

I walked back to my flowerbag, but this time I remained standing for the rest of the ceremony and Prayer calling.

When the time finally came to walk to the pyre, the assembly passed me and many bought flowers. Some who already had flowers bought another wildflower, believing them to have special meaning since I had been given a Prayer. Eventually, my flowers were all sold save one which I clutched in my hand. A beautiful and small white wildflower with a tall head and proud leaves.

Instead of leaving, as was my custom as the Passing ceremony gave way to the Lighting, I fell in line with the other villagers. As I joined them to place my flower on the pyre, I realized that instead of gaining looks of pity, as was my due, eyes began to gaze upon me with appreciation and acceptance. As someone worthy of consideration and Prayer. I stood as one with the villagers as we watched the body, Prayers and petals turn to ash. It was the first time I had let myself feel that I belonged.

After the ceremony was complete, deep in the dark of night, the villagers returned home. I myself retreated within the branches of the great sweeping willow at the edge of town. It was the closest thing I had to a real home and the trunk I had carved into over the years. None could tell without peering between the leaves, but the bark of the trunk had been smoothed away in swirling patterns of stem, leaf and blossom.

No moonlight pierced through the thick tangle of branches so, as I dumped out my coin purse onto the earthen floor, I felt along the ridges of each coin to identify its worth and take inventory of my eve. A rare smile tugged my lips into a soft grin as I lay down to rest and, for once in a long while, began to plan for my future.

No house could I afford as the haul was still small, but not trivial. I decided instead to go to market the next day to buy my own urn, some paper and lead. Now when I sold flowers, I would ask the buyer's name and write a Prayer for each one. Like the man whose Passing I had attended, I would leave a legacy behind in the form of Prayer names. For everyone at one point is in need of and deserving of Prayer.

*　*　*

Mary Therese Ellingwood is an aspiring fiction writer working full time as a mathematics professor at Central New Mexico Community College. Her short term goals include finishing several short stories across different genres in an effort to discover her writing voice. Her long term goals include completing two works-in-progress novels.

Social Consciousness Poetry   Gold Medal
Joanne Bodin

EYE OF THE HURRICANE

An illusion for our consideration, eye of the hurricane

has its own characteristics. Safe, in our place of calm,

we wait for the second wave to slap us out of complacency.

Thrust into an alternate universe, we are now the dystopian novels

we read. We are now the witnesses of a global coronavirus pandemic.

We are now that generation who tell our stories of resiliency, of fear,

of panic, of despair, of hope, of longing for a way of life that will be no more.

It's all a matter of perspective. Last night I sat outside on my terrace at dusk.

No sunset, no blue sky. Just a gray mist left over from an earlier rainstorm.

Honey locust tree branches still bare, waiting for their cue to bud.

Iris about to send out yellow blossoms. Flowering plum, crab apple send

aromas that blend in with night mist. Sound of a cricket and whisper of gentle

breeze. Perfect calm. It's all a matter of perspective.

*   *   *

Joanne Bodin Ph.D., is an award-winning author and poet. She has received numerous awards for her writing which include her novel *Walking Fish*, her book of poetry, *Piggybacked,* and her novel *Orchid of the Night*. Her poetry has appeared in numerous literary publications. She also teaches writing. See website. **www.joannebodin.com**

Social Consciousness
George McFall

Silver Medal

DESCANSOS

Beyond the cracked sidewalk and the patch of dry ground stood a ten-foot high cinder block wall, topped with razor wire, stretched out like a malevolent slinky. "Touch me," it said, "and I'll bite you."

The wall had been painted a dozen times. Tan overlaid pink, through which showed a patch of blue, then yellow.

A small shrine sat against the wall, candles in red glass jars, flowers, some wilted, some fresh, a wooden cross, some bedraggled teddy bears and three photographs—school pictures—of three young girls. Above the shrine scrawled in red paint on the wall's yellow face was one word: "REJOICE."

Ana passed the shrine every day as she walked to and from school. It marked the place where her younger sister, Martha and two of Martha's school friends had been shot dead by gunfire meant for a gangbanger trespassing on a rival gang's turf. A February wind whirled trash around the site. Plastic grocery bags, empty cigarette packs and food wrappers snagged on dry tumbleweeds and mingled with the sad offerings that neighbors and friends had left to mark the spot and to make some gesture—defiance, despair, or simply grief—in response to the madness that had taken over their world.

"Just in the wrong place at the wrong time," the police officer pronounced, as if stating the obvious was somehow a comfort for stunned families trying to comprehend the incomprehensible. The ambulance drove away carrying the small bodies to the morgue. Ana gripped her mother's hand. The officer offered to drive Ana's mother to make the official identification.

"She just told you who it is!" Ana stamped her foot on the porch. "Why should she have to go somewhere else to tell you again?! It's my sister. It's Martha. Didn't you listen?"

"It's okay, *hijita*, shhhhh," her mother said and smoothed the girl's hair. Ana marveled at her mother's quiet composure. Everyone in the neighborhood had been touched by violent death. Do you get used to it? Ana wondered.

"She's upset," Ana's mother said to the policeman. "Just give me a minute and I'll go with you." She hugged Ana to her and whispered, "It's okay, it's okay." Ana sobbed, her head on her mother's shoulder. "Why Mama? Why?"

"I don't know, hijita. Maybe God knows. You go in the house and wait for me."

"If you'd rather wait . . ." the policeman said.

"No, it's fine." Ana's mother guided her toward the house, passing her to the arms of two other women, Ana's aunts, then she returned to the waiting police car, sagged into the back seat and sat, unmoving, ready to be driven to the morgue to perform the worst duty of her life. She refused company other than the officer. "I want to do this myself," she said.

The police searched in vain for someone who could help them identify the shooters. The eyewitnesses gave a vague description of the car—black and long, like an Oldsmobile or a Buick.

Two neighborhood women witnessed the shooting. They'd been walking to a nearby grocery store. A young man hurried past them and crossed the street. They avoided looking at him directly, partly out of fear. The young man dressed like he belonged to one of the street gangs, though so many young people had adopted those same styles you couldn't tell which might be dangerous and which might just be trying to look that way. They didn't get a good look at the young man's face. They were sure they didn't know his name.

He wore a long-sleeved flannel shirt, buttoned only at the collar, over a white t-shirt and three-quarter length khaki pants. One witness remembered a baseball cap turned backward. They saw the three young girls walking toward the young man. Just girls on their way home from the elementary school a block away.

The women didn't notice the car at first. It came from behind them and from behind the young man. They paid no attention—there was usually traffic on the street at this time of day. Suddenly they heard the brakes screech. The young man turned at the sound, saw the car and ran. Gunshots. They didn't count them. One woman said that the gunfire sounded so different from the way it did on television.

The driver gunned the engine, the tires spun, squealing and smoking, and the car sped away out of sight—too fast for the witnesses to get the license number. They'd clutched each other in panic, hiding their faces in the folds of their clothes.

The young man, who had flattened himself, got up and fled limping in the opposite direction. The police found blood on the sidewalk and followed the trail until they lost it in an alley near a parking garage. The schoolgirls lay bunched together on the sidewalk, unmoving.

Ana and her friends built the shrine the day after the funerals for Martha and the other girls. Araceli's uncle worked at a flower shop and he gave her a bunch of blue and yellow flowers that they were going to throw out in a day or so. They were called nemesia. Martha had loved the color blue.

Sofia and Ava both brought small teddy bears from their rooms. Ana made a cross with nails and glue and some pieces of wood she found in the alley outside Chase's hardware store. She painted it white and carefully printed the names of the three dead girls in red and tied a strip of red ribbon where the pieces of the cross intersected. Other neighbors brought mementos and candles in little red jars. Ana hoped that the jars might keep the candles from blowing out in the wind.

She modeled the shrine after others she'd seen around town and on the highway. "Descansos" they were called. Mostly they marked the site of a fatal traffic accident. A few had bicycles painted white and affixed to the site. "Ghost bikes" Ana called them. She imagined their ghostly riders gathering after midnight, gliding on the bare wheel rims pursuing some ghostly mission—maybe completing the journey that death interrupted—and returning at daybreak to put the bike in its place by the road.

Most descansos featured crosses and some had personal items to evoke the memory of the ones who died there. One prominently displayed a fiberglass motorcycle helmet fixed to a cross of welded rebar. It surprised Ana a little that no one had removed the helmet, which looked expensive. People seemed to respect the descansos. Perhaps it marked the return, however fleeting, of a shared sense of honor.

One evening a few weeks after the shootings Detective Sergeant McKinney appeared at the house. Ana's mother brought him into their living room and he accepted the coffee she offered. He told them that the police had made some progress in the investigation, though it might not make much difference in the long run. They had identified the gunmen's intended target. His name was Billy Garcia, known also by his gang name, "Chill." Nineteen years old, he'd recently been living in California.

Chill had a pretty extensive criminal history for one so young, said the sergeant. Two years in a juvenile detention center for an armed robbery when he was fourteen. His sentence might have been longer but no one was hurt and Chill hadn't carried the gun. There were lots of other offenses, said the sergeant, but he didn't list them.

"We're sure it was him. He had a fairly recent gunshot wound in his left leg. That corresponds with what the witnesses saw and we were able to match his blood with samples taken from the blood trail we found leaving the scene."

"Then you've arrested him?"

"No," the sergeant said. "I'm afraid he's dead. A car accident. He was high on something, driving a stolen car and crashed at an intersection. Nobody else even got hurt. The other driver ran the red light. Go figure."

Ana's mother asked whether the police were any closer to identifying the gunmen. The sergeant said he would call her if they learned anything more but he was not very hopeful.

Ana's mother walked him to the front door. She thanked him for bringing the news. As he stepped onto the porch, she asked, "Where was the accident?"

"Ma'am?"

"The accident where this Chill was killed."

"The intersection at Paseo and the freeway," he said. "The light turned green and he started across. Drunk driver in a big Dodge Ram pickup ran the light and t-boned him. He was dead at the scene. It probably doesn't matter. I don't think he would've told us anything anyway."

Three days later an automobile pulled up and parked beside the concrete wall. Although the driver's face was in shadow, Ana could tell she was sad. There was something about how she turned away from the sun and rested the weight of her hands on the steering wheel, something about her silent composure. The driver stepped out of the car, walked timidly to the shrine, which stood out brightly against the backdrop of the block wall. Ana watched as the woman knelt and stretched her hand out towards the cross, adorned now with fresh yellow and orange flowers that Ana had placed there.

As she did the woman noticed Ana for the first time. She froze as if she'd been caught doing something wrong. She looked confused and apologetic and she pulled her arm away quickly. She stood as if uncertain what to do.

"It's okay," Ana said. "It's okay to touch them." She approached slowly and they looked into each other's eyes. The woman was like a frightened animal that might bolt at any second. Then she relaxed a little and sadness replaced the confusion on her face.

"I didn't mean to . . . to intrude. It just seemed so out of place, and I had to stop and . . . and..."

"It's okay," Ana said. "You can leave something if you want."

"I wouldn't know what to leave. I've never seen something like this before. It's so moving. What does it mean?" She picked up one of the glass encased candles and turned it in her hands reverently, examining it as if it were an artifact from an ancient tomb.

"They're called descansos. They show where someone was killed. Mostly it's car accidents. Sometimes it's other things. You can see them on the highways. It's something for people to remember when they pass the place."

"I don't know that I would want to remember something terrible like that," said the woman. "I think I would want to forget, or at least not have to be reminded every time I passed by." She replaced the candle and stood.

"My mother says it helps people remember the ones who died. And it reminds us that life is precious." She paused and added, "And it reminds us to be careful—to look out for others.

There are lots of descansos here; they seem to comfort people."

"Did someone die here?"

Ana stepped off the sidewalk and went to the cross re-arranging the flowers that she'd brought from the flower shop.

"My sister Martha and her two friends were killed here." The strength of her voice surprised Ana. She told the woman of the shooting, and how the three children had been walking home from school.

"They were just in the wrong place at the wrong time," she said.

"Oh, I'm so sorry." The woman impulsively reached out and pulled Ana to her. She held the girl close for a moment. Then, realizing she might have overstepped, let her arms drop and turned a half-turn away, looking again at the shrine.

"I'm so sorry, I didn't mean to—"

"It's okay," Ana said.

"We made this. Me and my friends. I come here sometimes. To put new flowers or just to sit. My sister liked flowers and I pretend I'm talking to her. I tell her about our family or school or things that happen in the neighborhood." A gust of frigid wind kicked up dust and threatened to tumble the cross over.

"Aren't you cold?" asked the woman.

"No," Ana said. "Thinking about her keeps me warm. We used to fight sometimes but we took care of each other. She was the happiest person you ever saw."

They sat silently, wrapped in their own thoughts.

"I'm Donna," said the woman. "Donna Horton. What is your name?"

Ana wondered what it was that drew her to this woman, someone she'd never seen before today and likely wouldn't see again.

"I'm Ana." She could see tears brimming in the woman's eyes.

"Why are you sad, Mrs. Horton." Ana recalled the silent composure she'd noticed when she first saw the woman in the car. She thought of her own mother waiting to be driven to the morgue in the back of the police car.

"I've lost my son," tears spilled onto her cheeks. "An accident. I've come to claim his body and take him back to California to be buried. I've been at the police station. Tomorrow I'll arrange with the funeral home to have him sent back on a train."

"I'm sorry," said Ana. Now Ana acted impulsively. She grasped both the woman's hands in hers and squeezed them.

"It must be terrible to lose a child. How old was he?"

"Nineteen. He wants to be—he wanted to be—an artist. He had talent. Mothers always say that, I know, but he really did. He got into trouble a few years ago, running with a bad crowd, but he was turning his life around. He was going to go to school and I had such hopes for his future here away from those bad people who influenced him. He was such a good baby, a good little boy. So happy all the time. I don't know why I'm telling you all this. I feel so lost."

"Where is your husband? He should be here with you."

Ana quickly apologized. It had just popped out. She knew as well as anyone that not all women with children had husbands to help confront the trials that life threw at you.

"I'm divorced. Years ago. He was my second husband. I was married to Billy's father before. He died not long after Billy was born. Billy never did have a real father to influence him in a good way. I always blamed myself for that."

Ana thought of her mother again. "Would you like to make a descanso for Billy? We could do it together."

Mrs. Horton grasped Ana's hands in hers. "Oh, I would." Then she hesitated. "But I'm going back to California. I won't be here to see it or look after it."

Ana said it wouldn't matter. Others would see it and that was the important thing. "Besides," she said, "I'll be here."

They listed things they would need. At Ana's prompting Mrs. Horton gathered a few of her son's personal items from the things she'd brought with her and that she'd collected from the police. She withdrew a small jack knife that had belonged to her own father, which apparently meant something to Billy. In her wallet she carried a small photograph of a pudgy, dark-haired toddler beaming at the camera. Ana said they could put it in a baggie to protect it. It would fade in the sun, but the descanso wasn't expected to last forever.

At the florist shop where Araceli's uncle worked they bought some fresh flowers and a gold ceramic cross about eight inches tall mounted on a wooden base. Ana told Araceli's uncle what they were doing and he found her a small garden trowel in case she had to dig in the hard- baked dirt.

Ana said that they would need something to put Billy's name on the cross and Mrs. Horton fished a bottle of red nail polish from her purse. She said Ana would have to direct her how to get to the accident site.

"It's at the intersection of a street called Paseo and the freeway. Do you know how to find it?"

Ana nodded, her heart beating as if it would come out of her chest. "You'd better get your coat," she said to Mrs. Horton. "There's a chill." Ana scrutinized her companion for a reaction but saw no change in her expression.

"I thank you so much for doing this. You'll never know what it means to me."

At the fatal intersection Mrs. Horton pulled the car off to the side out of the traffic. The concrete overpasses for entering and exiting the freeway swooped and arced above them like a scene from a futuristic film. They set up the descanso in a triangle of ground separated from the road by a concrete curb. With the garden trowel Ana scraped some dirt and rocks and piled them around the base of the cross. They arranged the flowers and, using a strand of metal wire they'd found in the dirt, attached them to the cross along with the plastic baggie containing the photograph and the jack knife. Mrs. Horton removed the nail polish from her purse and using the brush provided with it, wrote her son's name on the gold of the cross.

Tears ran down Mrs. Horton's face. She gripped Ana's hand as they returned to the car. "Wait!" Ana grabbed the nail polish bottle and ran back to the shrine.

Kneeling next to the cross, she removed the cap and dipped the brush into the polish. On the back she wrote one word, red letters on a gold background: "REJOICE!"

* * *

 **George McFall** is a former lawyer, hod carrier, carpenter, classical radio DJ, drug store clerk and building materials salesman among other things. Currently a husband, father, grandfather, friend, he wanted to be a writer when he grew up. Still working on that one

Social Consciousness Poetry   Silver Medal
Mary Dorsey

ONCE UPON A TIME WHEN WE COULD...

Once upon time when we could…
Touch.
We didn't.
Choosing instead a
superficial hug.
Anxious to be on our way.

Once upon a time when we could…
Talk.
We didn't.
Choosing instead to
let out fingers to write a message
devoid of any emotion.

Once upon a time when we could…
Work.
We complained.
Upset about hours,
co-workers,
conditions and pay.

Once upon a time when we could…
Help.
We didn't.
Too busy to see the suffering of
our neighbor.
Our own wants much too important.

Once upon a time when we could…
We didn't.
Then…
The plague that did not
discriminate against victims
came.
And the world turned upside down.

The only way to
Touch.
would be through glass or
not at all.

The only way to
Talk.
would be to say hello or good-bye
through an i-pad.

The only way to
Work.
Some from home or not at all.
While we longed to go back.

The only thing we could do
was help.
Becoming more aware of others.
Creating acts of kindness.

Once upon a time when we could...
We didn't realize our
abundance of simple blessings.

Now that we have...
May we turn what we could...
into what we do.

*   *   *

 I'm **Mary Elizabeth Dorsey**; early 70s.; born, Stratford, Ct. moved to Albuquerque, 1975; retired RN, 2X leukemia (AML) survivor, had own stem cells transplanted to save my life; been writing since childhood; walk every morning; love animals, live with my beloved feline fur babies. Hope you enjoy my contribution.

Social Consciousness   Bronze Medal
Lynn Andrepont

AN EXTRAORDINARY INCIDENT

George awoke at 5 am. No alarm clock sounded. He heard no rooster crowing. No faint morning light had yet begun to fade away the night's blackness to grey. His wife had not yet stirred beside him. It was like every other morning.

He arose from bed, washed and shaved, dressed, fed the chickens and did a few more routine chores before he walked the gravel road in the early dawning of the new day, the same five blocks he walked every day through his aging, tattered neighborhood of small, wood-framed, post-depression houses, each with its tiny front porch, some screened in, and then across the newly paved highway to the country grocery store at the edge of town where he worked behind the meat counter. He owned a car, an old second-hand 1950s Buick that he polished like clockwork every Saturday afternoon because he only drove the clunky black behemoth to church on Sunday mornings, or perhaps to visit relatives when his wife insisted.

At noon, he removed his bloodstained apron, washed his hands, and walked home for lunch, carrying the neatly wrapped cut of meat that his wife would prepare that afternoon for supper that night.

He and his wife ate their lunch together in near silence. His wife briefly recounted her morning, but George spoke little. When George stood from the table and reached for his hat, his wife would tell him that afternoon's chance for rain. She always listened to the noontime weather report as she prepared and laid out their lunch and never failed to inform George what he could expect in the way of possible rain each afternoon.

"We might get a stray shower," she warned through the screen door as George stood upon the front porch, preparing his pipe for the walk back to work, "a 20 percent chance."

On his return walk to the grocery store through the neighborhood, he waved to Mrs. Marks, who each day could be found at that precise time wearing the same faded floral sunbonnet, pruning her rosebushes or doing some other garden chore in her well-manicured front yard.

"What's the price of your ground sirloin today, Mr. George?"

Mrs. Marks called everyone by their first name, and, to her, all women were "Miss so-and-so," whether married or not.

"Same as yesterday, 75 cents a pound."

"And the chance for rain today?"

"The wife says 20 percent."

George had been the butcher at the neighborhood grocery store since it first opened in 1940, twenty years earlier. Prior to that and after prohibition ended, George had been a bartender, and before that, when first married through the first years of the depression, he was a cotton farmer, a sharecropper. Life was much harder then. He and his young wife worked their hands raw picking cotton and still nearly starved to death. They lost their firstborn to a fever when he was just a baby. Perhaps this was why George was content with his current circumstances, the security of unfailing routine and the comfort of knowing that each day would be much the same as the last. Now, at nearly 60, with his surviving two children grown and on their own, he had no intention of retiring from his job. He still marveled at the abundance of food delivered daily to the store, a different product each hour of the day it seemed, beginning with bread, baked that morning, filling the air with a warm yeasty aroma just as the store opened, fresh fish on ice that was driven up from the gulf coast mid-morning, produce in the afternoon, followed by canned goods and then the arrival of the refrigerated meat-truck.

Retirement wasn't even something George thought about...but then he wasn't much for making plans of any sort. Every day started and ended much the same way.

Although George's son, now married and living miles away with his own family, had enlisted in the U.S. Marines after high school, George himself was never in the military. He was too young at the time to serve in WWI and too old for WWII, but somedays he wished he could be like the neighborhood veterans who sometimes gathered on the benches set out under the covered veranda in front of the store, telling and retelling their battle tales over ice-cold bottles of cola in the summer or steaming black coffee in the winter, commenting on the make and model of each of the cars that drove past along the highway. George watched them, the veterans and the cars, from behind the meat display and through the large storefront window, painted with the week's specials that never seemed to include ground sirloin. Through a small open window behind the meat counter, he could hear the men laughing. He listened to their stories. Someone might wipe a tear from his eye or pull out a handkerchief and feign a coughing fit to hide being overcome by emotion. They recounted distant places, foreign people, bloody skirmishes, and deeds of valor and sacrifice which sometimes created vivid pictures in George's mind.

In reality, George wasn't much for conversation. Perhaps that was why he had lost his job long ago as a bartender. The boss had told him to talk it up with the customers, tell them a joke or two, keep them engaged, so that they felt at home and would drink more. Generally quiet and reserved, George didn't have the right disposition for small talk, and he was too soft with the regular, overly rowdy drunks. He lacked worldly experience and barely knew how to read, though he had completed school through the eighth grade, rare for a boy his age from the south Louisiana backwoods where he was born and still lived, although area towns, including his, were now rapidly growing with more people moving from the farms into towns.

When he noticed Mr. Richard building his new store on the main road out of town, he offered to help with the carpentry. George was a skilled woodworker and that ability eventually led to his job behind the store's meat counter because George was also skilled at sawing and slicing up the pork and beef carcasses delivered whole to the store.

"George, you are the most consistent meat cutter I've ever known," Mr. Richard had told him. "You hardly even need to weigh your cuts—each is that close to the last one. I've never seen anything like it."

At closing time, George again removed his apron. At the end of each work week, he brought his dirty aprons home to his wife to wash. Mr. Richard offered to have them laundered for him, but George was used to his wife washing the clothes he wore, and it just wouldn't feel right to wear any article of clothing that his wife hadn't washed herself.

There had been a brief shower late that afternoon and the gravel road home was still damp, which was good because it meant less dust in the air. George didn't like hearing his wife complain about the cars that would pass in front of their house, filling the air with dust that somehow found its way into the house and on to the furniture. He never saw any dust on the furniture because his wife always managed to do the dusting, every day, before he arrived home.

After finishing supper and evening chores, George sat in a rocker on the back patio to smoke his last pipe of the day, watching his chickens scratch in the dirt before they all headed off, in unison, softly clucking, to roost in their coop for the night. If the sky was clear, prior to retiring to bed himself, he would search for familiar stars and constellations. He heard the customary sounds coming from within the house, his wife putting away the supper dishes, the radio or television. The sweet smell of gardenia blossoms in nearby shrubs mixed with the pungent scent of his tobacco smoke. On weekend nights, if the breezes blew in just the right direction, he heard sultry blues and flashy jazz notes, live music from the old dancehall located across an open pasture in the far side of town where the Negros lived.

As the couple prepared for bed, George's wife sometimes told him bits of popular news from the day. Perhaps she'd heard some broadcast about such things as space rockets, race riots, the Cold War, political problems in distant parts of the world like Cuba or Asia, or she described scenes from the television shows she'd watched, especially from her favorites, *Bonanza* and *Gunsmoke*, but George seldom took much interest. The troubles of others, whether real or fictional, all sounded the same to him, and little of it seemed to have any consequence, directly, on him or his quiet life. Every morning for George would arrive much like the previous one.

One unusually warm Wednesday, the last Wednesday in October, a customer George had never seen before came into the store. The last Wednesday of every month was the day George brought home to his wife staples and non-perishable groceries, in addition to the meat he would bring to her each day for their supper. These were incidental items…the kinds of things his wife didn't grow in her garden or make herself…like laundry bluing to get his aprons bright and white, waxed paper, molasses, and popcorn. He seldom carried cash and never bought from any other grocery store; items purchased from Mr. Richard were discounted and subtracted from his monthly paycheck.

Just before the man in uniform entered the store, Dottie, the checkout girl, had been speaking pleasantly with George as she tallied the price of the items he had placed in his Wednesday box.

"Looks like your wife's making her famous popcorn balls for Halloween, so I guess my kids, dressed to scare the dead, will be knocking after dark at your house again this year, you can be sure."

Dottie's good-natured smile immediately turned to a frown when the soldier came through the door.

A distant relative of Mr. Richard, Dottie was proficient enough at the register but she could be a little too bossy to the stock boys and even to George on a bad day. George mostly avoided her, but he knew she liked chatting with the customers and wondered if that was another reason Mr. Richard had hired her.

The soldier, looking confident, perhaps even a little defiant, stopped abruptly when he saw Dottie and the expression on her face. He seemed then to raise his head just a bit higher.

"You need to leave, boy," she said to him, circling her finger in the air and then pointing to the door. "Just turn yourself around and go on back from where you came...right now."

George looked from the man at the door to Dottie, her face now growing red, not with embarrassment. It was more something like anger, indignation perhaps. No one else was in the store, and George knew that Mr. Richard was out back somewhere, behind the store, dealing with a delivery.

"Are you telling me, ma'am, I can't buy me a soda pop in here?"

"No, sir," she answered. "You got to go...get right out of here, right now, boy, you hear me!"

George noticed the man's crisp "dress blues" uniform. He was very likely an officer, judging by the insignia he wore. He had removed his hat from his head as soon as he entered the store. He was not a boy at all. Beads of sweat trickled down the side of the man's face.

"It's some hot outside today, ma'am. I just want to buy me a soda pop, then I'll be on my way."

"Boy, I done told you to leave," Dottie raised her voice. "We don't need no trouble here."

"Cola ok?" George suddenly asked him, thinking if that's all the soldier wanted, why not give it to him so he'd leave.

Glances passed from the soldier to Dottie and from Dottie to George.

"Yes, sir," said the man. "That would be just fine."

George reached into the box cooler next to the counter and pulled out a bottle of cola, popping the cap off using the opener conveniently attached to the front of the refrigerated chest.

"Go on and add this to my other stuff, Dottie," George said as he handed the bottle to the soldier, waving off the nickel offered to him in exchange.

Glaring at George, Dottie hit the keys of the cash register a little harder than necessary while George wondered why the soldier hadn't turned and left yet.

"Can I give you a hand with that box, sir?"

George hesitated, but the soldier placed his hat and the cola into the box, picked it up, and still managed to open the door, holding it open for George.

A single car was parked out front in the gravel parking lot, a shiny new white Cadillac Coupe de Ville.

George stood on the veranda waiting for the man to hand him back his box, say thanks perhaps, and be on his way, but he didn't do that. The soldier looked at George right in his face, right into his eyes. The soldier's eyes were black as night and seemed to hold the remnants of experiences and struggles George had only imagined during his own long lifetime.

"Mister," said the soldier to George, "that was really brave of you, you know. They're not likely to ever let you back in there now."

George glanced back through the store window at his meat counter, orderly rows of uniformly cut pork chops and mounds of ground sirloin visible inside the glassed case.

"I work here," said George.

"You *used* to work here, is my guess. Bet you didn't even think of that."

"No."

"Man, I'm sorry," the soldier moved towards the car. "Can I give you a lift?"

"Oh, no, I prefer to walk," said George, taking his box back and handing the soldier his hat and cola. "Thank you for your service, son."

The unusual warmth of this bright October day gave the neighborhood a colorful stillness George had not recalled ever feeling before. Before crossing the highway, he turned back to the soldier who had donned his hat and opened the door of his car.

"I guess," George said as he balanced the box with one arm and tipped his own hat with his free hand in a gesture of farewell, "we're all born to make some sort of sacrifice in our life, large or small, sometime or other."

Lynn Andrepont holds a Master's Degree in English from what's now the University of Louisiana at Lafayette. A former librarian, teacher, marketer, journalist, and editor, she now aims to publish her first novel, *Escape from Moon Village,* about a princess storyteller, her once-flourishing Archaic (3000 BCE) community, and its collapse.

Social Consciousness Poetry Bronze Medal
Sara Gray

EVOLUTION

For no one can love this world who has not been damaged by the actions of our species, yes us, the so called perfect peak of evolution. I could even forgo the beautiful words of poets, the lofty words of philosophers, the genius of scientists. I would trade music for the winds of the universe and the chirping of birds. How have we managed this earth, and what right had we to manage it at all? If I could take the earth in my hands I would pluck the ships from its seas and leave the waters to the dolphins, the whales, the plankton. If I could take the earth in the palms of my hands I would wrench the steel structures from its skin and smash its cars and trucks and trains with my thumb. Then I would rest.

Let natural forces take over. Too much cold? Too much heat? Volcanoes and earthquakes? Let the earth decide.

*   *   *

 **Sara Jean Gray**'s professional career was as a writer and desktop publisher in the areas of education and science and the environment. Two years ago a chance poetry workshop set her on a new path that keeps her from dwelling on the fact she is in Covid quarantine.

SECTION EIGHT

THRILLER/SUSPENSE

Creeeeeeak. Someone's coming up the stairs. The maid, your spouse or some nightmare that is creeping closer with each step.

Suspense/Thriller   Gold Medal
Nathan McKenzie

THE VISITOR

(Or Floating Lessons)

"Baby," my Mama used to say. "Life is nothin' more than a lazy river. The headwaters is birth and the gaping mouth is death, but you don't got to worry about that. No, you just got to learn to float and the river will do the rest. And floating is easy, baby. Floating is what life's all about."

I used to believe her, too. But now belief seems hard to come by. Looking into your face reminds me why. I could retrace every detail of your face in my mind if I wanted to. Your stubby little nose, the creases around your mouth, and your eyes that are as blue as the sea. Sometimes when I look into your face and watch the way your smile spreads out, I still believe Mama. But other times I wonder. It's the times when he comes and you go away with him that I find belief gives way to doubt. Those time are hardest of all.

"Just let go, baby. Let go and float."

"I can't, Mama."

"Can't do what? Can't float or can't let go?"

"Either."

"Baby, your problem is you can't let go. You're too afraid. Floating is easy."

If I close my eyes and think on certain things, I know she's right. The way the sun fell over the pavement that moment before I saw you, baptizing everything in its blinding light. Honeysuckle and lavender perfuming the air. The smile you gave me as you passed by and then were gone. The little sighs that you give when you're fast asleep, your breath sweeping across the pillow. But the focus only lasts for a moment, slipping through my fingers like water, before I must return.

"I want to tell you something," you say, an uncomfortable look on your face. "Something about myself. It's important that you know." We were engaged, but not yet married. I suck in a breath and wait expectantly. Fear enters my heart. *Tell me. Dear God, just tell me.*

"I have someone I want to introduce you to, an old friend." You give a sad little smile, a smile without teeth. I smile back because I don't know what to say. We make eye contact, he and I. No words are spoken, just the slightest gaze and then I turn back to you. I want him to leave, but I don't say it. I don't say it because I don't know how and I lack the courage because I'm afraid that I might lose you. I am silent. *Just float baby, it's so easy, you can do it.* I will keep silent.

You are walking down the church aisle in white, head to toe. The heads of everyone in the church turn and watch you. Silk rose petals crunch softly beneath your feet. Honeysuckle and lavender. Afterward we make love. Neither of us is any good at it because it's our first time. The noises you make cause me to laugh a little. You ask me why I'm laughing. I say it's because I'm self-conscious, which is also true.

"I hope it will always be like this," you say, a slight note of melancholy in your voice. I am distracted by the sound of the waves breaking along the shore. Tourists walking up and down the beach, building sand castles or sunbathing on beach towels. It's been a year.

"Me too," I say.

You give a half smile in response, the kind of smile that says you're searching for something that you can't quite find. I wish I knew what it was. Your pale blue eyes are hidden behind Ray-Bans, with tinting as dark as the paint on our Camry. A wave rolls in, casting white foam all over the beach. Tourist laughter. Sun-tanned bodies rush out into the water, others walk along picking up seashells. The Pacific spreading out north and south and disappearing at the edge of the horizon.

I lean over and kiss you on the cheek. You don't move. I ask about him, even though I know I shouldn't. Brows raise. "When was the last time?" You shrug but don't say anything. Turning over onto your side. Away from me. I apologize, then stand up and walk out into the surf where the roar of the waves blocks out all other noises. Silence.

"Spread your arms out, baby. That's the way. Spread them like you gonna fly," mama says.

I close my eyes and visualize the red hawks that circle around in the air. Their wings don't beat, they just circle around looking for prey. I am like that hawk. I spread my arms out and inhale.

"Good job, baby, you gettin' it."

For a moment I float on the water, as light as a hawk in midflight. Beyond awareness. Then my eyes open. Disbelief and fear. Weight returns to my body and my torso slouches and sinks. Arms flail, frantically grasping for the ledge on the side of the pool. Out of reach. My head sinks below the surface. I gasp for air and inhale water. Looking up, all I see is blue. The sky is inseparable from the water as it laps above my head. My back hits the bottom of the pool, then I feel hands reaching down and lifting me up. My mama's hands. My head crests above the water. Inhale. Sunshine and breath.

"It's been a long time," you say.

"Yes!" I smile. I know exactly what you mean.

He visits on the following evening, unannounced, during dinner. Pasta Primavera and breadsticks growing cold on the table. Doorbell rings. I already know who it is. He takes a seat. The conversation growing cold. I look at you, you do not look back. Staring down at your plate, with the food that you do not eat. I say "you look pretty tonight." You are silent. He never speaks. Until the candlesticks are burned down to waxy nubs. They are blown out and he goes away. I ask you if you want to go to bed. You are silent. The room is dark and cold, as cold as the uneaten food on your plate.

A week passes. Autumn. He visits again. His visits are now frequent. Sometimes an evening, sometimes a day. Browning cottonwood leaves pile up in the front yard. You whimper at night, into your pillow. I ask you what's wrong. You say you don't know, but that's a lie. And we both know it. Naked trees stand alone in the front yard.

Weekend. Out of town for work. "I'll be fine," you say. Kiss on the forehead. Open door and open road. You'll be fine. His name unmentioned. Hotel sheets that smell of bleach. Unknown halls and unknown rooms. You'll be fine. Ironed suits and cheap cologne. Handshakes and luncheons. Small talk and goodbyes. Headlights on the interstate at 9 PM Sunday night. Pulling into the garage at midnight. "I'm tired," you murmur in the darkness of the room. My hand on your forehead. Your pillow, damp with your tears. You tell me that he visited. Stayed all weekend. Just tired, need to rest. Close the door, please, sleep on the couch. There are no tears there. Just silence.

You sleep late, stay in bed. "Are you alright? What do you want? What can I do?" The questions come fast. Answers do not. You say you're fine. You need time. Just shut the door and walk away. Close the curtains like so. Blackout curtains. Turn off the light please. "I'll be back later," I say. "And then . . ." You do not respond. Your eyes are already closed. Just walk away. You've gone away.

Mama grew up in a tiny town in southern Louisiana. "So tiny that the mice got bored, one day, and picked up and moved on down the road," she would say. Her daddy was a preacher at a little country church, her mama stayed at home. They both passed on before she was fully grown and she spent her teenage years moving from one relative to the next. But before all that, when she was still very young, her family would take trips in the summer to a lake called Anacoco. That was where she learned to float. Laying her body down on the water, the body of a child, allowing herself to relax.

"Did you see any snakes?" I asked her once. "Cottonmouths or water moccasins?"

"Sure. I don't bother them, they don't bother me. See, all God's creatures are good down deep. Some of them gotta kill to survive, but there ain't no hate in it."

"I would have been afraid," I said. As a child I listened to her. Believed every word. As I got older I stopped listening. Sometimes, when I was still young, I'd talk to her about something I'd learned in school. Some injustice or existential terror.

"Ain't no sense in being afraid. Fear is like a disease, it'll eat ya from the insides out. Remember what I told ya 'bout floatin. You got to let go, baby. There ain't nothin' in this world to be afraid of."

"But Mama, what about all the hate in the world? Can't live without fear in a world with so much hate."

She paused for a long time before answering. Finally, she looked up at me and tugged on my sleeve. "Hate is like this. Nobody's born hateful, it's something folks put on over time. They grow into it little by little. If they wear it long enough they get to thinking that's just the way things are. But it's not. It can be taken off just like it was put on. Some folks never will, of course, not on their own. That's God's work. He'll take away all the hateful and broken things about us, all the calcifications of the heart. Maybe not in this life, but he will. We're all hateful and broken in our own way, baby. Every one of us. You remember that, it'll change the way you look at folks and their hate."

You show me the pregnancy test with its clear blue plus sign. I close my eyes. There you are walking across the campus. Baptizing light bouncing off pavement. Walking towards me for the first time, eyes the color of the sea. Honeysuckle and lavender. Eyes open. "Will you be alright?" You know what I'm asking, of course, but I can't bring myself to say that. You nod and smile. A smile that I believe for the first in a long time. Hope given way.

You grow big. Healthy. Jelly is squirted on your belly. Transducer applied. Looking through murky waters. Magical shadows. I hold my breath.

For a moment wondering "where, where?" Then a form emerges. A head. A pair of legs. The crescent sliver of an arm. I inhale. Sunshine and breath. You smile again. A girl. Three and a quarter inches.

"I hope she has your eyes," I whisper.

"I hope she has your courage," you say.

I am silent. *What courage?* Though I say nothing. I pat your hand "Maybe, but I hope she never needs it?"

Whispering in the darkness. Words passing, some landing, some falling away. You close your eyes. "I am tired," you say. "So, so tired." Bedrest, yes. Bedrest and care. Nurses coming once a week. Nothing to fear. Call the doctor if we must. I'll work from home. Never go away. Never, never.

"Sleep now," I say. "I'll stay awake a little longer, then I will come to bed." You sigh and roll over onto your side. I pause and bite my lip. Words bubble up. I suppress them. *Nothing to fear.* "I'll be quiet," I say. "Turn the hall light off so you can sleep. Just watch a little TV. If you need anything just ask." You don't respond. I flip off the hall light switch, wait by the bed. Listen to the soft hum of your breath. Breath sweeping across the pillow. Silence.

He comes again the next day. Stays a week. Doorbell didn't ring. No footfall on the porch. Just came to the open door. You say you expected him, though had hoped he'd stay away. "What can I do?" I ask. You sigh again and ask me to leave. Over the threshold, out of the room and down the hall. Close the curtains and shut the door. Lie on the bed in the guest bedroom. Eyes open, staring at the ceiling.

Wrestling with phantoms as the shadows dance on the far wall. Mind racing. Sleeping and waking. Sheets soaked with sweat. Searching. As he lies beside you in the bed. Whispering into your ear. Sleeping and waking. I walk down the hall. Fingers grasping at the cold walls. But they aren't my fingers. Feet slipping silently across the floors, landing on the frozen tiles. Not my feet. Door approaches. I listen in. A whimper. Crouching down. A moan. A squeak of the bed. Not my ears. I pull back. Receding into darkness. Waking. Staring up at the ceiling. *Just float, baby.*

You lie on the couch. Legs propped up on pillows. Rubbing your belly. Eyes looking though the open window. Golden hour. Shadow of an elm in the yard falling across your face. "It'll be soon now," you whisper to no one in particular. I sit in the recliner at the other end of the room. Eyes on you. You, still staring out the window. "Dear God, so soon," you say. I ask you if you need anything. You do not respond.

"You gonna be alright," I say, not knowing if it's a question or an answer.

Silence. Rubbing your belly. Inhaling and exhaling. Light fading in the window. Closing your eyes. Shutting me out.

"When I die," Mama would say, towards the end, after the cancer had laid claim fully and hospice nurses filtered in and out of her room at all hours. "When I die, don't put me in no velvet-lined box. I don't wanna lie suffocatin' in there till the good Lord sees fit to come and raise me up and carry me home. No. Set me free, baby. Let them cremate me till all that's left is ash and memories. Then take me down to the river and pour me in the water. Let me float on that water till Jesus comes for me. That way when you see the river, or ever stand at the edge of the ocean you'll think of me. Lord knows, wherever I am, I'll be thinkin' of you. Set me free, baby."

Whimpering softly. I turn and blink. Shuffling off the membranous fog of sleep. 2:46 AM. Cries from the baby monitor on the bedside table. I turn towards you. Breathing softly, your face pressed against the pillow. Pushing out of the bed. Down the hall, into the nursery room. Paper with balloons and baby animals covering the wall. Lifting baby into my arms and rocking slowly until all crying has ended. Breath sweeping across the pillow. I walk back to our room. Your face still pressed against the pillow. Faint smile on your lips, a look you never give anymore. Only in sleep. It will vanish when you wake, so I leave you be. Lyng on the bed, looking at the ceiling. Waiting for morning.

I look at you from across the breakfast table. Your eyes diverted. Staring down at the bagel on your plate. Toasted and uneaten. "You gonna be ok?" I ask. Silence. "I could take another week off work, if you want." I want you to want, but I don't say that.

"I'm fine," you say. "You're gonna be late."

I nod and kiss you on the cheek. *Will it always be like this?* Walking toward the door, patting my pockets to take stock of my keys and wallet. Trying to be quiet, don't want to wake the baby. I grab the door knob, but pause before twisting it. Turning back towards you, I ask if he'll be visiting today. I ask, even though I already know the answer. You give a shallow nod.

Yes, of course he'll be back. He will stay for a week or two, perhaps a month, who can say. And at night, before we go to bed, I will kiss you. I will kiss you, because that is what we do. Then you will go to bed with him. You will go and you will shut the door and spend the night with him, and I will let you because we have an understanding. For my part, I'll pull out the foam mattress from the hall closet and lay it on the floor in the baby's room. I'll put some sheets on it and find a pillow. I'll sleep there so that I can rock the baby when she wakes up and cries. I'll rock her until she goes back to sleep. I will be sad, of course, but I won't let it show. I promise.

What I will do is tell her about you. When I sit and rock her to sleep, I'll tell her all about you. You and mama. I want her to know where she comes from. Here's what I'll say:

"Baby, you never knew my mama. She passed on years before you were born. But she would have loved you. She would have fussed over you and held you in her arms the way I'm holding you now. She would have cooed to you and sung you lullaby's. But most of all she probably would have talked to you about floating, the way she always did to me. I never understood her when I was young, not really. Only now, as I hold you in my arms wondering what the future will hold for you, sweet baby, do I see it.

When you're young, the whole of life can seem like a gift wrapped up just for you. It's enticing to look at and you can't wait to unwrap it. As you get older you start to unwrap the gift, little by little. There are some beautiful things in the box, the kind of things you dreamed of. And there are also some ugly things, things you never imagined would be there. They are also part of the gift. Those ugly things, they give meaning to life too, and without them the beautiful things that are waiting for you in that box wouldn't quite mean as much.

Floating is all about the way you accept the gifts in that box. Can you just hold on to the beautiful things and avoid the ugly ones, unfortunately not. But you can't let the ugly ones hold you down and sink you, either. No matter what comes out of that box you gotta let go, you gotta float. When you can float you realize whatever comes out of that box doesn't matter so much after all. What matters is what's in you. And all of it is part of something much bigger going on, much more beautiful. That's the real gift baby girl.

My mama was a wise woman and a brave one too, a lot like your mama. The two bravest women I ever did meet. When you get older you'll understand your mama better. She's got a mind as quick as a jackrabbit, a laugh that you'll never forget and eyes that are as blue as the sea. But not everything has been easy for your mama. She struggles with depression. You'll learn more what that means as you grow up. It's not all the time and it's not always the same. It comes and goes like a visitor. Sometimes she'll go weeks or even months without him visiting, she'll laugh and smile and be fully herself. Then one day, he'll show up again, sometimes for no reason at all and she'll be different. Like the parts of her that we love are absent for a little while, until he goes away again.

There are treatments and strategies to keep him away. Your mama knows all about those. She's strong, and getting stronger. The important thing is that you know how much your mama truly loves you. No matter what, her love for you is as sure as the seas. Don't ever forget that baby. Don't ever doubt it.

My prayer for you, baby girl, is that you would float. No matter what lies in your box, good or bad, and there will be both, you gotta float. Never forget who you are and where you came from, that'll give you buoyancy. Let go, baby. When the time is right you'll know how to do it. Floating, after all, is what life's all about."

Nathan McKenzie has a Master's degree in Public administration. A member of Southwest Writers, he's featured in their last two publications. Currently he's working on two books, and needs a nap. He is thankful for all of the support and collegiality he has found as a part of Southwest Writers.

Suspense/Thriller   Bronze Medal
R J Mirabal

"NUESTRA SENORA DE DOLORES"
(OUR LADY OF SORROWS)

The dry heat woke Dolores Sanchez. Covered in sweat, her throat parched, she slipped out of bed like moonlight through gauze to avoid waking her husband, Bennie. Early July in Espanola, New Mexico, meant closing the windows against nights of heat until the morning chill came.

Dolores opened the bedroom window to let the cool outdoor air dry her skin. As she turned back to bed, she heard a moan outside. Her chest tightened. Her green eyes opened wide.

The full moon coated the valley, distant hills, and gun-barrel blue mesas with a silver sheen. The alfalfa field behind the Sanchez's home sloped down, its far edge the Rio Grande River. Along the banks, tasseled with willow bushes, a figure groped its way. Again, the moaning. It vibrated inside Dolores's head.

The form was dark, draped in a black shawl from head to mid-calf. It reminded Dolores of Mrs. Chavez, an old woman from down the road. The moaning, now insistent.

It seemed to call, "Katrina," Dolores's five-year-old daughter's name.

Perhaps one of the neighbor girls? No, that was an adult rushing along the river, a knife blade cutting into the sinew of the arid earth.

"Kaaatriiinaaa. Ooooh, my Kaatriinaa!"

A thick needle of despair burned through Dolores's mind in search of her heart.

She heard a thunk from Katrina's room. Had she heard the voice? Dolores rushed into her room.

Window open, the breeze animated the gauze curtains. Katrina's bed was rumpled and empty. Dolores flew to the window and saw Katrina dash across the field to the river bank.

Dolores' heart lurched as if some abyss yawned in front of her daughter.

"Kaatriinaa," came the refrain.

"Katrina, no!" Dolores screamed. "Come back here, right now!"

Dolores leaped out the window and ran through the alfalfa. Almost at the river's edge, she grasped Katrina's shoulders and slung her around.

"Katrina, why didn't you stop?"

Katrina's face, round and impassive as the moon illuminating it, regarded Dolores as she would a moth. Dolores shook her limp body.

Katrina collapsed and began to cry.

"Mommy, where am I? I had a dream about a big—"

"A big what?"

"I dunno, I forgot. I'm so cold."

Dolores carried her home. She turned once to look back. The riverbank, devoid of life seemed unimpressed by the incident.

* * *

"No, really, Dolores," Bennie said. "I never woke up. You're not used to our hot evenings, but in a few weeks when it rains it'll be cool again." Bennie dug into a mound of homemade butter and dragged it across a steaming tortilla.

"It's not about the heat. Katrina was sleepwalking in the field last night."

"Sometimes kids do that when they're insecure. She'll get used to living here, especially when school starts—kids are all the same, she'll make new friends."

"This is not insecurity. There was some woman walking along the riverbank calling for her—"

Bennie froze a moment, the butter dripped into the palm of his hand. He recovered and took a bite. "Come on now, are you sure Katrina wasn't the only one sleepwalking?"

"What do you take me for? I may be a little paranoid after living in L.A. for twenty-seven years, but I'm not that dingy. I swear I saw a woman in a black shawl and, well, I think she was doing all that moaning and groaning calling Katrina."

"It was only the wind. *Maybe* you saw the old lady from down the road, Mrs. Chavez." Bennie laughed and winked at Dolores. "You probably dreamed the whole thing. Your baby was sleepwalking, you heard her leave in your sleep, and your imagination ran away with itself. No matter," he said to her doubtful expression. "Mother's intuition told you she was in trouble so you saved her from waking up alone."

"Please, it's not my imagination. Nothing happened like this when the two of us lived in L.A.!"

Bennie's smile faded. "Your daughter is now my daughter, too. It's a sacred trust with me. You know that."

Dolores saw no purpose in continuing. "You're probably right, just the newlywed jitters."

Bennie washed the tortilla down with coffee. "Got to rush. Only six weeks until school starts and Espanola High's new assistant principal can't be late the first day on the job, sexy young wife or not!" He gave her a pinch on the butt, a wet kiss, and left.

Dolores sat in silence trying to believe the streaks of light across the table were more real than last night's moonbeams.

* * *

The afternoon burned itself out as ashen clouds and restless winds filled the sky. Struggling up the dirt driveway to the Sanchez home, a hunched form shuffled, weighed down with the shawl of widowhood.

"Dooloores? Dooloores?"

Inside, Dolores crept to the low window and, leaning against the wide sill watched Mrs. Chavez approach.

"Come in, Mrs. Chavez," Dolores controlled her voice and smiled. "It's nice to see you, but you shouldn't be out with a storm coming."

Mrs. Chavez's lined face formed a dozen smiles from forehead to chin. "*Ay Dios mio!* No! I've seen too many summers to be stopped by a feeble puff of wind. In New Mexico the clouds are only clouds. Half the time we don't even get a sprinkle!" She laughed in the same sing-song that characterized her speech.

"Sit down. Have some coffee."

"Ah, *que bueno.* Here," she handed Dolores a tortured paper sack. "Melons from my garden…."

"Oh no, Mrs. Chavez, I don't want to deprive you—"

"No, no, *querida,* I have more than I can eat. Something sweet and good from the earth for you and your *mejita.*"

Dolores recognized the endearing term that referred to Katrina. Last night's experience flooded back and she staggered slightly before she went to the kitchen.

After serving coffee, Dolores affected an air of off-handedness. "Was that you I saw last night, a little before midnight, walking along the river?"

Mrs. Chavez giggled. "No, no, *de versas?* I am an old woman. I go to bed with the *gallinas.*"

"That's odd. I could have sworn it was you. I saw a woman dressed in black walking along the river. It sounded like she was crying or moaning. I could have sworn she was calling 'Katrina.'"

Mrs. Chavez's look of merriment transformed to fear. She crossed herself mumbling a fervent prayer in Spanish.

Spellbound by this reaction, Dolores said, "What's the matter? Have I said something wrong?"

"*Dios nos ampare,* Dolores don't you know? This woman, she sounded crazy, no?"

"Well, maybe. Certainly, very upset."

"*Ave Maria!* You have seen *La Llorona* searching for her babies. She drowned them in her madness and now longs for them. She would even take someone else's child for her own. Such as your *mejita,* Katrina. She is all right, isn't she?"

"Oh yes. Katrina headed toward the river bank but she was only sleep-walking."

"That was not the walk of sleep. *La Llorona* calls."

"But who is this La Yo... whoever? Why isn't she locked up or put away?"

"She is of the old times and only visits this world searching for her lost children. Even when I was a little girl, she wandered the river banks. I've heard her call but prayed the rosary and...."

"Now wait a minute," Dolores said, skepticism growing. "You're talking about a ghost. I saw a human figure—"

"*La Llorona,* I tell you. *Es mas que un sombra.* Don't laugh at what you don't understand. Keep *mejita* indoors at night until the frost comes."

Dolores could become fond of Mrs. Chavez, the grandmother she never knew, but this superstition was hard to swallow even out of politeness. "Look, Mrs. Chavez, I know I'm a—"

Bennie walked in. "What a wind! *Buenos Dias, Senora* Chavez."

"*Gracias,* Bennie." Mrs. Chavez said.

As Dolores looked at the *senora's* face, she detected a troubling change in the old lady's expression from friendliness to inscrutability.

Mrs. Chavez tightened the shawl around her face. "I must go. It will be dark soon and I have animals to feed."

* * *

Bennie wiped his mouth, "Those enchiladas aren't bad at all. You're not quite the *gringa* I thought you were. Anyway, what did Mrs. Chavez want?"

"She brought some melons. She told me who I *imagined* I saw last night."

Bennie's eyes darkened.

Dolores when on nonchalantly, "It seems there's this La Yo, uh, Yoro..."

"*La Llorona.* I've heard that foolishness since I was a kid. It's just an old folks' tale that's been around for ages. All over New Mexico, Old Mexico, and God knows where else *viejecitos* talk about the old crazy woman and her despair. It came from Aztec myths—*Matlaciuatl,* a vampire. *Cuiapipiltin,* a goddess looking for her poor lost children, maybe even *La Malinche,* a conquistador's mistress lamenting her people's betrayal. It's just a bogeyman or bogeywoman, for cripes sake, to keep the kids indoors after dark." Bennie drank his iced tea as if it were gravel.

"So why didn't you tell me all this before, Mr. Folklore Expert?"

"It might alarm Katrina—and you. Besides, I don't trust Mrs. Chavez. I suppose she denied it was her out there last night?"

"Well, yes."

"There you are. She was doing her foolishness and didn't want some *gringa* and her kid bothering her. *La Llorona* is a perfect cover for her witchery."

"Are you saying she's a witch?"

"It's well known among the *viejas* around here that she prides herself a *bruja.*"

Dolores smirked. "Now look who's a sucker for 'old folks' tales!"

* * *

The sun was sharp as cactus thorns on the Espanola streets while low-riders bounced along at fifteen miles per hour. Stuck behind them in traffic, Dolores finally escaped the procession when she turned on to the road home.

Dust spewed up behind Dolores's car matching the turmoil in her mind. How could those women and the cashier at the grocery store treat her that way? Their disregard for an outsider pelted her spirit with a thousand needles.

Approaching home, Dolores saw Mrs. Chavez walking out of their long driveway.

She stopped the car. "Good morning. Sorry, I wasn't home. Hop in and come on back for a cup of coffee."

Mrs. Chavez continued on her way without any acknowledgment.

"Mrs. Chavez? Ma'am?"

But the old woman walked along the edge of the road, feet sinking to her wrinkled ankles in the sand.

* * *

It was past bedtime, but Dolores was not sleepy, her gaze drawn to the bedroom window facing the river. "Bennie?"

"Mmm?"

"I don't think I'm the only one who saw *La Llorona* last night."

"Are you still on that kick?" He put his hand on her stomach. "Let me try to get your mind off it—"

"No, Bennie, really! You didn't see her. If you would have… well, it was real. Anyway, I think I heard some women talking about her in the store. I asked them about it but they and that punky cashier acted like I was crazy. It wasn't so funny, though. I wish I could understand Spanish."

"I'll teach you a little, but I'm tired right now," and he sighed.

"Well, don't let me keep you awake, but you may be right about Mrs. Chavez. She was here today while I was shopping. I met her as she was leaving but she acted like I wasn't there—"

"*Ay, bruja!* Ignore it, it's her problem. If she amuses herself putting a hex on this house to protect against *La Llorona*, fine. Don't let it get to you. You only give her power by believing it."

"You should talk," Dolores said as she snorted.

Silence dominated for several minutes. Then out of the silver air came a moaning with a familiar timbre. Dolores couldn't breathe.

"Bennie, do you hear that?"

Deep breathing was her only answer.

Then, inside her head:

"Kaaatriiinaaa."

The same scene repeated. She got up, went outside. The breeze brought in air tasting like steel. The cloaked figure floundered along the riverbank.

The figure wailed. Spread arms imploring the heavens. Finally, the apparition slumped down among the tall weeds, as if a pile of discarded clothing. The despondent, lonely voice barely human.

Dolores marched down the path to the river, determined to confront the bewitched old woman. Then instinct took charge and she whipped her attention back toward the house and Katrina's window.

There, like a miniature moon, she saw her daughter's face. Dolores rushed back to the window.

"Katrina! Get back in bed!"

But as she reached the open portal, her daughter looked right through her. A dead stare, unaware of Dolores standing in front of her.

Dolores turned her gaze back to the riverbank. "Witch!" she called out.

As if caught in some immutable cycle, she felt the magnetism that drew her daughter two nights before. Like a dandelion seed in flight, she swooped across the field toward the grieving figure.

As she neared, the shape moved on. Thirty feet away, Dolores saw it was not Mrs. Chavez. The loose clothes couldn't hide the lithe figure with the energy and fluidity of a young woman.

Nothing seemed familiar about this lady of sorrows, but the patterns of movement followed a path etched in Dolores's subconscious. Was it like Mrs. Chavez of forty years ago? Her bent frame could be that tall and slender if it were uncoiled. The bowed legs could be that straight and robust.

Dolores looked skyward for some kind of answer. The moon laughed breathlessly. Later, she couldn't remember returning to the house and putting the comatose Katrina to bed.

* * *

Dolores followed her morning routine as if nothing had happened, though her sullen mood hung like a thick vapor around her shutting out her husband and daughter.

She busied herself with housework trying not to think. Finally, out of resentment for being *only* Bennie's housewife, she thought about applying for a New Mexico teaching certificate and substituting the coming year. Perhaps, in another year she could teach full-time.

* * *

While watching television that night, Dolores mentioned her plans to teach again.

Bennie didn't seem to absorb it. "You think we need more money?" Then he turned to her. "What did you say?"

"I said—"

"I know what you said, but what you *mean* is you're going to put me in a spot. If you teach at the high school, we'll have to go before the school board to get special permission for you to teach at the same school with me—"

"I didn't realize—"

"Oh, I know it's archaic but the school rule says no husband and wife in the same building."

"That's stupid."

"I didn't make the rule. But if I want a chance at the head principal's job when he retires, I can't go around playing politics in broad daylight!"

"Oh, but it's OK behind closed doors is it?"

"Now wait a minute…."

Dolores wondered if Katrina, in the next room, heard Bennie and her arguing. If she did, it could only bring back the horrible screaming, hitting fights between her real father and Dolores. The scene would be salt on unhealed wounds.

Dolores heard the back-screen door open and slam shut as the girl went outside to play in the fluttering silence of twilight.

Dolores had enough. She flounced off to the bedroom and slammed the door. It was their first serious argument. Her wounds, though not as delicate as Katrina's, unleashed a flood of bitter memories.

Her reaction was to become depressed, then sleepy. She escaped by lying down for a nap. Things would be better in an hour or two.

In the midst of a dream of stainless-steel mosquitoes, she realized she had been asleep a long time. Dolores sat up, alert but unsteady. It was still dark and Bennie had curled up against her.

Moonbeams crawled across the back of her head. Midnight.

She turned to drink in the moonlight with her eyes.

"Kaaaatriiiinaaaa."

It was a reoccurring nightmare with few variations. Undaunted, she went to Katrina's room.

The child had never been to bed. The smooth bedspread mocked Dolores.

"Oh my God! Don't take my baby!"

She flew out the window and across the field as if suspended on the air, powered by her imagination.

"Kaaatriiiinaaa."

But now, the difference in that voice permeated Dolores's racing brain. It was definitely the voice of a young woman and there was no sense of longing in the tone but rather the joy of victory. The call of a mother who has *found* her child.

"Katrina?" Dolores sobbed. Then, "Katrina," more bravely.

Reaching the riverbank, she found it empty and quiet. Then Katrina's laugh shattered the opalescent air. Turning to her left, several yards away Dolores saw the black figure reaching out to Katrina.

"No, Katrina! Don't go to her. Please, my baby."

The figure gripped the girl.

"Mommy!"

"Yes, baby," Dolores ran forward and sobbed confronting the figure, the face in deep shadow under its shawl.

That face, only slightly lighter than the clothing, regarded Dolores. The figure released Katrina like casting off a gum wrapper. It stepped toward Dolores.

In the last moment the moon penetrated the blackness of the hood and Dolores saw the eyes—solid white shining with the satin sheen of a pearl. The hands rose weightlessly, boney fingers each tipped with tin fingernails echoing the moonlight, a net of bloody rivulets dripping off their edges.

Dolores's body lost all energy as the truth coalesced when her mind faded to black.

* * *

She stroked Bennie's back. "You don't want to go to sleep right now, do you?"

Bennie let out a quick breath. "Boy, I tell you. Since you decided to settle down to just being my wife... You've been a real hot number in bed."

"Complaining?" she asked coyly.

He grinned like a teenager in the back seat with a girl for the first time. "Complaining! I'm locking you away so no one can steal you."

As they snuggled, a moan of anguish reverberated across the night, swallowed by the ceaseless flow of the Rio Grande. She rose, strolled seductively to the window, and regarded the dark night, the moon in its last quarter.

A black shawled figure whimpered and implored the heavens along the riverbank. It turned to face the adobe house from across the field, but swift hands closed the window curtains.

Panic crossed her face for a moment. Without a sound, she glided out their bedroom and peered into Katrina's room.

The girl was in bed asleep though she grunted, fidgeting slightly. Bennie came up behind his wife and stroked her shoulders gently.

"I thought you were over this funny business."

Her voice was meditative. "I'm all right, now. I just wanted to see my daughter."

In the subdued light and shadow, she caught a glimpse of her reflection in a mirror on the wall to her left. She delighted as she saw her pearlescent eyes shine like satin usurped by her gleaming teeth. Her hands reached to grip Bennie's face possessively.

Bennie looked down. She laughed inwardly when his amorousness faded as his attention was drawn to her hands.

Her silvery fingernails glinted with a net of sinuous rivulets of sweat dripping like blood.

*   *   *

RJ Mirabal pursues, music and volunteering. RJ belongs to Southwest Writers and SCBWI. His fantasy trilogy books were Finalists in the NM/AZ Book Awards. His *Trixie* book made Finalist for the 2020 Next Generation Indies and 2020 NM Press Women Awards. His newest book is a Young Adult dragon story.

SECTION NINE

HISTORICAL FICTION

This category brings life into focus with all its complexities in a totally different time and place into focus. If your taste run towards family rivalries, riveting battles and intrigue, then this is the category for you.

Historical Fiction
Dana Starr

Gold Medal

HILLS AND VALLEYS

8 April 1912

Blood oozed from the cut on Benjamin Lynch's lip. He couldn't stop running long enough to stanch the flow. His brother-in-law was on his heels, spoiling for a fight.

Benjamin rounded the corner at the Pig Whistle Pub. The sidewalk along the quay was crowded with pedestrians: women in elaborate wide-brimmed hats, men smoking cigars, children carelessly licking ice cream cones.

The street was empty. With no hesitation, Benjamin ran into the road. He noticed the pile of horse manure in time to jump over it. The brute chasing him wasn't so fortunate.

Benjamin spared a backward glance when he reached the other side of the road. What he saw made him smile, causing him to wince in pain. He took a handkerchief from his pocket, pressed it to his throbbing lip and hurried away from the man sitting in shit in the middle of the road.

Relieved to be rid of the overgrown oaf, Benjamin slowed his pace after two blocks. He wasn't afraid to fight. He'd been a fighter his entire life; however, striking his wife's brother was out of the question. Her family despised him enough with no violence in the equation. He reached home unaccompanied.

* * *

Theodosia was ironing a dress in the kitchen. She took one look at her injured grandson, with blood dripping from his face to his shirt, and rushed to his side. "What happened to you?"

"Rachel's brother threw a rock at me." The old woman steered him to the bench at the kitchen table.

"Keep your voice down. Rachel's resting," she said before moving to the cupboard. She retrieved a cloth, poured water on it, and handed it to him.

"Something's burning," he said. "Oh, bollocks."

His grandmother scurried back to the steaming, flat, black iron she'd left on the sleeve of the dress. She moved the heavy iron to the cooker before examining the damage. Holding up the fabric, she frowned at the copy of the iron burned into the sleeve. "I guess I'll have to turn this into a short-sleeve dress."

"I'm sorry," Benjamin said.

Joining him on the bench, she rested her arm on his. "The dress is the least of my concerns." She unconsciously patted his ink-stained hand. "I thought Rachel asked you to stay away from her family."

"She did, but I had to try to reason with her father one more time." He looked down at the paper-thin skin on her hand, the hills and valleys of veins as pronounced as the image of the iron on the dress.

"You two are my family now," said Rachel, "and this little one."

Benjamin and Theodosia turned at the sound of Rachel's voice. The young woman stood in the doorway, hands resting on her pregnant belly. The sadness she saw in her husband's eyes equaled her own. "Are you okay?"

"I'm fine. It looks worse than it is."

"Tell me what happened," she said, approaching the table.

"I wanted to talk to your father, but your brother wouldn't let me inside the gate."

"Which brother?"

"The big one," he said.

"They're all big," she replied.

"I think it was Aaron. I told him he'd be an uncle soon."

"What did he say?"

Benjamin couldn't make himself repeat the ugly words he'd heard. The last thing he wanted was to heap more hurt on her. "He didn't say anything. He just picked up a rock and threw it at me."

Rachel sat across from her husband. She studied the pattern on the tablecloth. The room was so quiet the ticking of the clock was abnormally loud.

Tick. Tick. Tick.

She sighed heavily and looked at her husband. "How can I still care so much about people who care so little?"

Tick. Tick. Tick.

Unable to answer her question, Benjamin grasped her hand and squeezed. The despair on her face was too much to bear. He turned his gaze to his grandmother.

"I have an idea," Theodosia said, desperate to ease the tension. "Come on. We're going to the inn for high tea."

* * *

The next morning, Benjamin woke before Rachel. She was nestled behind him, snoring softly. He felt two soft thumps on his lower back. Rolling over, he spread his left hand on her stomach. His child kicked him again.

He could hear his grandmother preparing breakfast. He rose reluctantly, dressed for work, and entered the kitchen. "Good morning," he said. "Did you sleep well?"

Theodosia stopped slicing bread and looked at him. "I didn't sleep at all and you know why."

"Gran, I'm not changing my mind. If I get the job, I'm leaving tomorrow."

"But what about Rachel and the baby?"

"They are why I need to do this," he said. "Once I get established and save more money, I'll send for them . . . and you."

"You can't even imagine how much I'll miss you." She reached to adjust the newsboy cap on his head.

He smiled at her and said, "I'll miss you too, but I have to make a better life for Rachel and little Ben."

"I'm not convinced she's carrying a boy," Theodosia said.

"Well, I am," he said, reaching for a slice of bread.

She swatted his arm. "Put that back. I'm making toast."

"I don't have time for toast. I've got newspapers to sell." He kissed her on the cheek. "Ouch, my lip still hurts."

His silly expression reminded her of his younger years. She'd raised him alone.

Benjamin's mother died giving birth to him. His father, Theodosia's son, dealt with that sad fact by drinking himself to death. Theodosia was Benjamin's only living kin. She was a widow who made ends meet as a dressmaker. They had each other and little else when he was a child.

At nine-years-old, Benjamin met a boy who always had at least one loose tooth, freckles, and a ferocious appetite. Ernest Corben, his best friend, was the youngest of nine children and always hungry. Even if Theodosia didn't get quite enough to eat, she made sure to save some food to share with Ernest.

Both boys started selling newspapers as children in order to survive.

Thanks to the triumvirate of desperation, talent, and perseverance, Theodosia and Benjamin managed within a decade to attain a certain level of comfort. Benjamin wanted more. A lot more. His ambition motivated him to work hard. But his country's class system stifled him. And his in-laws infuriated him. They'd disowned their only daughter for falling in love with a Catholic of limited means.

Benjamin carried an armful of newspapers to the corner he'd fought tooth and nail to call his own for ten years. Males, young and old, had tried to take his spot and steal his customers to no avail. Ernest was waiting for him, grinning like the cat that ate the canary.

"I have brilliant news," Ernest said.

"I got the job?"

"You got the job." Ernest extended his arm for a handshake. Benjamin dropped the bundle of newspapers and hugged him instead.

"I'm gobsmacked. How can I thank you for the recommendation?"

"No need to thank me," Ernest said. "I need the help, and you're the perfect man for the job."

"I can't believe we're going to America," Benjamin said.

"I can't believe it either. I'm really going to miss Theresa and Edward."

"I haven't seen them in so long," Benjamin said. "Edward must be walking by now."

"Yes, he is. He turned one last week."

"Please bring your family to the house tonight. Gran would love that."

"On one condition," Ernest said. "She has to make her famous shepherd's pie for me." He looked at his pocket watch. "We're leaving in a little over twenty-four hours."

"Say, that's a dandy. Where did you get that pocket watch?"

"Theresa gave it to me for our anniversary." He held it out to show Benjamin the elaborate E and T on the back of it. "She had it engraved with our initials."

Benjamin held the watch in his palm, admiring the scrollwork. "That's impressive," he said.

"So is your fat lip," Ernest said, pointing at Benjamin's face. "What happened?"

"I tried to talk to Rachel's dad yesterday."

"Did he hit you?"

"Of course not," Benjamin said. "He's a rabbi. He punches with his words not his fists."

"Who hit you?"

Benjamin stared at the watch in his hand. He didn't want to answer the question. He didn't want to relive the hurt and humiliation he'd felt. He didn't want to try to explain the unending compulsion he had to make things right with Rachel's family.

"I really don't want to talk about it." He handed the watch back to Ernest. "I've got to get busy. I have a lot of newspapers to sell."

"There's no time for that. You need to meet with Abraham. He's waiting for you in the lobby at the Criterion on Oxford Street."

"I have to sell these newspapers first."

"I'll do it for you," Ernest said. "I was always better at this than you anyway. Don't keep him waiting too long."

"I don't deserve your friendship," Benjamin said.

"Don't be a wanker." Ernest clapped him on the back. "Get going."

"Seriously, thank you for giving my family a future." Benjamin barely got the words out around the lump in his throat. He walked away from his mate, headed in the direction of Oxford Street.

Ernest picked up a newspaper and held it up. "Extra! Extra! Read all about it. *Titanic* sets sail tomorrow!"

Benjamin turned and looked at Ernest. They smiled at each other.

* * *

Entering the lobby of the Criterion hotel, Benjamin didn't recognize Abraham Mishellany right away. They'd only met once in the print shop that employed Abraham and Ernest. "Thank you so much for this opportunity," Benjamin said. He stuck his hand out to shake the hand of his new boss. It didn't escape his attention that the man's hand was as discolored as his own as a result of years of contact with ink.

"Ernest speaks very highly of you," Abraham said. "Have you ever sailed on a ship?"

"No, I've never been out of Southampton," Benjamin replied.

"Let's hope you get your sea legs quickly." He chuckled and gestured for Benjamin to sit. "You'll be assisting Ernest with typesetting. We'll be printing the Atlantic Daily Bulletin for the passengers." He lit a cigarette and continued, "We'll print other things too, mainly daily menus for the dining rooms. Do you have any questions?"

"Only about a hundred," Benjamin said.

Abraham smiled. "I'll try to answer all your questions, but first I'll need you to fill out this paperwork." He gestured to the papers on the table bearing the logo of the White Star Line.

An hour later, Benjamin returned to an empty house. He couldn't wait to share his big news, but he couldn't find his wife or grandmother. He found a note propped against the iron sitting in the middle of the kitchen table. He read it and ran out of the house.

"Sir, please keep your voice down," said the woman behind the desk.

"I'm sorry," Benjamin replied, "but I've been all over this hospital and I can't find my wife."

"There you are," said Theodosia, rushing to him from the hallway.

"Is Rachel . . . is she . . ."

"She's alive, but she's lost a lot of blood. She's in surgery now," Theodosia said.

"What about the baby?"

"The baby is breech. The doctor is performing a procedure he called a cesarean."

"What's that? Is Rachel going to be okay?

"Ben, I don't have any answers." She put her arm around her grandson. "Let's go to the waiting room."

He paced and checked the clock on the wall every few seconds. He would've sworn time had slowed to a crawl. He was staring out the window, looking but not really seeing the flowers on the lawn when the doctor entered the waiting room. Benjamin turned to see an exhausted man approaching him.

"Are you Mr. Lynch?"

"Yes," Benjamin said.

"I'm Dr. Ford. Your wife survived the surgery. We're trying to get her vital signs stabilized. She's in critical condition."

"What about the baby?" Theodosia said.

"She's very healthy," the doctor said, "and she's got quite the set of lungs. I'm surprised you can't hear her in here. A nurse will let you know when you can see them both."

Theodosia looked at her grandson. Tears streamed down his face.

The moon was up by the time Benjamin got to see his wife. He sat in a chair next to her bed. "She's so beautiful, Rachel. I wish you could see her."

He picked up his wife's limp hand. She didn't open her eyes. "Please wake up. I love you so much." He kissed her hand. "I can't do this without you. Please wake up."

A nurse woke him in the middle of the night. He'd fallen asleep in the chair. He asked, "How's she doing?"

"About the same," the nurse replied.

At sunrise, Theodosia walked through the door with a basket in her hand. Benjamin was talking softly to Rachel and stroking her hair. He looked at his grandmother with sorrowful eyes. "She won't wake up."

Theodosia set the basket down. "You listen to me, young man. I spent most of the night praying." She hugged her grandson. "Rachel is going to be fine. We have to have faith." He held the woman who raised him tighter and longer than usual. His stomach growled. "I brought you some breakfast," she said.

"I'm not hungry."

"That's nonsense. You need to keep up your strength." She unpacked the basket. "I just saw little Theo. She's the most gorgeous girl in the world."

"So, you've named her after you?"

"Of course, she looks just like me," Theodosia said.

Benjamin attempted a smile. "I forgot to tell you. I got the job." She gave him an incredulous look.

"I'm not going. Of course, I'm not going. Everyone I love, everything I need is here," he said.

Her body flooded with relief. "That's what I've been trying to tell you all along." She handed Benjamin an English muffin. "I need to run an errand. I won't be gone long."

* * *

Theodosia approached the imposing house with trepidation. Rachel had talked about her family home, but Theodosia never imagined it to be so grand. She let herself in the gate and stooped by the flower bed lined with pebbles. She picked a large one. It was hefty in her hand. She put it in her pocket and knocked on the door.

A large boy opened the door. "Hello, Aaron. I need to speak with your father," she said.

"Who are you?" he asked. "And how do you know my name?"

"I'm Theodosia Lynch. Your sister is married to my grandson."

The boy smirked at her before shutting the door in her face. She took a deep breath, wrapped her right hand around the pebble in her pocket, and pounded on the door with her left hand. She pictured Rachel clinging to life and pounded harder.

Aaron opened the door again. He stepped onto the porch, towering over her. "Lady, you need to leave."

She took a step back before tossing the pebble a few inches in the air and catching it. The boy stared and she did it again. It grazed his chin the second time. She caught it and said, "I need to speak with your father right now."

"Go away," he said.

"You're not the only one who knows how to throw a rock." She pointed at a window near the door. "It would be a shame to have to replace that window."

The boy hesitated. "Wait here." He turned and went inside, closing the door behind him. She hummed the tune to "It's a Long, Long Way to Tipperary" and slipped the pebble back into her pocket. She was determined to wait all day if that's what it took to speak her mind. Halfway through the second chorus, Rachel's father opened the door.

"Your daughter has a daughter," Theodosia said. The man opened his mouth to speak.

She shook her head. "No. You're going to listen for a change." She stroked the rock in her pocket. She'd never really intended to use it to cause harm. Touching it gave her courage. "Rachel almost died in labor. We're not sure she's going to make it. She needs her family, all her family."

A woman who looked like Rachel stepped around the man in the doorway. "Please take me to my daughter," she said.

The two women were halfway to the hospital when the Rabbi caught up with them. Theodosia reached for the rock in her pocket. The man reached for his wife's hand. No one spoke. They resumed walking. Theodosia let the rock slip from her fingers to the ground.

* * *

Benjamin was giving his daughter a bottle for the first time when the *Titanic* departed Southampton. The evening the ship struck the iceberg, Rachel emerged from her coma. She was surrounded by Benjamin, Theodosia, little Theo, her parents, and her seven brothers, including Aaron.

12 June 1932

Benjamin held his arm out for his daughter. Theo looped her arm through his. He kissed her on the cheek before they slowly headed down the aisle. Her many uncles and aunts, her grandparents, her mother, and soon to be mother-in-law stood as the bride approached her groom. She was marrying her best friend, Edward Corben.

Dressed in a gown of her own design, she was almost as talented a dressmaker as her namesake had been. Edward gave her the locket around her neck. She gave him a pocket watch engraved with elaborate scrollwork and the initials E and T.

1 September 1985

Theo was talking to her daughter on the phone. "Darling, I've got to hang up. It's time for the news and you know I don't like to miss it."

"Okay, bye Mom. I'll talk to you tomorrow."

She set the phone down next to the antique iron she used as a paperweight. The same iron Theodosia had used in the same kitchen. Theo moved slowly into the parlor. The dreary, wet weather bothered her bursitis. She settled herself on the couch next to Edward.

The TV screen filled with an image of the ocean. The announcer said, "Dr. Robert Ballard made history today. He discovered the wreckage of the *Titanic* utilizing the *Argo*, an unmanned submersible equipped with powerful lights and cameras to aid in the search."

Theo couldn't believe it. Her entire life, seventy-three years, the *Titanic* had loomed large in family lore. She held her husband's hand. The news announcer said, "The *Argo* captured video from a portion of the debris field."

They watched as the *Argo* circled a boiler, from the *Titanic's* engine room, embedded in the sandy surface of the ocean floor. Edward squeezed Theo's hand. The *Argo* floated by elegant plates, teacups, and a beaded purse.

Dipping down into the valley between two hills it glided by a pair of leather boots and hovered over what appeared to be a pocket watch. The couple stared as the camera focused and zoomed in on the initials E and T.

*   *   *

Dana Starr writes for Pajamas All Day at danastarr.net. Her essays have received honorable mention in the 2018 Erma Bombeck Writing Competition and 2019 Women on Writing Competition. Her fiction will appear in two anthologies in 2020. She's a former copywriter and currently an aspiring humor writer.

Historical Fiction
Lynn Doxon

Silver Medal

A GENERAL'S DILEMMA

"Five more miles, men, and you can sleep in the Fort." My troops were weary. We had marched over two hundred miles in the ten days since General Washington sent us north with orders to occupy Fort Ticonderoga.

The sun was setting behind the mountains as we approached Fort Ticonderoga. I stopped to assess the fortifications while the men marched on. Five different Generals had commanded the Fort in the two years since the British had surrendered to Benedict Arnold and Ethan Allen. Each commander had ordered significant improvements, then left before their completion. Snow and rain had eroded Schuyler's earthen Fort across the river on Mount Independence. A floating bridge joined Ticonderoga and Independence. The pilings of the permanent bridge were only partially completed. The old French boom and chain barely held together. West of Ticonderoga General Gates had ordered abatis installed along the former French line and built new blockhouses at both the French line and Mount Hope. It was too dark to make them out clearly.

I rode through the gate unchallenged. That would change immediately. New cannons to replace the ones Knox took to Boston were lying inside the walls, not yet mounted on the wagons. Wooden huts replaced the tents the men had slept in last summer.

"Major General Arthur St. Clair here to relieve General Wayne," I announced to a passing lieutenant. "Where can I find the General?"

"Mad Anthony haint been here since March, Sir. The Colonels would be havin' their supper in that buildin' yonder."

Three months without a commanding General. I shook my head wondering how bad the conditions here would be. I strode into the dining room. Cilley, Scammell, and Hale, the Colonels who had accompanied me, were ladling venison stew into their bowls. Three other colonels had finished their meal. "Stay seated, gentlemen. Can you apprise me of the current situation?" I asked as I took a seat at the table.

"Colonel Francis, Eleventh Massachusetts, sir. Welcome to the Fort. We have two Continental regiments, mine and Marshall's, but they are not at full strength. Militia units come and go. I am unsure how many are currently present."

"We started the winter with seventeen hundred men but have lost a third to disease, weather, and accidents. Marshall added. "Only about a thousand are fit to fight now. Our hospital is constantly filled to overflowing,"

"Seth Warner, Sir. Green Mountain Boys. Gates thought the Fort was impregnable, particularly with the new Fort Independence across the river. But we see some weak spots,"

"What are they?" I asked.

"Mount Hope and Sugarloaf. Mount Hope overlooks the Fort from the west. If the enemy occupies it, they can fire on us or gain the advantage in skirmishes or a siege. We built a fort there, but no troops occupy it. The greater danger is Sugarloaf, which overlooks both Ticonderoga and Independence. If they get cannon up there, we are sitting ducks. General Wayne said they couldn't, but I have climbed it myself and found three paths passable to horses and artillery. General Wayne claimed that Fort Ticonderoga could not be taken without much loss of blood. I'm afraid we don't have enough blood among us to hold onto it, General."

"Thank you, Colonel. I will look at the lay of the land in the morning. For now, is there any of that stew left?"

* * *

I set out to check conditions for myself shortly after sunrise. Livingston, my aide de camp, followed me with paper and quill. We had only about a month's worth of food. Barrels labeled salt pork had cracked. The brine leaked out, and the meat putrefied. Our only meat was the small herd of skinny cattle grazing outside the Fort. The cooks were scraping the bottom of the flour barrels. Only rum and ale were abundant.

A stack of muskets lay on the floor of the armory. I was elated until I picked up one after the other, and they all but fell apart in my hands. Not one of them would fire. Ammunition of all sorts was in short supply. There weren't enough cannonballs for even one per cannon. The blacksmith told me there was no iron left for mounting the guns. We had enough lead to make musket balls but not enough gunpowder to get us through a battle, let alone a siege.

I walked to the gardens planted between the Fort and the river. Only a few small carrots were ready to harvest. Summer came late to this part of New York.

The Mount Hope fort stood on high ground to the west, and the old French line was a perfect defensive position. If I could occupy those, we could withstand a considerable force. But that was a forlorn hope.

After a light lunch, I crossed the floating bridge to Fort Independence. Brigadier General Matthias Alexis Roche de Fermoy met me at the end of the bridge. "What are you doing here?" I demanded.

"I command Fort Independence," he said.

"Washington would not have assigned you to this Fort after you abandoned your position at Trenton. Your actions appear to favor the British more than they do the Americans."

"I do not favor the British." he huffed, puffing out his chest. "It was much too cold to be out in weather like that. The Continental Congress gave me this command, not Washington."

"General Washington is the Commanding General of the Continental Army, a force for which you volunteered. I will inspect the earthworks."

"This is my fort," he whined.

"A Brigadier General does not instruct a Major General," I said, riding forward.

The breastworks were well built, and the abatis installed correctly. The fortifications were strong. I could see the abilities of Horatio Gates in the Fort's layout, but Fermoy's men were another matter.

"Your men are sleeping in the middle of the day. The British could attack at any time."

"The British cannot take this Fort. It is impregnable."

"The British don't believe that, and neither do I. You will keep your pickets alert twenty-four hours a day."

"I take my orders from the Continental Congress."

"The Continental Congress approved my appointment, so you take orders from me."

It was little more than putting a silk waistcoat on a hog, but I ordered daily drills and the rebuilding of the earthworks.

* * *

The next week General Schuyler, now Commander of the Northern Amy, arrived. I was pleased that I at least had a proper guard in the gatehouse.

"Arthur, how are you?" he said as he came in. "And how is Cousin Phoebe?"

"She is well. The birth of our little Maggie was a tough one, but she is well recovered."

"Why didn't Washington send the ten thousand troops I asked for?" he asked.

"Come inside so we can speak freely, Phillip."

I poured two mugs of ale, and we sat at the table in my quarters. "Washington does not believe the British will attack from the north," I told Schuyler. "He thinks they will come inland from Boston. He also thinks Ticonderoga is impregnable."

"Maybe, with ten thousand men. Not with this garrison. When I was here last year, it was only the weather that kept Carleton from taking the Fort, and we had twice as many men. I have reliable reports that a large British force left Quebec weeks ago heading upriver. Perhaps it would be advisable to bring all the men to Ticonderoga and abandon Independence."

"The earthworks at Mount Independence are more defensible," I said. "We might see the British sooner from that side. The abatis provide protection we don't have on this site, and the cannon are properly mounted. Even there, we do not have enough ammunition to repel a major invasion. We need to plan for a possible retreat."

"I am afraid you are correct, Arthur. Fight as long as you can. Wear the British down. The New England states are pushing hard for a stronger force here at Ticonderoga. I have asked them to send militia and supplies. But if it comes to it, there are two ways to retreat, by water to Skenesborough, or by foot on a rough road through the little village of Hubbardton."

"We will do we can. I wish I knew what we were facing. Every scout I sent out was either chased back by Indians or failed to return."

I managed to get the men into a reasonable formation to see Schuyler off. He promised reinforcements from Albany.

I contemplated my options. There was little chance of success. Two thousand soldiers could not defend the Fort against a British assault. If the British mounted artillery on Sugarloaf and warships on the lake, it would be a massacre. If we retreated, New Englanders would never forgive us. I tossed and turned all night, weighing my options. I finally concluded that I could not let these boys die here. If the British did come soon, our best chance was to force them into skirmishes in open ground. Making a stand here would mean inevitable defeat and needless deaths.

I continued my review of the fortifications throughout the day, pushing the men to complete the unfinished improvements. If Schuyler's militia and supplies arrived before the British, we might have a chance. If nothing else, morale would improve if the men were busy. I sent a company under Captain

James Wilkerson to Mount Hope to guard the old portage road, the most likely approach for a northern army.

As I explained my expectations to the officers at dinner, I heard raucous laughter from outside.

"Is that something we should investigate?"

"Oh, no. That is just Lieutenant Andy Tracy telling stories. His father is an Irish storyteller, and he seems to be following in his steps."

After the meal, I stopped at the edge of the circle of firelight to listen to the stories. The men were having a good time. I hoped it wouldn't be the last.

* * *

After another week of disciplined labor, Fort Ticonderoga was looking better and fewer men were spending the day drinking. I assembled the men to compliment them on their progress when a scout ran through the fort entrance.

"Sir, the British are at Three Mile Point with two warships, eighteen gunboats, and three sloops. I do not know how many men are on those ships, but they appear to be British, Canadian, Hessians, and Indians."

This is it, I thought. I set my jaw and faced the men.

"The British approach. Double patrols and be on alert until we know their strength. Check your arms and remain battle-ready. Dismissed."

Within the hour, we heard fife and drums through the woods. I called the men back from Mount Hope. The British appeared as Wilkerson's company reached the old French line. The men took cover in the earthworks. I hurried to the front. "Hold your fire. Fire only on my command."

The British fired a volley from a safe distance. Captain Wilkerson fired back. A British soldier fell. On hearing the gunfire, the entire company opened fire. The British scattered immediately, but my men shot three volleys before I could stop them.

"Wilkerson!" I fumed. "When I give you an order, I expect you to follow it."

"General, don't you see that I have killed the first Redcoat of the engagement. They were close enough for us to hit them."

"Your duty is to follow orders, not to seek glory for yourself!" I yelled. Wilkerson stalked off. The British soldier still lay on the ground.

"Retrieve that soldier," I ordered. "We can at least give him a decent burial."

Four men ran toward the soldier, who lay still on the field. As they approached, he jumped up and tried to club them with his rifle. They subdued him and brought him into the Fort.

"He's drunk, not wounded," the men reported.

"Put him in the stockade until he can answer questions."

As I watched them haul him off, I wondered how much information we could get from him. The battle was upon us, and I had no idea of the strength of the enemy.

At supper, I spoke with the officers. "Impress on your men that they MUST follow orders. We picked up one drunken sot off the field. If we are unable to get any useful information from him, the ammunition fired today has been wasted."

"Sir, the prisoner is conscious," a sentry called. "But he is refusing to talk."

"Livingston, get me that Irish storyteller. Tracy, was it?"

Lieutenant Tracy reported a few minutes later.

"Lieutenant, I'm putting you in the stockade."

"Sir?"

I smiled and said, "I need you to pretend you are a Loyalist spy. Put on civilian clothes and get friendly with the prisoner. Share this flask of whiskey with him, but don't get him so drunk he passes out again. Get all the information you can."

"Yes, Sir. This is the best assignment I have gotten in this army."

* * *

In the morning, Lieutenant Tracy came to report.

"Once he believed I was a spy, he answered all my questions. General Burgoyne leads five thousand six hundred regulars. Hessians, militia, and Indians bring the troops to about ten thousand. Eighteen vessels came down the Lake. General Carlton has more troops at Crown Point.

"The prisoner himself has been out with scouts. In three days, they took six prisoners and killed more. The Indians were to harass us continually. While they did that, the rest would surround us and cut off our communication."

"Thank you, Lieutenant. Get some breakfast and some sleep now."

Even if the prisoner was exaggerating about the number of men, they outnumbered us by five to one. Even a brief stand could be suicide.

That evening at dinner, my officers and I quietly celebrated the signing of the Declaration of Independence.

"It is hard to believe that less than a year ago, I read the Declaration to the men for the first time," I said. "So much has happened since then."

"This new nation has had quite a start," said Colonel Hale.

"That it has," replied Colonel Cilley. He stood, glass in hand, to propose a toast. "What is that? Do I see a campfire on Sugarloaf?"

We rushed to the window. Fires burned atop Sugarloaf, and men moved in front of them.

"We will hold a council of war at seven in the morning. Livingston, tell Fermoy and his senior officers."

* * *

At first light, I saw cannon on Sugarloaf. It had come down to the choice between death or retreat.

All the colonels were in my quarters promptly at seven. The only officer missing was General Fermoy.

"Livingston, can you see what is delaying General Fermoy?"

He was back five minutes later. "He is starting across the bridge now."

We waited, but Fermoy did not appear. What could he be doing? Finally, I started without him.

"This is our situation," I began. Just then, the door opened, and General Fermoy walked in.

"It is very disrespectful to begin a council of war with your co-commander not present," he said.

"There is no co-commander. We waited for twenty minutes." I retorted.

"Ah, these New England Puritan timekeepers. Every moment must be exact."

"I am neither from New England nor a Puritan. Please be seated. As I was saying, Gentlemen, and General Fermoy, the British have ten thousand troops—British regulars, Hessians, Canadian militia and Indians. They dragged cannons up Sugarloaf and will soon be able to open fire on Fort Ticonderoga and Fort Independence at the same time. We have two thousand eighty-nine able-bodied men. That includes one hundred twenty-nine unarmed artisans and about nine hundred untrained militia. We can fight from Ticonderoga or move everyone to Fort Independence."

"We must move all the troops to my fort," Fermoy said.

The Colonels hesitated. Finally, Colonel Warner spoke. "Even at Fort Independence, we cannot hold out long when we are outnumbered five to one, and cannonballs are raining down on our heads."

"We are already almost surrounded," Colonel Francis said. "It would take little effort for the British to cross the neck of the peninsula and cut us off completely."

Colonel Hale nodded. "A retreat should be undertaken as soon as possible."

"How can we do that?" asked Colonel Cilley. "The British already have eyes on us from all sides."

I breathed a sigh of relief. I would not have to convince the Colonels. "We will retreat under cover of darkness. All the invalids, camp followers, and supplies go to Skenesborough on boats. Hale, take charge of that operation. Bring anything that floats to the docks. The British won't see them from either Sugarloaf or Mount Hope. Have the men prepare secretly and quietly. Destroy any cannon or supplies we can't take with us. Fermoy, do the same at Fort Independence."

"That is the coward's way out," declared Fermoy. "We must make a gallant stand and become the heroes of the war."

"We will do the army more good if we live to fight another day," Warner said. "My Green Mountain Boys can outfight the British any day in a running battle in the woods, but they are unprepared for the kind of defensive stand you are talking about."

"Warner is right," I said. "Begin preparations."

The officers left one by one. When they were all gone, I went to the Quartermaster.

"Divide the rations among the men, then package the remainder for the boats. Butcher eight of the cattle as quietly as possible and distribute the meat among the men. Drive the remaining cattle into the woods."

"Do you know what this will look like on your record?"

"I can save the army and lose my reputation or save my reputation and lose men. I know what I am doing. If all turns out as I hope, it will benefit the nation."

"We appreciate your willingness to do that."

"Get to work. There is much to do before nightfall."

The Fort seemed only a little busier than usual. Two hundred boats and canoes lined the docks. In the huts, the men melted lead and formed musket balls, sorted supplies, and packed haversacks.

We loaded the boats after sunset. One by one, they took off into the dark lake. As the last boat shoved off, I ordered the men across the bridge.

A messenger approached me. "Sir, Colonel Marshall wanted me to tell you that they have not started the evacuation of Mount Independence."

"What!" I jumped on my horse and crossed the bridge as quickly as I could without knocking soldiers into the water. I pounded on the door of Femroy's quarters. He opened it, rubbing his eyes.

"What are you doing? The night is half gone, and you have not begun to evacuate."

"You surely can't expect us to march all night with absolutely no sleep."

"That is exactly what I expect."

He turned back into his hut and closed the door.

I rode to where the regiment awaited orders. "Spike the cannons, strike the tents, gather your supplies, and march after the Massachusetts regiment."

I ordered the Ticonderoga garrison to help. After two frenzied hours, the men were ready to retreat. Fermoy finally emerged from his quarters, threw his saddlebags over his horse, and mounted up. As he did, I saw flames through the open door.

"You idiot! You set fire to your quarters? What better way to alert the British. Damn you. Damn you to hell."

He galloped away. I was beside myself with fury. The building blazed, lighting the night. The British could see the rear guard of the army as they climbed the hill. In the water, the flotilla of boats was lit up by the blaze. Fermoy had to be a British agent.

"Colonel Francis, form a rearguard to hold back any troops that follow us

As I rode over the hill at the rear of the retreating army, I looked back. Frasers Highland Regiment was forming a bridge of flat bottom boats along the French boom and chain. We would have delayed them more if we had not repaired it. The crossing would be slow, and then they had to negotiate the marshy ground around East Creek. We still had a chance of escaping. Yet Fermoy's fire had cost us a four-hour lead.

I rode forward, encouraging the men as Washington always did. I would undoubtedly be vilified for abandoning Ticonderoga and might be court-martialed for disobeying, but the men were alive and able to fight. We now had to divide the British forces and fight them in the woods. Some of Burgoyne's troops would hold Ticonderoga. Fraser's Highlanders were already following us. Burgoyne would most likely go south toward Albany.

This was a fight I knew we could win.

*   *   *

Through the process of tracing her family tree, **Lynn Doxon** became interested in the stories of her ancestors, the incidents of their lives. In this story, she fictionalizes a pivotal event in the life of her sixth great grandfather, Arthur Sinclair.

Historical Fiction   Bronze Medal
Linda Triegel

NIGHT OF THE BELLS

The first time I heard the bells was during the big storm of 1892. Pito Vargas drowned in the arroyo within sight and sound of San Miguel Mission, but only the bells saw or heard him. Rational people called it coincidence that his violent death and the strange midnight clamor of the bells should have occurred at the same instant. Father Benedicto called it superstition and cried shame upon his flock for avoiding the mission after dark.

Don Carlos Cantrell laughed. It was just like the Mexicos, he said, to be afraid of their own church. Don Carlos was not a religious man. He had come to the territory, an ambitious young American named Charles Cantrell, thirty years before, and built his great rancho with his own muscle and sweat. No Spanish-talking god, he said, had helped him to do it.

But Carlos had his pride and he took good care of his people. He built their homes and nursed their sick and saw to their children's education. He even gave them Sundays off to go to mass—and to confession for the excesses of the Saturday night before. None of this, however, endeared him to San Miguel. San Miguel tolerated him only because he had married Maria Elena Dominguin.

Everybody knew Elena. She was the best of San Miguel, the end product of its heritage. The territory had been, over the centuries, Spanish, Indian, American. It had been ruled by great chiefs, by priests, soldiers, royal federal governors; but San Miguel was and had been and in its heart always would be Mexican. Mexican and Roman Catholic. The mission was the beginning and end of San Miguel. It had not been built for the town; the town had grown up around it.

Every Sunday Elena attended mass—early in the morning at her own chapel at the hacienda and again at noon in San Miguel. Her Mexican servant brought her to the church in a closed carriage; the long black mantilla that covered her hair hid much of her slim figure as well, and inside the church she kept her head lowered over her rosary, so that no one could see her face. But everyone knew that it was a beautiful face —the skin the deep ivory of her Spanish ancestors, the eyes as black as the hair, the full red lips moving in prayer. If she had not been so real, so human—even those who dared not touch her hand could taste the odor of the sweet musky perfume that drifted from her skirts as she passed—San Miguel would have placed her up over the altar of the church and worshipped her and not thought it sacrilege.

Don Carlos did not attend mass, but it was his custom to meet his wife afterwards and escort her home. One Sunday, in the sixth year of their marriage, he came to meet her and found she was not alone.

It was true that Elena was never really alone. Her servant Manuel went everywhere with her; he drove her carriage, waited while she paid her calls, carried her boxes, books, letters, opened doors for her, held her chair. But no one noticed Manuel anymore, as they would not notice Elena's shadow in the presence of the lovely reality.

On that Sunday, another young man stood by Elena's carriage, talking to her with the ease of long friendship and the intentness of years of talking to be made up. He was a handsome man, fair where Elena was dark. He wore the short jacket and fitted trousers that marked him as a "foreigner"—an American. He was Doctor John Carter.

John and Elena had played together as children. I remember watching them from my office window in the days when I was still practicing law in San Miguel. Seeing them together, those days did not seem so long ago, and seeing Elena smile, I wondered how I had not missed her smile before this. John had left San Miguel just before Elena's marriage, to go east to study medicine. Now he had returned to set up his practice.

Manuel waited patiently for *los señores* to finish their conversation. His hat pulled down over his black eyes, the reins held loosely in his brown hand, he seemed oblivious to all that was happening around him. There was a kind of arrogance about him. Pito Vargas had had it too, I remembered—as if they were not servants at all, but kings in disguise.

Elena laughed at something the doctor said, and threw back her lovely head. The mantilla slipped from her smooth black hair and fell to the ground. The doctor immediately picked it up and handed it to her, and it was this gesture that Carlos saw first.

He rode slowly up to the carriage and reined in his horse. He took off his hat to his wife, but did not seem to see the doctor. He half-stood, his elegant tooled boots thrust against the stirrups, only his hard eyes moving over the scene. Then he lowered himself and sat rigidly in the saddle.

"Vamos, Manuel."

Manuel turned his head slowly towards Elena. There was only a suggestion of inquiry in his voice.

"Señora?"

Carlos looked sharply at the Mexican, who paid no attention to him.

The animation faded from Elena's eyes. She sat back in the carriage. "Está bien, Manuel. Adelante."

The doctor smiled once more at Elena and moved out of the way. The carriage started off down the street. The residents of San Miguel returned to their homes, their shabby little stores, the clusters of adobe huts that ringed the town, the small farms in the barren hills. Father Benedicto, from the steps of the mission, looked thoughtfully after Elena's carriage, then back at John Carter. I could guess what he was thinking.

* * *

An influenza epidemic struck the villages around San Miguel that winter and spread even to Don Carlos' rancho. It was not a serious form of the illness, but to poor people unused to such civilized ailments, it was disastrous. Doctor John worked without ceasing, without sleep, often without food for days on end. We all did what we could, but Doña Elena, because they were her people, did more than any.

I remember her sitting up all night with a sick child, growing stiff in the same position by the bedside, her eyes weary from the feeble light and the closeness of the room. She scarcely spoke two words all night, even when John urged her to go to bed. She refused. He did not force her, but stood back to gaze down at her with admiration in his own tired eyes. Then he left her. At last, when she saw the child would recover, she judged it time to leave.

"Manuel, por favor...."

She held out her hand to be helped up, then, exhausted, had to be carried home.

But the influenza was not so deadly as the plague that followed it to San Miguel. This disease had been there before, but now it came in a particularly virulent form, as if it were a complication of the physical malady. Its hold was the stronger for its victims' diminished resistance. It was at first no more than an unspoken idea, then a question asked tentatively of a friend, inevitably an evil thing that penetrated every corner of San Miguel.

It was rumored that Doña Elena had taken a lover.

Considering the circumstances, the rumor was perhaps understandable. The marriage of Maria Elena Dominguin, the sixteen-year-old aristocrat, and Charles Cantrell, the rich American *ranchero,* had been one of convenience only. Carlos was a proud man, petty and possessive. He was sensitive about his origins and what was here called his *machismo*—his manliness. He did not pretend to understand Elena or her people, but it was good for his pride to possess her, and he treated her well. He gave Elena the freedom to go where she wanted, do what she would. She was allowed to pick her own servants and to run the hacienda as she pleased. Elena in her turn had evidently weighed Charles Cantrell carefully against the advantages of a great hacienda and the title of Doña before her name and been content with her choice.

Carlos had even, in his way, been faithful to Elena. Since he did not go to confession, even Father Benedicto could not be sure that he was, but it was not unusual for such a man as Carlos to openly keep several mistresses, and Carlos did not. To me, although I never said it aloud, it seemed unnatural that Elena should be happy with such a man, a man not of her own kind, and I was not surprised when the rumors began again. And now that there was an object to fasten them on, no one remembered that John had not been there when the rumors began in the first place, nor that he was not of Elena's "kind" either. But such is the unreason of calumny.

Carlos pretended to see nothing, but he set his henchmen to watching the doctor. Less openly, Elena too was shadowed. What Carlos never realized was that he need not have taken the trouble. San Miguel did not love Carlos Cantrell, but they would love even less the man, whoever he might be, who compromised their Elena and—the highest crime of all—was caught at it.

John and Elena had no opportunity to be alone, for Manuel was always with her, even when she was not surrounded by other servants and family. But the lack of evidence only made the supposed crime the more terrible. The atmosphere of suspicion grew heavier with the passing uneventful weeks and months.

* * *

In the spring there was another storm. The day had begun warm and airless, and the very calm should have been warning enough of what was to come. The cottonwoods near the arroyo fluttered ominously, and dust hung suspended over the road leading out of San Miguel.

It was the 19th of March, the fiesta of San José Obrero, but Father Benedicto's sermon that morning had little to do with Joseph the Workman, the husband of Mary.

"My children...."

Father Benedicto spoke in a hushed voice, but every member of his congregation heard him. He leaned forward, his hands supporting his lean body against the pulpit, and fixed his fierce black eyes on each of them in turn.

"What is it that ye fear? Is it the night? The bells? Is it the church?" His voice sank to a whisper and the ancient beams of the church strained to hear him; the cool shadows crept forward from the altar. He raised his hand and brought it down upon his open Bible with a force that made the candles flicker and sent the shadows back into their lairs. "Or is it another kind of fear? Is it—can it be—a fear of self?

"Of hidden shameful passions—passions that can do more destruction than any natural force? Think! Think of the power of greed. Of lust. Of vengeance and pride...."

Don Carlos had asked to see me that afternoon on a matter of business. When I arrived at the hacienda, I was surprised to see Elena preparing to go out. A family in an outlying village needed food, she said, but on such a day as this, and nearing dark, I would not have expected her to feel obligated to go personally. I offered to accompany her, if she cared to wait, and for a moment I thought she would accept my invitation. She looked at me as if there were something she wished to say, but something else—in my face, in her reserve, I know not—inhibited her.

I watched her drive off with Manuel. Shortly after, I heard several horsemen set out in the same direction, but paid them no heed except to think it a curious day for so much travel. It was a curious day in many ways. There was some unknown thing hanging in the air over San Miguel, as heavy as the growing storm clouds, but I myself was too obtuse to catch the look, the gesture that signaled an inner storm.

Carlos had called me to ask my legal advice and, when I heard what was on his mind, the feeling of an impending crisis grew stronger still. He wished to know what constituted legal proof of infidelity. I had never until that moment felt any anger towards Carlos, but suddenly his abominable pride became too much to bear. I told him I could not help him and, taking advantage of my years, I told him why and left. But even as I did, I knew that my anger would change nothing.

Had my visit not been cut so short, I would not have reached my home before the storm broke. As it was, I barely succeeded in crossing the arroyo before it filled. The heavy round raindrops hissed as they struck the hard dry earth, and their steady tattoo quickly blended into a dull roar as the water came down in solid sheets, filling every crack in the parched earth and running coffee-colored and foaming in the arroyo.

I reached home and made up a fire as quickly as I was able. Then I changed my clothing and settled into a chair in front of it, prepared to sit out the storm. But I was not permitted to rest. I chanced to look out of my window just as a bolt of lightning struck the big cottonwood nearest the arroyo. For an instant as brief as that lightning flash, I thought of Pito Vargas.

Then there was a second flash and I saw, illuminated against the mutilated cottonwood, the figure of a woman, her skirts whipped around her by the wind and rain. She ran towards me. I rushed outside to bring her in. Both soaking wet, we confronted each other. Her hair hung down in wet, bedraggled strands and the hem of her dress was caked with mud, but it was the look on her face that terrified me.

"Doña Elena! What has happened?"

She seized my hands and looked up, her beautiful dark eyes frightened, imploring.

"Forgive me! But you must help me! John—"

"The doctor? Where is he?"

"I do not know! I could not find him, but I must have help! They have…"

Suddenly, from the mission, we heard the peal of the bells through the storm. It was not so much a peal as one long ring and an echo, as if the voice of the big tenor bell had been choked off.

Elena stood very still, staring at the window. Then she covered her face with her hands and moaned piteously, as if in great pain. She fell to her knees, crossed herself, and bowed her head. I understood then, finally, what had happened.

Father Benedicto found him the next morning with the bell rope around his neck. Doctor John signed the death certificate that read "accidental strangulation," not because he believed it, but because there was no way to prove it otherwise.

They buried Manuel in the cemetery, next to Pito Vargas, the first victim of the bells.

Linda Triegel grew up in Connecticut and moved around a lot before settling in Albuquerque. She started writing after college and eventually published 12 romances under her pen name, Elisabeth Kidd, as well as short stories and travel articles. Her first cozy mystery, writing as Elly Kirsten, is *Civil Blood.*

SECTION NINE

HUMOR

You'll find something to smile about here. Or at least shake your head and forget about that to-do list you had.

Humor   Gold Medal

Robert Speake

ONCE UPON A TIME IN THE GARDEN OF EDEN

YOU COULD SAY THAT THE RECORDED HISTORY OF MEN'S OPPRESSION OF WOMEN IS ROOTED IN MYTHS, in particular the Abrahamic religions creation myths of Adam and Eve in the Hebrew Bible's Book of Genesis and the Fourth Chapter of the Quran.

The Judeo—Christian version of the creation myth was finally written down—by male scribes—most likely in the 6th century BC, around the time of the Jewish Babylonian Exile. It was only scribed after several millennia had passed and thousands of other men, who could neither read nor write, had orally embellished it and passed it down through the generations.

If you've ever played the party game of passing a whispered phrase around a circle, you can imagine the chances of generations of illiterate oral storytellers screwing up some details of the creation myth, adding their own maleness to it, or even getting its messages wrong entirely.

But devotees of the Bible, as written, don't see it that way. This particular creation myth, as you may recall from Sunday School, goes like this:

One day, Adam, who God had created from dust a few decades back, was hand tilling some fallow ground to plant some veggies in the strictly—vegetarian Garden of Eden, where there were also lots of fruit trees to pick for dietary variety.

At this point in the original story of Humankind, Adam is solo, the very first human being ever created by God. No Eve. God tells him it's OK to plant anything he wants and to eat any fruit from the trees except one: The apple Tree of Knowledge of Good and Evil.

As the myth has it, God invested his first son Adam with innocence and didn't want him corrupted by knowledge or evil, apparently in the belief that they were one and the same. Some of today's fundamentalist religions and politicians—and their followers—still think they are.

One day, after creating all other life, God decided to give Adam a Woman, who turned out to be Eve. The myth says God did it because Adam was lonely, but that beggars belief, too. How could you be lonely if you've been alone all your life? More likely, God realized He needed some way to carry on the human race that Adam couldn't do all by himself, so He created Woman, Eve, to begat their son Cain who, after he murdered his gentle shepherd brother Abel, may have begun the begatting of all other human beings down through the millennia to us.

But since Cain clearly was bad seed, Adam sired another son, Seth, when he was a biblical 130, and some other kids, maybe as many as 28 (he and Eve lived over 900 years!) including some girls to help with the begatting. But that part of the Genesis story completely ignores the little detail of incest having played a major role in the creation of the human race.

But let's assume the biblical scholars are right, that the story of our creation is an allegory, not the literal truth, and move on. Sorry, fundamentalists.

Even more unlikely than God creating Woman just to see that Humankind got made, the male scribes who wrote the myth down thousands of biblical years later needed to explain, metaphorically, how the countless generations since Adam and Eve that all required Woman came to be. So they wrote that God created Eve out of one of Adam's ribs—another plot—point in the story that beggars belief, biologically—speaking—and the First Couple's next few years passed, without any backstory worth being in the Bible.

We rejoin the myth when they were in their golden years, whiling away their days lying around in the grass naked, enjoying the good life in the apparently moderate Mesopotamian clime in Eden, eating raw fruits and veggies, drinking from the Tigris River, which was clean back then. They had no jobs or kids—yet— or financial cares or any of the other myriad of woes we have today. And they didn't realize they were naked either. So, life was good in paradise.

Then, one day a serpent—a slimy creature the Genesis scribes must've used for dramatic effect—sidled up to Eve and said, "Have you noticed how ripe the apples are in that tree over yonder?" nodding its creepy head towards the forbidden Tree of Knowledge of Good and Evil. Eve, being Eve, according to the male scribes, said, "Why, no, I hadn't. Let me check that out."

With that, Eve walked over, reached up, and plucked a nice juicy red apple from one of the lower branches. It was as tasty as the snake said it was and its juices ran down her chin onto her comely naked bosom. Eve turned to

Adam, smiled seductively, and said, "Here, take a bite." Adam hesitated a bit, then, well, because it was Eve, his woman, took a big manly bite and the juices ran down his naked torso to his naked loins, too.

That's when the First Couple first noticed they were unclothed and frantically searched around for palm fronds to cover their privates. And God obligingly gave them some garments from some stash to hide their nakedness.

Thus was born Original Sin and human shame, which the ancient male scribes laid entirely onto Eve, for taking the first bite out of the forbidden apple.

Then the scribes have God banish Adam and Eve from the Garden of Eden forever and, symbolically, the entire human race from the promise of life after death in paradise. The descendants of the serpent were confined to forever crawl on their bellies, while those of Adam were doomed to work hard their whole lives and die and those of Eve were destined to be the only sex to suffer the excruciating pain of childbirth and to always be subordinate to men.

That last punishment by God of Woman held in America until the first wave of feminism washed over the land in the 1950s AD. Since then, a cold war between the modern versions of Adam and Eve has waged incessantly, leaving divorce as common as marriage now.

God's banishment of the First Couple from the Garden of Eden came just in the nick of time, before they had a chance to sample the fruit of the other big—dog tree in the Garden, the Tree of Life, which would've given them eternal life. In which case they'd be a lot like God and thus be free of His total lordship over Humankind in all matters, large and small, from world wars to the common cold.

According to one quirky modern Islamic scholar, even the Quran doesn't really promise an afterlife in paradise, with 72 virgins for every devout Muslim man. Apparently, some Islamic scribe centuries ago mistook the words "white raisin" for "virgin" in an indecipherable old parchment, so the promise is 72 "white raisins" for every devout young suicide bomber. The story's hilarious, but it's contradicted many places elsewhere in the Quran. In either case, it's not likely he, or she, after exploding a suicide vest in a crowded market, will end up in paradise.

Still, according to the ancient male writers of the Book of Genesis, it's all Eve's fault and, by extrapolation, it's the fault of Womankind that we have so much shame and misery today.

Which is all the excuse Men ever needed for believing that their own miseries can be traced back to the Original Sin of Woman, instead of to themselves.

Now, as comical as the Judeo—Christian creation myth is, once you tease out its faulty logic as a story, it's very likely the very first written source of women's oppression in human history. Let's look at the two most powerful reasons why that's so important.

First off, the scribes who hand—wrote the creation myth have Adam being created first, which suggests that he was more favored in the eyes of God than Eve. Which is to say that men are more important to God than women.

Even worse, the belief from the creation myth that men are better than women in all ways is surely the most misogynous lesson taught to boys in Man School at the feet of their adult male authority figures, teachers, coaches, troop leaders, even their fathers, especially them.

Superiority breeds contempt, contempt spawns oppression, and oppression silences the oppressed, in this case Woman.

The second big reason for thinking the male Genesis writers ascribed all of Original Sin to First Woman Eve, purely for manly reasons, has to do with free will, a topic that has been hotly debated by deep thinkers since at least as far back as Aristotle. Neuroscience has now entered the argument, trying to prove that the brain's neuron networks automatically operate and that we actually exercise our "free will" a split—second after a network fires.

But let's assume we do have free will, which just about everything really important about human beings is based upon. Couldn't Adam have refused to take the forbidden fruit from Eve? Of course he could've. Didn't he have a choice as to whether he took a bite out of it or not?

Of course he did. That he did has reverberated down through the ages. No Eden for us. Ever. Even if you believe that mythological allegories contain truths, they are, after all stories, and all good stories have internal logic. And the story of creation fails that test on multiple counts, especially ascribing Original Sin to women and human superiority to men.

Islam's version of the Abrahamic creation myth in the 4th Chapter of the Quran says Adam and Eve's sins of biting the forbidden apple are theirs alone and aren't hereditary. We say something even better: We say Original Sin doesn't exist: No one is born with any sin in them. That comes later, in lives so utterly imperfectly lived, swimming like fish our whole lives in the dark mythological waters of male superiority over women and their ridiculous inferiority to us.

One only has to compare the superb county—wide coronavirus pandemic responses of the female national leaders around the globe to those of their halting and hapless male counterparts to see how ridiculous the notion of male superiority truly is, nowadays, and surely always was.

Still, even the most absurd of beliefs dies hard and this one has been around for all of recorded history, and probably far back into prehistory. So it's rooted deeply in the human psyche, including, unhappily, the women of the world's fundamentalist religions brainwashed by the great leaders of those faiths into believing women are justifiably inferior to men.

After more that 40 years, the Equal Rights Amendment to the United States Constitution has finally secured it's magic 38th state, Virginia, needed for ratification, yet the deadline for that passed decades ago. Congress can waive that, but the decision is in the hands of the men there.

How ironically absurd it is that equality for women still rests in the hands of men, the way it always has, as far back as the Garden of Eden, where the made—up male God gave the made—up Adam rule over everything in his made—up domain, including his made—up wife Eve.

Too bad women don't start wars. They could sure use one right about now. On us men.

God forbid, though, that it could take a hot war for women to achieve equality with men.

Then they'd be just like us.

*   *   *

A freshman essay class turned **Robert Speake** on to writing. "Prof" assigned topics like "Compare Jesus Christ to a Popcorn Ball." Robert was oddly the class star. On his last piece, Prof scrawled, "You write well." After a long engineering career on three continents, that remains Robert's Pulitzer. And the writing life is finally his.

Humor Poetry
Charles Powell

Gold Medal

CAN NOT

Not even a little bit
Can't even come close
Can not do it
Not at all
None
Not
Can not

I can't swim
Can't dance
Can't sing
Can't ride a bicycle
Can't play any music instrument
Can't multi-task
Can't throw a football

I can't speak a second language
Can't knit or crochet
Can't drive stick
Can't play pinochle or bridge
Can't somersault
Can't whistle
Can't play tennis or golf

Not
None
Not at all
Not even a little bit
Can't do it
Can't even come close
Can not

*   *   *

Charles Powell : grandfather, Air Force veteran and retired postal worker. With a BS in Social Science, he's been published in SouthWest Writers *Sage* and the *Fixed And Free Poetry Anthology*. He's also enjoyed success with prose and poetry in several SWW writing contests. Raised in Chicago, Albuquerque's been home 34 years.

Humor   Silver Medal
Rose Marie Kern

THE LAMB CAKE

Every year at Easter my Mom made a chocolate lamb cake using a mold. She slathered it with vanilla icing and pressed coconut flakes on the outside. The baking mold had openings on the sides in case you overfilled it, and usually we kids would be glad to munch on the parts that seeped out and baked on the cookie sheet.

One year my 11 year old sister, Bunny, got a new puppy a week before Easter. Like most new puppies it had a few accidents which she always cleaned up.

Dad had to work late on Good Friday and came home after Mom and the rest of us were already in bed. Quietly he made his way into the bedroom, which was illuminated only by moonlight through the window. As he walked around to his side of the bed he saw a dark, ropy puddle on the floor.

Very quietly he said "Oh God…what the..." Then, "Phew!" He stood up and went out of the bedroom and over to the foot of the stairs as though he was really hoping that someone was awake. He walked back to the bedroom, gagged, then upstairs to the kitchen, then back down, where he threw a kitchen towel on top of the pile and opened the window over the bed. He undressed and for once did not kneel down next to the bed to say his prayers.

Mom was on her side and it was all she could do not to break out laughing, but she just pretended to be asleep, listening to Dad gag, choke, groan and try to breathe heavily into his pillow. He finally got to sleep and she reached up and closed the window because it was getting cold. A little while later he woke up…gagging…and opened the window again. He put his face right up to the screen and breathed deeply a few times before laying back down and burying his nose in the pillow.

According to Mom this went on all night, she would wake up and close the window. He would wake up and open it again.

Early the next morning Mom got up at her usual time, which also woke Dad. As she got up, Dad said, "Mother, do you smell anything?"

She said, "No, Honey", which he did not believe.

"Well if you look over on my side of the bed, Bunny's puppy left us a present."

With a serious expression, Mom went around the bed, then, unable to hold it any longer she yelled "BUNNY!"

My sister knew what was going on and she pelted down the stairs to the master bedroom. Dad said, "Come over here and see what your dog did."

Bunny went over and knelt on the floor and poked her finger into the pile. Dad got agitated, "Don't do that, go get something to clean it up!"

Bunny lifted the pile off the floor – and ate it.

*   *   *

Before making her home in Albuquerque, **Rose Marie Kern** grew up in a large Catholic family in Indianapolis. With a plethora of stories to call upon she is contemplating a book about this lively group she will entitle *The Kern Kids*. Stay tuned for more fun with goats, rotten apples, stone monasteries, and camping at Starve Hallow.

Humor Poetry
Charles Powell

Silver Medal

HOW COLD IS IT?

It's hair raising cold
It's eye fogging, nose frosting cold

It's ear aching cold
It's breath freezing cold
It's teeth chattering, arm shivering, finger numbing cold

It's leg shaking cold
It's knee knocking cold
It's toe curling cold,
It's body trembling, bone chilling, heart pausing, blood stopping cold

That's how cold

* * *

Charles Powell : grandfather, Air Force veteran and retired postal worker. With a BS in Social Science, he's been published in SouthWest Writers *Sage* and the *Fixed And Free Poetry Anthology*. He's also enjoyed success with prose and poetry in several SWW writing contests. Raised in Chicago, Albuquerque's been home 34 years.

Humor   **Bronze Medal**

Bonnie Hayes

LISTEN UP, All you traffic-weary Suburbanites and bone-chilled Urbanites!   *Before you rashly schedule that moving van one dreary winter morning or smoggy summer afternoon, consider the dangers. This cautionary tale is for YOU!*

A SOUTHWESTERN SPECTRAL SPECTACLE

The "Newcomer Meets Ancient Dead Indian Elder Phenomenon" is a documented hazard here in New Mexico. Often commented upon but poorly understood, it is no laughing matter. It can cause irreversible psychic damage and have lifestyle—threatening consequences. There is no vaccine, no silver bullet, and no known cure. Like an inflammatory disease, once it is contracted, it just has to run its course. Here in "The Land of Enchantment" no one is entirely immune, and many never fully recover.

You are a high—risk candidate if you have suffered any of these events in the last year:

- A divorce or bereavement
- A corporate downsizing
- A midlife crisis
- A close encounter with a health professional
- An unwelcome relative living with you for more than two months
- An unscheduled meeting with an extra—terrestrial and/or IRS agent

Any single one of these risk factors predisposes you to be a wretched victim of this endemic Southwestern malady. If you have two or more of them, your moving van is probably already headed this way.

While this move seems harmless – perhaps even sensible – it is not. New Mexico is no place to try to regain balance in your life. It's hard enough to maintain your balance in this State even with years of practice and no major personal crisis. And, You, poor soul, are clueless about what that imbalance will demand of you.

Exercise extreme caution after arrival. You will be exposed.
New Mexico is simply "too different" a place to support gentle transitions. Let us assume that you can tolerate the physical challenges: the lack of oxygen (altitude sickness), the dry air (dehydration), and the peculiar effects of those mood—altering green chile endorphins (euphoria) that we ladle onto all of our food. All of these factors will compound your distress by producing bizarre and mysterious symptoms. But they are just diversions. You are destined to become a casualty in a very casual land because you are utterly oblivious to the real threat.

The Culture Shock.
It strikes from day one. New sights and sounds, disturbing ideas, and a barrage of unfamiliar cultures, complex metaphors, and contradictory worldviews assault you. You are pummeled from all sides, all day, and all night. You are completely out of your element. Naive, bewildered, and defenseless—you are far too vulnerable to survive a protracted exposure to New Mexico.

Do not underestimate the disruptive power of this experience.
The lack of sleep from the indigestible spicy food may wear you down, but it is the relentless sensory overload that will do you in. It's too much, too fast, and it is overwhelming. The predictable discombobulating of your moribund belief system will soon manifest dramatically.

Prepare for a major mental meltdown.
The crackle of the neural synapses arcing in your brain and the musty smoke from the short—circuiting of your never—tested ideology can be detected by an experienced observer from across the room. You won't see it coming, but we veteran New Mexicans recognize the signs

It is not subtle.

You have a wild, haunted look and you are babbling about wolves and spirits, your past life, cosmic convergences, miraculous interventions, alternative realities, and aliens that descend to earth on beams of light. Worse than all of that, you have forgotten the price of your favorite latte on the Starbucks Menu! You are in acute philosophical distress.

The World, as you know it, is disintegrating.

You have not the will, the skill, nor the experience to fend off a challenge to your old version of reality. Every waking hour your flaccid traditions, customs, and habits try to compete with all the new and exotic alternatives. Disoriented, having no way to sort all the new information, and completely at a loss as to how to screen it or evaluate it, you buckle under the load. The intensity of the distress and the perceived level of threat escalate rapidly. Your decrepit defenses are forced to make a last stand.

It is not going to be pretty.

What you are experiencing is the collapse of a belief system; a system which has been unexamined, neglected, and unappreciated for a lifetime. Like watching the demolition of an aging skyscraper, the event has a unique fascination and a monumental quality. Perhaps you would have been fatally injured if you had not moved out, but you are still profoundly shaken by the sudden, rapid destruction of something you thought was enduring. You wander around in the rubble–dazed. With silent screams, your brain arouses your Subconscious Special Forces—your *"Dream Team."*

Your inept Dream Team responds to the call.

From the neglected bunkers in your brain, gut, and nervous system, the covert forces of your mind and body (inactive and unexercised for almost an entire lifetime) galumph into action. With the best of intentions and no perceivable plan, your *Dream Team* mounts an intense *Nocturnal Campaign.* It is a last ditch effort to assimilate all your new experiences into your fossilized belief system. *It is doomed from the start.*

But your Dream Team gives it their best shot anyway.

Night after night, in vivid 3D Technicolor, *Your Team* churns out distorted alternatives and sends up weird possibilities. They valiantly try to integrate all the confusing symbols and conflicting beliefs into something sensible. Your neglected introspective work of a lifetime has been collapsed into a few months of frantic, hysterical self—absorption. It is simply too much, too complicated,,, and too late.

The Integration Initiative not only fails—it backfires—DISASTROUSLY.
You are defended by the untrained and led by the disoriented. Hastily constructed paradox barricades crumble. Secret bunkers are exposed. It is a complete rout. All of your bewildered, covert Special Forces have nowhere to go and no place to hide.

They stumble around, shell—shocked.
Firing off stray rounds of metaphors and strafing all the symbols, old and new, they turn your interior mental landscape into a no—man's—land. In the infernal internal chaos, they lose track of who is "Them" and who is "Us." It is a high—stakes, alternative reality, free—for—all.

Everyone is losing—especially YOU.
Unused to communing with your own psyche, frightened by the bizarre images, and hearing internal voices that you have ignored for decades—YOU FREAK OUT! You violently reject responsibility for any of it. One morning, you wake up, in a cold sweat, and, in desperation, pass the buck to—*whom else but—**The Hopi Grandmothers.***

Whatever happens after that morning—it's all entirely THEIR fault. Because, now, a bunch of old, dead, Indian women are, presumably, running the whole show.

It is obvious to any onlooker that <u>Something</u> has snapped into place.
Yesterday you were flopping around like a whacked trout. You weren't sure if you were a reincarnated Biblical character, an alien from another dimension, or (my personal favorite) an Anasazi Spirit Walker.

But Today? TODAY! You are full of purpose, or focus...or something.
One thing is indisputable...whatever "IT" is...you are most definitely FULL OF IT.

So... what happened last night?
You saved yourself, that's what. Somebody had to do it. Your old belief system was in ruins, your reality was reeling, and your identity tottering. Your puerile instincts and latent character flaws had to rescue you. As a stopgap solution, they slapped together a wobbly *"NEW YOU."* (What good are knee—

jerk reactions, honed by a lifetime of denial and self—delusion, if they can't create a self—serving personal myth in an emergency?)

We could smell it coming, but anyone can see it now.
The fashion metamorphosis has begun. You are flaunting a new look and singing (or chanting) a new tune.

But—First Things First.
Before you can theatrically proclaim your new status as the *"Chosen Channel for the Ancient Indian Ancestors"* you need to perfect your new uniform. You have a shiny new persona, complete with an imposing personal myth. A befitting costume and accessories are needed to perform your new role properly. You quickly acquire the requisite three or more pounds of turquoise and silver jewelry and the bits of stone, bone, and feathers to adorn yourself.

Once you are conspicuously dressed for success—you assemble everyone who is willing to attend (or unable to escape.) In full regalia, with great ceremony (and considerable pompous oratory) you announce your newfound purpose and mystic identity. You claim you are *"A Channel for the Ancient, Sacred Hopi Grandmothers."*

A bona fide "CHOSEN ONE"... yep, that's YOU!

You humbly repent the misguided ways of your past.
You make an elaborate production of casting off the trappings of your former life. You disavow the evil, materialist culture you have transcended. You congratulate yourself profusely and swear that you have moved beyond the childish need for approval and status.

(You pause, graciously, to acknowledge your audience's applause and adulation.)

You impress everyone with your bulleted, prioritized lists.
A detailed, itemized account of all the things you are going to change about yourself and your old, pedestrian ways. To project your new identity to the admiring world, you change your name. It's a romantic notion that might have merit, if anything had actually happened to justify calling yourself, *"Winged Soaring Eagle."*

However, there is one, indisputable change—the FERVOR of your new conviction.

You absolutely, adamantly believe that...with those Ancient Hopi Grandmothers at the helm...Everything is going to be PERFECT. Your inner life will be blissful. Your outer life will be harmonious. Your whole world will be wonderful and beautiful and serene... *Forever!* (*Sorry to disappoint you, Honey, but it ain't that easy.*)

"The Land of Enchantment" has cast its spell on you, and you are <u>stuck</u> in it.

We know this for a fact because we've seen it (and/or done it) all before. We can't tell how long this phase will last. But we have no doubt—*there is no stopping you now.*

YOU ARE READY TO LAUNCH! Properly suited up and tightly scheduled, you sally forth to implement your Personal Freedom Agenda and execute your Medium and Long Range Goals. Complete Liberation from all the restrictive norms of your former mundane life and a total Spiritual Awakening are scheduled for the next vernal equinox. The Event is to take place in the ruins of a sacred archeological site (to be booked A.S.A.P.)

You believe you have dedicated cable access to The Great Beyond (with a free lifetime service contract.) Therefore, you presume that our local indigenous tribes will be honored by your very presence. Clearly when a sanctified, elected spirit (such as Yourself) graces their ancient holy places with your superior spirituality and manifest destiny, all their dusty old symbols will be raised to *"A Whole New Level."* When anyone *dares* to question your motives or suggests you don't belong there, you are surprised and indignant.

YOU are beyond reproach, divinely guided—directly connected through a mystic link to THE TRUTH. You know this with certainty, because...THE HOPI GRANDMOTHERS told you so—Personally!! And, EVERYONE KNOWS that those SACRED ANCIENT ONES possess ALL THE WISDOM of ALL THE AGES. Obviously, they must also have ALL THE ANSWERS! Whatever instructions THEY impart, therefore, are beyond reproach, divinely inspired, and incontestable. Who can argue with that logic?

And what is the advice they are downloading?

Why it is <u>EXACTLY</u> what you have always wanted to hear! Imagine that! What a coincidence...and how convenient. Who would have thought that tribal elders from one of the most traditional, ceremonial, conservative societies on the planet would be telling you to abandon all your family commitments, forget your financial obligations, kiss off the people you have wounded or wronged, and get naked and/or high. These certainly aren't the kind of message that their real descendants get from those old ladies. And those living descendants are skeptical as I am.

We point out these anomalies, as a courtesy.
To anyone who is a Native American Want-A-Be, we caution, don't attempt to join a *real* Native American community. None of their traditions or communal demands on your time and resources will mesh with your fantasy of being a "Free Spirit" or a "Wild Indian."

Predictably, you soon discover that living Elders and real Tribal cultures cramp your style. Even the spectral Elders are becoming a bother and all your Sterling accoutrements a burden. It is time to break free of their restraints. However, before you fire the old ladies, you wring one more obliging epiphany out of them. It is the last inspired directive from the Grannies from the Great Beyond. You claim they instruct you:

"OH! CHOSEN ONE! Return now to the Source of All Being for YOU have risen to A NEW LEVEL OF CONSCIOUSNESS!"

Now you can summarily dismiss the guides. (Who needs stodgy old Indians anyway?)

Exit the Hopi Grandmothers—Stage Right.

On to the Next Act: Buy the sackcloth loincloth or the robe spun from organic Angora goat hair, because now you are going to be *"Communing DIRECTLY with NATURE."*

Vibrating at a much higher frequency than we lesser mortals, you tune into your newly activated telepathic rapport with all living things.
Suddenly, you are able to connect empathically, with all the innocent wild creatures—especially the fashionable, sexy ones. Wolves, pumas, bobcats, and bears—all these ferocious predators will instantly recognize You, a Transcendent Being, as their Cosmic Cousin. They will snuggle up to you like

cuddly bunnies in a Bambi movie, their killer instincts overwhelmed by the aura of love now emanating from your Pure Radiant Self.

It is "Transcendence," with a capital "T." You are euphoric—Positively sparkling with Positivity. Your projections of love and harmony will create a fantastical world where all strife will disappear like a wisp of hemp smoke in a stiff breeze In *Your* "GLOWING VISION," not only will the lion lie down with the lamb, ALL the Earth's creatures will be dining exclusively upon bean sprouts. (This Disneyland fantasy of "Nature" can only be maintained by someone who has never been anywhere wilder than Central Park or the farm's petting zoo.) .

You can't tolerate reason in this phase either.
In fact, anyone who dares to doubt you is a *"blasphemous heretic creating discordant vibrations. And, You are also now absolutely intolerant of any such unenlightened non—believer who presumes to question your ability to manifest Your Perfectly Perfect World.*

Sadly, you are not alone.
We have many victims here in the Southwest who are trapped in this extreme stage of the disorder. Remission is rare. Some of them have been stuck in this chronic deluded state since the early 60's. They all espouse that, unless foiled by us unbelievers, You purified avatars, "Children of the Light," will succeed in transforming all of society by proxy.

It will happen overnight.

One miraculous day, we will all wake up—share the planet very politely—love everyone—and "Live Happily Ever After." It is the phenomenon's nadir, but, to YOU, it feels...

MAGICAL!!
PEACE! BROTHERHOOD! SISTERHOOD!
UNCONDITIONAL UNIVERSAL LOVE FOR ALL!!
RIGHT HERE! RIGHT NOW! IN THE LAND OF ENCHANTMENT!
YOU ARE AT ONE WITH THE COSMOS AT LAST!!!*
* * **
*Please extend our sincerest condolences to your family.
* * *

The End

*   *   *

Bonnie J. Hayes
Creating two 6'x6' Siemosauri in her garage for the "Dino Stompede" Natural History Museum fundraiser, motivated this artist to find a creative outlet that did not require a hazmat suit nor risk exploding the furnace. She is now fuming (organically) at her computer, inspired by her family's gallows-humor tradition.

SECTION TEN

SPIRITUAL/PHILOSOPHY

This category encompasses many different paths all on the way to finding a deeper meaning for each of us.

Spiritual/Philosophy   Gold Medal
Francis Rose

JEREMY'S JOURNEY

Jeremy fluttered his wings and launched upward from the pine bough where he had spent the night. Small and brown, Jeremy was not very remarkable in the bird world. He was quick enough to escape the claws of pigeons who thought he would make a good dinner and he was good at finding small bugs and worms as he peered between blades of grass.

Jeremy liked to sit on telephone wires and chirp with the other birds. He enjoyed singing and flying through bright sunny afternoon. He twittered as the dogs in the yard beneath would bark at him. How stupid they were!

What Jeremy did not like was wind and rain. On days when the sun was hiding behind the rain clouds, Jeremy and the other small birds tried to find a place where they could hide. His feathers were not made to cast off the water, so he would shake himself, then huddle close to a tree trunk or under the roof of a house.

The worst came when the winds grew cold. Jeremy went to find food, but most of the bugs and worms were hidden underground. The berries were all gone from the bushes and the seeds on the ground were hard to find. He had to fly out of his shelter to eat, but as soon as he could he would go back to perch beneath the eaves of a large old house. He would fluff up his feathers so that he could stay a little warmer and bury his beak under his wing.

In the winter time, Jeremy could see into the windows of the houses. He saw the dogs as they played with the humans. The humans always had food and water set down for the dogs and they were always warm.

Jeremy thought to himself. "I wish that I was a dog. I wish I was warm and never had to worry about finding food." Jeremy shivered as an icy breeze cut up under the eaves of the garage where he was sheltered.

That night Jeremy was so cold that his body died. He didn't feel any different really. He could still fly. He opened his eyes and saw a very bright glow that looked like the sun. He flew towards the glow and felt light and warm.

"Hello, Jeremy." A calm voice spoke to him from the middle of the glowing light. "Do you know where you are?"

Jeremy shook himself. "Am I in summertime?"

"In a way," the voice said. "Here it is always summer."

"Can I stay?" asked Jeremy anxiously.

"For a little while." the voice answered.

"Is there a branch nearby to land on?" Jeremy asked.

"No, but you do not need branches anymore."

"What do you mean?"

"Look at your feet." The voice instructed.

Jeremy looked and was astonished. He had no feet! He had no feathers! He had no wings or beak!

Jeremy's body was all aglow–just like the light ahead of him. "What happened to me?" Jeremy said.

"You simply left your feathers behind. You have come here to be with me." As he spoke the glow brightened and expanded.

Jeremy was not afraid, he was happy. He drifted towards the glow until he became part of it. Suddenly he began to sing with as much joy as ever he had sung on a lovely summer's day.

All his experiences, all the feelings he had ever had, good and bad were shared with the great glowing spirit that had called him. For a time they sang together of fat juicy bugs and eggs hatching. They crooned about cold winds and gray wet days. They rejoiced in flying over trees and seeing reflections in the streams below. They became one.

Finally the song dimmed. Jeremy pulled away from the Great Spirit and in doing so he felt alone again. But he knew he was a piece of this divine one, even when apart.

"Thank you, Jeremy, for bringing us your memories and your knowledge of the skies of Earth."

"Are you ready to continue your life's journey?"

Jeremy loved being here, so close to the Great Spirit of which he was once part. But he still had many tasks to perform before he finally became one with all the other wisps of Spirit that had split off so long ago. His job was to live separately, to learn, to understand life, and to add his experiences to that of all the other souls that made up the Great Spirit.

"Yes, Great Spirit, I am ready to continue my task."

"And what form would you like to take this time?" the Great Spirit inquired.

Jeremy thought for a moment. Here in this place he remembered that he had been a fish, he had been a spider and he had been a bird. He remembered the dogs in their nice warm house.

"I should like to be a dog." Jeremy decided. "A big dog" He added.

With these words the spirit of Jeremy was pulled into a dark warm place, where he slept until he was born.

* * *

"I swear that dog is going to drive me crazy!" The lady put her hands on her hips as she watched the big German Shepard barking at the birds in the back yard. "Joe! Joe! Get in here!"

As Joe bounced into the kitchen he jumped and danced around the lady until she had to laugh. Joe did not remember that he had once been a bird named Jeremy, but he barked as much as birds sing and he loved to leap in the air outside and woof at the birds on the telephone wires.

Joe thought birds were lucky, they could fly anywhere they wished. Joe hated having to stay in the yard or being put on a leash. Joe had to learn to do the things that the Lady told him to do. He learned that the sounds she made meant that he was supposed to do things or go places. Obedience was a very difficult thing, and Joe often envied the birds as they flew around and did as they pleased. He looked across the fence to where a horse named Ruby lived. She was beautiful and very large!

He ran outside again, right up to the fence and began to bark at Ruby. Oh how loudly he could bark!

The Lady sighed as he came back to be petted. "You know Joe, I have never heard a dog that liked the sound of his own voice as much as you do, and I have never seen one that would jump so high just for the fun of it."

She laughed as she scratched behind his ears. "Maybe you should have been a bird."

Joe cocked his head and looked at her funny, and his soul laughed.

* * *

 **Francis Rose** was born on the feast day of St. Francis of Assisi in St. Francis Hospital. With such a beginning how else could she live but to empathize with the creatures around her? Jeremy's Journey is being illustrated for a picture book soon to be available.

Spiritual/Philosophy Poetry   Gold Medal
Carl Hitchens

THE SUN RISES

A*ckquechkq*, the Sun, rises-
lifting off the ground
from behind a craggy foothill
of the Sandia Mountains,
washing a faint glow
over the colorless atmosphere
encircling the land

A*ckquechkq* climbs the backside
of Sandia's rocky eminence
Its light getting squeezed
between mountain walls,
building up pressure to break free

In slow mo, it peeks
over the silhouetted cliff,
setting off an eruption
of fiery red and gold light,
splintering into sharp spears
that stab my eyes,
burning away the shadows
of yesterday's dark clouds

pausing for a brief landfall,
to catch its breath
on a nearby mesa,
before launching again
on its meridian transit

en route to the vaulted tapestry
of white-clouded blue yonder,
where Earth and Sky consummate
their cosmic marriage—
pollenating the world
with life and regeneration

We, like the sun
rise and set each day,
revolving around the axes
of our self-awareness,
pointing true north, we hope
toward preservation and survival

We, like constellations of stars
on the celestial sphere,
mark the passages of our lives
sunrise to sunset
equinox to equinox
solar year to solar year

Each morning we lift off
into the dawn of potential,
arc around the orb of aspiration
and set down in twilight's reflection
of losses and gains

We are light and energy
We are wind and rain
We are seasons that come and go

We are reason tied to imagination
combined into gravitational tension
by which we survive the unimaginable

Like the sun
we endure out of habit
and by habit we endure
Like the sun
we are galactic synergy

Here at the junction
of earth and sky
of time, space and matter
We are A*ckquechkq* in the flesh.

*   *   *

Poet/storyteller/essayist/blogger, **Carl** **Hitchens** strives to act as a voice of cultural-social-political examination, critique and criticism. In describing creative inspiration, he says "every artist is sound-personified, a blind beggar acutely listening for the alms of truth falling into the bowl of enlightened awareness."

Spiritual/Philosophy   Silver Medal
Lisa Durkin

TEACHING AND LEARNING
ONLINE IN A COVID-19 WORLD

COVID-19; who saw that coming? One week we were dealing with our usual struggles, like remembering the password to our Amazon account, and the next week we sat wide-eyed, isolated at home, listening to proclamations about quarantines and wringing our hands over the number of ventilators hospitals needed but didn't have. Parents are especially struggling with social distancing. Not only do they wonder how they're going to make ends meet in a looming recession accompanied by vast joblessness, but they must also contend with their own kids who have to learn online in the living room rather than in a classroom.

Ask any teacher, and they will tell you that a few of those kids act like crazed monkeys. One mom ranted on YouTube, "If we don't die of Corona, we'll die of home teaching!" Another mom gave a tearful testimony, "It's 11:15 and I'm hiding in my son's room. I feel like this is really hard." My favorite was the dad who explained to his son's teacher, "Remember when I talked with you earlier this year and said, 'you don't know my child?' Well, now I know, I don't either."

The world changed when Coronavirus shut down schools for over 54 million students. The minute a government official declared, "School is cancelled," by far, most students danced in jubilation, because to them, that meant starting summer vacation three months early. Some of these students and their parents have virtually dropped off the map, out of touch with schools. Truancy was an obstacle before the school shutdown, and now it's Mt. Everest. What will the graduation rate mean this year, or a diploma for that matter?

I've been involved in education for three decades, most of which has been in a science classroom. Kids in my district were fortunate, because this year they were provided individual computers. That meant our school didn't have to scramble for a month to purchase and distribute computers to our kids like other districts. My students were already well versed in our online teaching platform. A week after the school shutdown was announced, we were expected to have online lessons prepared. Our students didn't get to dance a jig for very long, it seems.

This unprecedented turn of events involved many surprises but also situations that Captain Obvious would have predicted years ago. After schools were canceled, classroom teaching had to be abruptly converted into distance learning.

As a nation, we weren't ready for it. Teachers suddenly had to learn new computer applications to make their lesson plans engaging and meaningful. Many households didn't have the electronic capacity to handle Google Classroom platforms and Zoom virtual meetings. Some families are hard-pressed to provide their children food, much less high-speed Internet. Distance learning definitely doesn't level the playing field between haves and have-nots. As much as kids love their smartphones, completing assignments on handheld devices is ridiculously difficult.

As one might expect, students from challenging demographics are also the kids missing most of their assignments. These are the same at-risk kids who weren't turning in their work before the COVID-19 crisis. Students who were failing before are still failing.

For students without Internet access, our district provides hot-spot locations where they can park and work in their cars. As a result, most of my students have logged on to our online learning platform. They can work on their assignments, but here's the catch. They don't.

Depending on the course, anywhere from one-quarter to one-third of my students have neglected to turn in any assignments since the announcement. It isn't only at-risk kids who are ghosts. Plenty of affluent students have already trotted off to an early summer vacation. They make teen-age excuses. They complain they suddenly don't know how to log on to a computer or they are unfairly assigned more work than what they would have been expected to do in the classroom. When a kid has to motivate themselves, it probably seems like more work.

There are many legitimate reasons kids don't persist with online learning. Students who struggle with reading are deeply impaired when a computer is their only means to learn. Schools also provide many students with a source of emotional support and solace. It's astounding how many kids wrestle with demons like addiction, family dysfunction, and mental illness.

The reality is far more tragic than many people would expect. School is a safe place for them. Another more subtle hindrance is that some children haven't learned the soft skills necessary for success, like conscientiousness or a work ethic. When faced with distance learning challenges, many students turn to each other, or the ever-abundant online cut-and-paste services for their answers. Master Google to the rescue! Cheating is so rampant with distance learning; it renders many lessons as pointless. Monitoring for cheating is a serious problem. Finally, children may simply lack supervision.

For teachers, COVID shelter-in-place has its delights and challenges. Although we can now get up at 8:00 and teach in our jammies, producing every single lesson online involves a steep learning curve. Our district has supported its teachers with daily email filled with a plethora of applications, instructions, clever pedagogical ideas, and websites. We have technicians at the ready to give a helping hand. Nevertheless, producing online lessons is frustrating, tedious and difficult.

A distance learning expert, Liz Kolb, advises that teachers need to use the 3-E model for student mastery. We need to first **Engage** students in mindful tasks that focus on learning outcomes. Students need to be active and socially engaged through co-use (collaborative teams).

Next, instruction must be **Enhanced** by focusing on higher order thinking skills and knowledge gathering. Teachers must be mindful of connecting prior knowledge to acquired knowledge.

Finally, teachers must **Extend** knowledge by providing opportunities for authentic tasks and contexts. This sounds great! I love it!

Here's the reality: putting technology in the hands of students comes at a high cost. Students need interaction, and the "co-use" tools are mainly Zoom conferences, discussion boards and messaging services. There are games and simulations, and those are awesome. But, as one of my students told me, "I can't learn this way! I need a teacher to teach me, not a computer to teach myself." The instructional time, where a teacher visits individuals or groups of students who are working hard to master concepts and skills, cannot be replicated with a computer screen. Even fancy software that projects the teacher in 3-D, cannot mimic those vital conversations. We are not Vulcans and we are not on the Starship Enterprise.

The biggest reason that most educators are in the field is because they love kids. Even though we are no longer managing a few wild monkeys in the classroom now, we also don't get to see our kids, talk with them, and entertain them with oh-so-witty teacher humor.

Learning and laughing with kids is the heart and soul of classroom teaching. To do otherwise smothers the flame of what it means to teach. It kills me when my kids email with pleas about their confusion, fear and frustration, and I can't smile with encouragement, or high-five when they finally get it. Students can't raise their hands with clever questions and answers during most computer lessons. Gone are the hands-on activities and laboratory experiments.

There is only so much a teacher can do to meet a variety of learning needs using a screen and keyboard. Although we are moving through the curriculum at a faster pace, it's mostly because I can't stop and check at the moment it's needed to see when the lesson is derailed and bring it back on track. Where work-at-your-own-pace sounds like a great idea, some kids are weeks behind.

They need the pressure of keeping up with their peers. They need each other, and they need teachers. It is vital that students have relationships in order to learn and to grow into healthy, well-functioning adults.

Teaching is an art as well as a science, and it's also a sales job. How does one sell something so fundamentally important, to anyone, without talking with them? Amazon can sell Cheeze Doodles and flat screen TVs online, but education isn't a product. It's a means to experience the world in a meaningful way, and more importantly carry on the knowledge, skills, and values of our people. We can't expect anyone to learn in isolation, no matter how comfy the couch is.

* * *

Lisa Durkin is a high school science teacher in Los Lunas, NM with an MA in Science Education from New Mexico Institute of Mining and Technology. During the past 31 years she has taught over 3000 students. Lisa is the President of the New Mexico's Coalition for Science and Math Education.

Spiritual/Philosophy Poetry   Silver Medal
Charles Powell

BAD WANTS COMPANY,
SO DOES GOOD

When I feel the smallest, the weakest, the most insignificant and vulnerable, the most impotent,
insecure and unsure and unimportant, uncomfortable and saddened,

My most dejected, deprived, discouraged, dispirited, disadvantaged, disappointed, depressed,
ashamed and unhappy

I'm also more likely to be suspicious, distrustful, fearful, angry, selfish, defensive and bitter
My judgement of others is more apt to be insensitive, harsh and severe

On the other hand, when I feel the strongest, the most significant, effective, potent, content, fit,
secure, forceful and certain;

My most important, confident, fortunate, satisfied, pleased, positive and joyful

I'm also more likely to be considerate, pleasant, patient, peaceful, helpful, cooperative, friendly,
forgiving, thoughtful, trusting, calm, kind and generous

*　　*　　*

Charles Powell : grandfather, Air Force veteran and retired postal worker. With a BS in Social Science, he's been published in SouthWest Writers *Sage* and the *Fixed And Free Poetry Anthology*. He's also enjoyed success with prose and poetry in several SWW writing contests. Raised in Chicago, Albuquerque's been home 34 years.

Spiritual/Philosophy   **Bronze Medal**
Desiree Woodland

GOODNIGHT MOON

Shafts of light cut sharply through the southern facing windows of the greenhouse. Dust particles danced and swayed like fairies celebrating the last rays of sun before evening. I sink into the comfortable green couch that was my family's refuge in times when children's tears needed comforting, sprained ankles and fevers required rest, and just plain old snuggling was required. I wait for my son, Ryan, to finish dressing for bed, and join me for our nightly story time ritual. No longer a toddler, he was a busy five year old, with legs sturdy enough to win races with his older sister, climb the cottonwood tree behind our house, and ride his bike to the end of the street by himself.

Are you ready yet, little man? I call, hoping my voice carried up the stairs. Soon, I hear small footsteps running down to join me. I scoop him up, noticing he has chosen his light blue t-shirt with Alvin and the Chipmunks on the front, and I wrap him in the cocoon of my grandmother's colorful afghan. He smiles and works his arm out to encircle my waist and lay his head on my shoulder.

Life will never be better than this, I think to myself. I close my eyes to savor the love of this precious moment. Surely, heaven will be like this.

I tilt my head to kiss the top of his blonde head and linger to breathe in the fragrance of shampoo and soap. Little boys can get so sweaty after a day of playing outdoors, but tonight freshly bathed, I revel in his scent.

"I want *Goodnight Moon*," he says in a husky little boy voice. Of course, I want *Goodnight Moon* too. Such a simple book, but the repetition has always tickled Ryan's funny bone. Tonight, is no exception. When we get to the part where the little old lady whispers hush and bids goodnight to mush, he cannot contain his laughter. Giggles roll over him as he repeats the words again and again. "Goodnight to the little old lady, goodnight moon and goodnight mush"…

This precious memory is tucked away in my heart.

Ryan died by suicide at age 24, and I struggled to make sense of it. Grief had spun my life out of control, and I needed to hold onto something bigger than myself. The moon in the night sky became a symbol that supported me during the most intense sadness. Each month I watched as the moon completed its phases and I was filled with a sense of mystery and the overwhelming peace that I craved.

The moon was a shining beacon to my heart, a powerful sign that one day all will be well. Psalms 89:37 says, "It shall be established forever as the moon, and [as] a faithful witness in heaven. Selah." KJV. God is present in the seemingly random events of our lives, as well as tragedies that make no sense, but he has set signs in the earth as reminders of his eternal faithfulness.

Even now, nearly 14 years later, when the moon is full, I often go outside and gaze upward and think about God's faithfulness. Sometimes, with tears, sometimes without, I whisper to Ryan; goodnight dear son, never goodbye, but see you later. Goodnight sleep well. I will see you in my dreams, and one day I will again hold you in my arms.

*   *   *

Goodnight Moon is by Margaret Wise Brown.
For further reading: Psalm 8:3, Genesis 1:4 KJV

Desiree Woodland lives in Albuquerque, New Mexico. Following Ryan's suicide, she wrote as a way to heal and published a memoir called, *I Still Believe*- mental illness and suicide in light of Christian faith. A retired teacher, she holds a master's level certificate in grief and loss.

Spiritual/Philosophy Poetry Bronze Medal
Frank Stephens

WELSPRYNG

Before and beyond speech,
grief overwhelms.

Four years,
still this promethean pain of your passing in my arms,
my guttural howl of anguish
and incomprehension
at this fresh void in the crowded vacuum-
where I thought no more could grow.

I surround you with powerless arms,
and try to squeeze life back in,
but feel you flow from me
bearing some unknown,
unknowable,
shade
into a dark synaptic mystery,
which only memory,
brief, incomplete, imperfect memory,
can ever illuminate.

I scream my song,

silent,
empty of meaning,
save in the rests between notes,
in the space between words,
where borrowed breath
encounters infinity of selection.
Yet I do choose,
yet we choose,
and from these choices spring
literature and lies,
poetry and propaganda,
all the joy and folly
of this creative beast,
this passing presence,
this transient accretion of essence,
emergent,
de profundis,
into brief, nascent awareness.

Before consciousness, beyond cognition,
this seeking sourced in sorrow.

      *   *   *

OTHER BOOKS BY SOUTHWEST WRITERS

Available on Amazon and at local Albuquerque bookstores

The *2019 Annual Writing Contest Anthology of Short Stories and Poetry*. If you liked this book, check out last year's winners too!

Kimo Theatre: Fact & Fiction. The KiMo Theatre is an iconic structure in Albuquerque, New Mexico that was built in 1927 to be a silent movie palace. SWW Members combined their skills to produce a book full of first person stories, historical data and photographs. The unique Pueblo Deco architecture combined with its history of theatrical and film events make it stand out as a historically fascinating place that is still in use today.

The *Sage Anthology*, a collection of short stories, poetry and articles about writing by writers first published in the *SouthWest Sage* newsletter.

The *Storyteller's Anthology* was the first collection of stories by SWW members including Anne Hillerman, and David Morrell

SouthWest Writers is a non-profit organization devoted to helping both published and unpublished writers improve their craft and further their careers. SWW serves authors worldwide in every fiction and non-fiction genre through meetings, classes, workshops and by providing writing opportunities.

SWW has a database of professionals who offer services to potential authors including editing, web design, mentoring, formatting, illustrations, cover art, blogging, and information about self-publishing. For more information go to:

www.southwestwriters.com

Made in the USA
Middletown, DE
18 September 2020